FALLING

SHARE YOUR THOUGHTS

Want to help make *Falling* a bestselling novel? Consider leaving an honest review of this book on Goodreads, on your personal author website or blog, and anywhere else readers go for recommendations. It's our priority at SFK Press to publish books for readers to enjoy, and our authors appreciate and value your feedback.

OUR SOUTHERN FRIED GUARANTEE

If you wouldn't enthusiastically recommend one of our books with a 4- or 5-star rating to a friend, then the next story is on us. We believe that much in the stories we're telling. Simply email us at pr@sfkmultimedia.com.

SFK
PRESS

FALLING

REBEKAH COXWELL

Falling
Copyright © 2021 by Rebekah Coxwell

SFK
PRESS

Published by
Southern Fried Karma, LLC
Atlanta, GA
www.sfkpress.com

ISBN: 978-1-970137-06-4
eISBN: 978-1-970137-07-1

Library of Congress Control Number: [TK]

Design services provided by Indigo: Editing, Design, and More.
Cover design by Olivia Croom Hammerman. Cover images: Medieval lady in long dress. Black and white silhouette by Eroshka from Shutterstock.com; knight courtesy of Pixabay.com.
Interior by Jenny Kimura.

Printed in the United States of America.

DEDICATION

To Samuel Luay and Melody Marie, my favorite humans.

To those battling depression: you are not alone.
National Suicide Prevention Lifeline: 1-800-273-8255

To all the healthcare workers that help us
win our battles: thank you.

To the military personnel that gave their lives:
faithful souls, rest in peace.

To those military personnel who still serve: thank you.

TABLE OF CONTENTS

PART I

PART II

PART III

PART I

The Fall

DAI UENO
2010

I FELL.

The air rushed past my ears with a high-pitched squeal. My ears stung as they cut through the air. The last image I saw was of her gold irises. My last thought, the song: *What will you do when you are alone?* Then the high-pitched squeal was inside of me, in the middle of my forehead and spreading, nails on a chalkboard, tearing me in half. The buzzing under my skin was gone, yet my whole body rang. I couldn't hear. Anything but the squeal. The song was drowned out.

This is death jumped up from my subconscious, but I wouldn't have time to process it.

My body hit the water; it felt like falling onto a sidewalk made of dry ice. It hurt instantly, like my balls had known exactly what the impact would feel like before it had happened. The shock burned its way up my spine like a hot metal rod, then settled in my stomach. The sour taste of stomach bile sat at the back of my throat like vinegar. The water rushed up my nose. My mouth opened in a silent scream as though the water could escape. The numbing cold forced my eyes open.

I sank. There was soft darkness reaching for me, pulling me to its chest. It promised a quiet sleep. I reached out toward it, but my arms spun me around, and I looked up and saw my jacket, a lonely shadow drifting off to my right. Then the cloudless night sky—there was a sliver of moon and a shit ton of stars scattered across it. My arms shot up, fought to reach for it against my will.

I redirected my arms to dive deeper, inhaled through my nose so I could take in enough water to drown myself. It felt like snorting rubbing alcohol. It burned so bad I couldn't keep my eyes open, and my hands clawed at my throat like they'd scratch open an exit for the water I'd aspirated. My legs betrayed me. They kicked my body up to the surface. My head broke through. My eyes opened. My arms reached out for the side of the lake. My hands grasped anything that could save me: grass, weeds, the compacted clay.

I pulled myself up and out of the river, then sat on all fours, heaving, until I coughed and the water in my lungs rushed out of me. I retched what didn't come out with that first cough. Then I had the urge to lay my face on the ground. I was tired after struggling. I had only enough energy to move my body to the side of my vomit. Then I laid my face down on the cool ground, and my body followed. I closed my eyes.

UENO DAICHI
1932

Ueno Daichi is not my name. That name belongs to a body long dead in a trench next to a barbed-wire fence in Germany.

I was born in a shack on a tiny plot of land in Central California in January 1920. It was cold that year, and in certain parts of Southern California, frost would be reported. As I was growing up, my father spoke little to me. He explained in broken English that he wanted me to live the American Dream, as, unlike him, I was an American citizen. He refused to speak to me in Japanese because Americans only spoke English.

My father would sing in Japanese while he tended our sugar beets. I would try to work as close to him as possible so I could hear the words he used. Sometimes, I'd repeat after him. If he caught me, he'd stop singing, so I learned to be as quiet as possible and listen before I opened my mouth. The only other time I heard him speak in Japanese was at night, after he was sure I was asleep. He would kneel next to his pallet, fold his hands, and pray. Later, I would learn his nightly custom was American; only the language he spoke was Japanese.

I would lie still as a corpse and listen.

During the day, my father sent me to school; in the evening, I helped him on the farm; at night, when he would get water from the well for dinner, I would take out letters he had hidden in a suitcase under his pallet, and I would look in wonder at the foreign symbols, imagining what mysteries they told me about my father's homeland. In school, I said nothing; it was how I was used to communicating, so it was what I did.

My father was an honorable man. We cultivated our sugar beets and sold them to local markets, and even though my father would not be able to buy the farm that he would work for thirty years, he would start work before the sun came up and work long after sunset.

One day, I came home from school and found his slack and lifeless body lying in the middle of two rows of sugar beets. My body created a shadow over his. His right hand grasped the dirt of the land that would never love him in return, and his left arm was thrown over his face as though he were covering it from the sun or hiding it.

I often think back on that day. I should have dug a grave for my father, buried his body, and continued to grow the sugar beets as I had been taught, but it disgusted me to see him clutching the dirt as though he had fought to keep working until the last beat of his heart.

Shamelessly, I turned my nose up at our one-room home, which felt like a cage, keeping me silent and alien from everyone else in this country. Looking down at my father's body again, I saw myself dead on the ground in his place. The vision crawled up the back of my neck, and all the hairs on my body stood petrified. I couldn't touch him, so I turned and ran, leaving my father's body to rot.

DAI

The Dream

2010

UNFIRE GOES OFF AROUND ME. THE WORLD SHAKES under my feet. I see a bright flash in the corner of my right eye. I look over at my right arm and see it is encased in a dull metal. There are scratches and dents, as though the armor has been used before, but my war is still coming. I feel it in my chest, which is covered in the same iron. Looking down at myself, I realize I am wearing a full suit of medieval armor. In my left hand rests a broadsword. The hilt wraps around my iron-covered hand, and though it feels so heavy I might drop it, I do not, and instead, I shift it to both hands, grasping it tight, waiting for my enemy. On my hip, I feel my solitary wakizashi. And though I wish to drop my broadsword and reach for that blade, I fear I will not pull it out fast enough. I will not wield it correctly. It will be useless alone.

Sunlight reflects off of my double blades, and I am blinded. I switch the sword to my right hand, and I blink until I can see. My vision is limited to a contained portion of the world, so I must be wearing a helmet, as well. I look down at my broadsword once again, and I know if I get close enough to my enemies, I can cut them down. I just have to get close enough.

There is an impact. A dry, hot heat. My body flies through the air. My helmet is ripped off. I see the full world around me for the first time. It is a bright blur of colors. My eyes tear up, and the water flies out the sides of my eyes and behind me. It is the only thing I can feel.

I sail. I keep waiting for my stomach to drop, but all I see is the sky I am being thrown toward. The high-pitched tone is distant from me, like it exists behind a wall. My eyes dry, and there is nothing left for me to feel.

I am pulled away from the sky. The air cuts past my ears familiarly. My stomach drops. That high-pitched squeal breaks through the wall and makes me cringe, makes my teeth grind past each other trying to drown it out, and there it is again: déjà vu. *This is death.*

I am relieved, but I close my eyes so I can't see it coming.

I hit the ground; it doesn't hurt. I only know I have landed because I don't feel the air stinging my ears anymore. The tone is gone.

There is a laugh. I open my eyes. Below me and in the distance stands a rigid-backed man with a scowl on his face and his daishō kinetic in his left hand. He gives directions to five young men in forest-green military garb, who operate a rusted Type 38 75mm field gun together. The wooden wheels have spokes missing, bullet holes, and patches along the outer rim to keep the gun stable if it has to be moved. But it won't have to be, and I have no doubt my grandfather will pull out his wakizashi and katana without hesitation, if need be. Despite using an outdated weapon created fifty years before his war, my grandfather will still keep himself and his five men alive. Then he will go on to start a hundred-billion-yen company.

My grandfather speaks. Quick. Bulleted. I cannot make out the commands he is shooting. A half-beat after his mouth closes, hands reach out to adjust for new coordinates. A quarter-beat, and then ammunition is loaded. The man next to my grandfather nods and picks up ammunition for the next bar. A half-beat rest, then the bang of a fifth hand firing the field gun. For the finish, they all laugh once in unison, or, rather, they all audibly push air from their diaphragms as one unit. One harmony. Then my grandfather speaks, starting the next bar.

Trapped in my suit of armor, I wonder if it is the second part of my grandfather's name I am missing, if it is the katana I am missing, or if it is something inside of me that is broken. What is the key? What did my grandfather know at my age?

Ashamed, I can no longer look at him, so I look up at the sky above me. A Lockheed YO-3 flies overhead, silent. I know without a doubt in my mind that my father is inside it. Armed with only a camera, he is still more accomplished at my age than I. He is flying to my mother. Going to a distant country to work for a commanding Japanese man so that he can be invited to dinner and fall in love with the man's daughter, the tall woman with the smile as wide as the sky and as beautiful as the stars. Their love will bring them everything they have both dreamed of.

I try to get up, but the armor is too heavy, and I am stuck. I look around the best I can from the ground, looking for my brothers in arms, those I can lead through battle, those I can get up for. There is no one.

I am trapped—alone—in an outdated piece of technology with an outdated weapon. My right hand closes, expecting the metal hilt of my broadsword, but instead, it clasps empty air. I reach down for my wakizashi, but it will not be unsheathed. I struggle with it, pleading, begging, but I know it is stuck because I am not yet worthy.

I stretch out my fingers, searching for my broadsword again. This time, I feel the top of the hilt at the very tip of the middle finger of my right hand. I reach out as far as I can. I reach until my arm aches and it feels as though my muscles will snap. It is not enough.

I am alone on this hill, in the middle of a battlefield, with no weapon to hold on to. I know my enemy is coming for me. If I listen hard enough, I can hear them—or it. I have no memory of how I got here. I have no memory of how I am supposed to leave.

But I believe:

I can be a great leader if I have someone to protect.

If I have the right weapon, I will fight proficiently.

If I'm fighting a war, one I believe in, even in this suit, I will be valiant.

DAICHI
1932

I WAS BIG FOR MY TWELVE YEARS; ALREADY THE HEIGHT OF many grown men. Most at that time were unwilling to hire Japanese people, and I spoke little to no Japanese, so I lived on what I could find in dumpsters behind restaurants and shops. During this time in my life, I didn't think of anything but finding my next meal and where I would sleep that night. This ended when I was thirteen and a shopkeeper found me rifling through his trash in the alley behind his shop. He told me that if I was hungry, he knew a place that would hire someone like me.

AS I GOT out of the car in front of the hundreds of acres of land owned by Mr. Martin, the shopkeeper gave me some kind of warning, probably something similar to *I'll send you to jail if I see you behind my shop.*

Chump, I thought. *Why would I go back to your shop to get caught again?* I gave him a vague agreement anyway and looked around. A few dozen people worked under the California sun, their backs hunched over, their skin the color or approaching the color of leather, their hands reaching out and harvesting or pruning the crops. They reminded me of my father, but I had nowhere else to go, which was why I walked up the drive to Mr. Martin's house.

DAI
2010

I OPENED MY EYES, AND THE POUNDING ACHE IN THE middle of my head told me I was awake. In my mind's eye, I was smiling—crazier than I had ever smiled in my twenty-one years—but in actuality, my mouth was tightly clenched. I thought hard about opening my mouth until I did it, slow and dumb, like after a dentist is finished with you. A strange sound came from my gaping hole of a mouth. It sounded like a croaker struggling on land. I closed my mouth.

I lifted my hand. My mind commanded it, and my hand followed a second later, heavy and dumb like my jaw. I dropped it and looked to my right so I could focus my eyes next.

The first thing I saw was my mother's face high above me. Clouded and gray. She grabbed my right hand in hers. Her hands were not cupped; she did not sing. She squeezed. Hard. Her face broke, and the rain started to fall.

Thunder came from my dad. "Why didn't you tell us the drinking had gotten this bad?"

No lightning followed. Only the insistent squeeze of my mother's hands, getting tighter. I did not look at her face. I was too exhausted to take in the storm.

My heart monitor beeped steady, steady. A nurse walked up to the door and looked through the window, but, seeing the storm inside, she walked away.

My mother's thumbs started to rub my hand. Frantic. You could hear the rain falling, then. My father turned to my mother and rubbed her back. He didn't say anything for a while. I knew at any moment, they would go outside the room and become the Klimt painting above our fireplace at home. My tall, noble mother would collapse in my father's arms. Her face would maintain its beauty despite the tears. My father would hold her up and put his face into the crevice of her neck, right next to her clavicle. His facelessness would not matter because he had her. Would gold erupt from their clothes? Would the nurses jump back in confusion, the doctors adjusting their glasses and taking notes?

My father raised his head. His mouth moved. My heart monitor picked up. *Ohno. Ohno. Ohno.*

I thought my heart monitor was strange because I couldn't hear what my father was saying. I turned my head to watch the line tracking my heart travel up, travel down, and even out. Up, down, and even out. Even as it sped up and the line moved quicker, it had a pattern, and I had no idea what it meant. What any of it meant. Everything around me seemed like disconnected details and events that I felt sure I should understand—that should make sense and that I should have context for—but instead, it seemed like I was opening a door into a room with a movie playing in another language. I had no idea how it connected to my life, though it had to; I felt it. And there were other doors. Whole buildings full of doors that somehow pertained to my life, but I couldn't decipher even one.

My mother's hands squeezed another degree tighter. Her thumbs dug into the top of my hand like she might push them through to my palm. I looked back over at my father. His voice registered this time, like distant thunder. "It's a nice inpatient facility. Think about it."

I nodded, agreeing that it was, probably, a nice facility.

My father nodded, his mouth set, believing we had come to an agreement. He put his hand on my mother's squeezing hands, and her thumbs stopped. She released me. Then she let my father help her up and lead her out of the room.

Through the porthole in the door, I watched my mother's head lean toward my father. Though I couldn't see her hands, I imagined they clung to him. Grasped his shirt as though it held the key to fixing me. My father turned his face into her neck.

I lay back and squeezed my eyes shut so that the only thing running through my mind was the sound of the heart monitor, reminding me that I was, unfortunately, still alive.

DAICHI
1932

MR. MARTIN AND HIS FAMILY OWNED A SIGNIFICANT portion of the farmland in the San Joaquin Valley. Mr. Martin's father, Mr. Martinsson, had been one of the founding members and sponsors of the Japanese Exclusion League, which became the Asiatic Exclusion League. Mr. Martinsson was old money from Sweden, and he had decided to come with the influx of Swedes wanting to join in the American gold rush of industrialization that the rest of the world had noticed. Mr. Martinsson had chosen California not because of the nuggets but because of the gold rays of sunshine and the fertile soil. What better place to make his fortune apart from his father?

He'd found that the U.S. was faster paced than expected; to make money at the rate he'd wanted, he would have to start with capital, so he'd written back home for a loan. When the money had arrived, he'd started buying land. His father and his before him had taught Mr. Martinsson that landowners thrived. But he had not been able to farm all of the land he'd owned by himself, so he'd hired workers. At the time, like Sweden, Japan had recently opened its borders to the world and had started to industrialize within the U.S., and an influx of immigrants had moved there for better opportunities as farming had become more and more obsolete.

Many American landowners had gone to Japan and brought back contracted workers who had wanted to immigrate to the U.S. Mr. Martinsson had gone to Japan and brought back ten contracted workers. Then he had been able to afford twenty. Then, Japanese, Chinese, and Mexican laborers had started to come to him for jobs.

Mr. Martinsson hadn't been prejudiced. In fact, unlike his landowning peers, he'd referred to the lot of the laborers—excluding the Mexicans—as "Orientals" instead of the terms his friends had used, like "Chink" or "Jap." What Mr. Martinsson had known, though, was that there were starting to be more "Orientals" than there were of him or even his landowning friends in the League. He had watched them from his window as they'd talked to each other in a language he had not understood, and they would work sixteen-hour days out in the sun and then make time to educate their kids in that jungle culture they had come from. And most of his best growers had been Japanese or Chinese, so if they had decided to revolt, how would he make his money? It could only be a matter of time before those "Orientals" took over. So, he'd hired locksmiths to install extra locks on his doors. He'd had rifles placed strategically around his house in hidden compartments or on the walls, within easy arm's length if he stood up. He'd hired a few kids here and there to report to him what their parents were up to.

He'd hired them, but he'd also worked to rid the state of the horde of them. He'd done what he could, and in 1913, the Alien Land Law had made it easy for Mr. Martinsson to attain his goal of making his own money through farming, as Japanese persons could no longer own land in California because they could not become citizens. Land Japanese persons' homes were built on had now become cheap because the land-owners had had the "Japs" living on the land to contend with, but Mr. Martinsson had figured it was only a matter of time before the League was able to rid the state of all "Orientals," including these "Japs." He'd only had to wait it out; then he could move good upstanding citizens into the houses as renters and sharecroppers so that he could make a profit from the land *and* from the homes, and he could finally have a good night's sleep, knowing his future was guaranteed.

MR. MARTINSSON HAD done everything he could as a good upstanding citizen to have as many future upstanding citizens as possible. Sadly, his wife had only been able to have one child: Alexander Martinsson. Mr. Martinsson had felt giving his son the name of a conqueror would encourage Alexander to be intelligent and to make his own wealth. Just as he had done.

For his son's wedding present, he had given him three small farms adjacent to each other and cultivated by a "Jap" family living on each piece of land. He'd told his son to be careful and to keep an eye out. A month later, he'd died—a heart attack while walking through one of his farms. Four workers had picked him up and carried him up to his house. They'd laid his body on the porch, as they had all been taught early on in their employment that hired help not specifi-cally employed as in-house staff would be shot for entering. Mayor Perkins had been a regular visitor and confidante of Mr. Martinsson's, as had the chief of police; it so happened that Mrs. Martinsson had made an almond caramel cake that was to die for.

MR. MARTINSSON'S FUNERAL had been a large occasion. The mayor, police chief, senators, and McClatchy brothers had been just a few of the hundreds in attendance.

ALEXANDER MARTINSSON WAS a different man from his father. He'd changed the family name from Martinsson to Martin, so the family would sound less foreign and more American. The delineation between himself and his workers needed to be clear—it was the only way this system would be successful. Mr. Martin was not afraid of the horde of "Orientals," whom his father had feared. In fact, he believed they were here to stay. He believed that instead of ridding the state of these persons, the best course of action was to harness their power.

He'd built a big white house on the hill overlooking the farms he had been given by his father. He believed that in every system, there had to be a leader, and it was important no one in the system forgot this. Then he had hired the families who lived in the houses. He'd bought more land around them and next to them over the years, and he'd hired Chinese, Japanese, Filipino, and Mexican wage laborers to work the land, as his father had done.

MR. MARTIN LET the workers who did not sleep in one of the three houses sleep in a temporary camp on the other side of the farm. Next to that temporary camp, right over the boundary line of his property, was another temporary camp, where those who waited for a job opportunity lived until Mr. Martin was ready to hire someone new. Both camps were nearly identical, with shacks made of what could be found discarded around the farm—usually tarp, or, if enough could be found, tin cans. Hulking in the valley between the two camps was a valley oak. It stood about eighty feet tall and had been on the property for as long as either Mr. Martin or his father could remember.

ON MY FIRST night, I was not allowed entry to Mr. Martin's home. I finished my walk up the drive at a big white door whose height had to be at least seven feet, as it towered at least half a foot above my head. I was afraid to knock once I faced the big white door. The sun was setting, and the shadow covering half the door gave it a menacing quality, as though it was cut in half as a warning. I felt eyes on me. I looked up at the second floor, and a serious-looking man in a fancy jacket stared down at me with a glass in his hand. I stared back up at him. After a few minutes, he brought the glass to his mouth and took a sip, and then he turned and walked from the window. I assumed I would have time to figure him out. In the meantime, I needed to find a place to stay until morning.

I looked down at the fields below. Experience told me I needed to find a place before the sun went down, so I started to walk farther into the farm. It was the end of the workday. Everyone seemed to be finishing up, standing and taking that end-of-the-day breath. The kind that woke a mind numbed to finish a long day of work, for a second, and then the physical weariness was back. But the weary clarity of the next day turned them into dead men, stumbling back to their graves: houses made out of garbage and branches; tents ratty with holes; trucks set up with bedding in the back to provide a starry open-air bed for dead eyes. It stank of filth and waste. I missed my father's one-room home. I could not lie among the corpses, so I climbed the valley oak. I settled onto a thick branch and leaned against the trunk. I closed my eyes.

I WOKE TO the same feeling I'd had the night before: I was being watched. I took my time waking up. I moved the muscles in my legs as little as possible. I flexed my fingers and stretched my arms. Once I felt my body was awake enough to jump down if I needed, I opened my eyes. The man I assumed to be Mr. Martin stood below me, staring up at me as though he were still two stories above my head. He smiled after a second and motioned that I should come down, and then he walked toward his big white house. I assumed he was telling me to follow him.

STANDING IN MR. MARTIN'S office, which was the size of the one-room house I had spent my childhood in, I felt small. This was not common, as I was as tall as most men, even at the age of thirteen. In front of his redwood desk, my palms so slick I was sure my sweat would start to pool on the floor, I felt like a small child. He stared at me for ten minutes, waiting, I assumed, for me to say something. I did not, as I had nothing to say.

Finally, he smiled big, then motioned I that should come forward. I approached and stood to the side of him. He said he liked me. Then he asked if I spoke any English.

I nodded.

He looked at me again, though this time he seemed to be looking for something from me. "You don't say much, eh?"

I shook my head.

He smiled. "Good, good." He stood up and came so close to my face that I could see the pores on his forehead. I felt as though I should be afraid, being so close to him, but I was not, despite my sweat-covered palms. He raised his left palm and slapped me good-naturedly on my right cheek. "I need a boy to do some odd jobs around the farm. Can you tie a knot?"

I nodded.

Mr. Martin walked over to a wall of large wooden filing cabinets that I had not noticed when I had first walked in. He pulled a piece of paper out as well as a folder. He brought them over to me and had me write out my name in English on the folder, and then he handed me the contract to sign. When I was finished, he put the contract in the folder, walked over to another cabinet on that wall, and slipped my folder inside.

He closed the drawer, turned, and walked over with his hand in his pocket. He handed me a two-foot piece of cotton rope. I tied the farmer's knot my father had taught me. Mr. Martin smirked, pulled it loose, and then tied a noose and handed it to me. I untied it and copied what he'd done. He patted me on my shoulder. "Good," he said.

MARY CHAPMAN
1968–1978

I WANTED TO BE A FLOWER CHILD. DANCING AND MUSIC, drugs and sex. My dream was to create a commune that had at least one person from every race on this Earth. At the age of eight, I knew without a doubt that I hated the institution of marriage and swore I would love freely. None of my ten children would know who had fathered them. I would name each of them after flowers, boy or girl. Everyone in my commune would be mothers and fathers to my children. We would all love each other and that would be enough.

But I was a good little Black Christian girl named Mary who went to her parents' Baptist church every Wednesday and Sunday. Who babysat kids in the neighborhood after school while their parents finished up their shifts and came home for a few hours before their graveyard shifts started. My momma only worked two jobs, so she'd come home at seven p.m. and check in on us. I'd watch multiple kids at a time at my house. I'd call them sleepovers, and I'd have the kids hold hands like I'd seen Dr. King do, and we'd all sing spirituals while walking around the house. Sometimes, I'd stand on my bed and say as much of the "I Have a Dream" speech as I could remember. I'd quaver my voice just like him. All the kids, young and with boogers hanging from their noses, would look up at me, enraptured.

In 1975, I was fifteen and desperate to dance. I wanted to feel the passionate desperation of the unfulfilled dream from Dr. King's speech on that dance floor, mixed with coke and body sweat all squeezed into a brightly colored, skin-tight, bell-bottomed jumpsuit. I wanted a fro twice the size of my head and to snort so much coke I couldn't feel my face.

In 1978, I was finally old enough to run off to college and burn my bra. I had missed the chance to jump onto a smoke-filled, rainbow-colored bus or to become the next Donna Summer, but I would find my rebellion.

Then my father died. My mother had no one and now needed to make up for the lost income from the two jobs my father had worked, so I got a waitressing job at a diner in town and settled for wearing a short fro and my uniform without a bra.

MARA CHAPMAN
2010

I STOOD OUTSIDE DAI'S HOSPITAL-ROOM DOOR, TRYING to recall the laughter he had given me. I willed myself to go in. My hands shook. I raised one of them anyway and smoothed the top of my hair with the back of it, though it was gelled into a tight bun. This was my chance. To be seen. To have those shoulders to myself. I was sure it was those shoulders I had fallen in love with. That had told me what kind of man Dai would be. Those too-square, new-to-sixteen shoulders had promised to one day fill out. To be the kind of shoulders that would support arms wrapped around me when I cried. That would protect a child from anything. That would open the world up. Just for me. They'd start my life. They'd take my fear. That was what those shoulders would do. I would know I was beautiful and never cry again. Shoulders like his could do that and more, I'd known just by watching his arms wrapped around Layla, his hand resting on her hip, tentative, as though anything she wanted would be granted. She needed only ask, or better yet, shift those hips ever so slightly to either side, and he would oblige. Anything. Everything. A boy with shoulders like that, with intuition like that, could only grow to be a great man. I was sure.

And then I was at his deathbed.

DAI
2010

S TANDING IN FRONT OF THE PORTHOLE DOOR, ACROSS the room, was Mara. Her hair was tightly bound back, her hands clasped in front of her, fingers interwoven and squeezing each other so tight it seemed like they'd snap any second. And an encapsulated silence. Like she was screaming behind a Plexiglas wall. If you listened hard enough, you could hear it. But you didn't want to. You didn't want the sound to break your heart. Didn't want that sound to climb down your throat and start screaming from you, too. Usually, I told a joke, made her mouth open up so her hiccupping laugh could tumble out and sit on the back of my neck like cool green grass in summer. Tickling and comforting. Ready to dissipate that itching under my skin like a cool salve. And where had that melody gone? It felt like the last time I had heard it had been at the lunch table, when our six-year-old selves had barely been able to contain the joy we had shared.

And then that yellow dress she wore. It made me hesitate. Want to reach out for her. Made me feel like she and it were reaching out to me.

I couldn't remember why the color of her dress had made me hesitate. Why her lost laughter had occurred to me. Her eyes widened like she saw this stream of thought unraveling in front of her. I felt like she had stripped me of my face and was pulling back the interconnected muscles to see what was behind it. I looked away from those x-ray eyes of hers. The artery in her throat quivered like it might yawn open and scream. Her fingers were squeezing each other harder and harder, but her legs, resolved, brought her to me. As they always did. As I knew they always would.

Mara didn't say a word. Not one. It caught in my throat, this moment, like that silent scream she had, and I thought: *I have never seen her like this.*

She slapped me. I didn't feel the impact, like the room had been pulled back into my dream. Then the sting warmed up my cheek a degree every second, like a burn, and brought with it the memory of the air rushing past my ears. Stomach bile rose up the back of my throat and water collected at the corners of both of my eyes. Her dress was like a blur of sunlight and I wanted her to touch me, hit me again, or to climb into my hospital bed and pull me to her chest. I wanted her to tell me everything was going to be *okay*.

I didn't like this feeling. Like falling from a bridge twice as high as the one I'd fallen from, too fast to make sense of any of this. Like falling indefinitely, not knowing when it'd all end. So I cleared my throat and jumped out of the hospital bed and bowed as though I had completed the performance of my life. I kept my head bowed because it seemed like the right thing to do, since I was already doing it, and I couldn't bring myself to look at Mara's face again. She panicked after a few seconds and started to clap for me. I swallowed the bile back down.

The nurse returned and snapped at me to get back into bed. I would've told her to go fuck herself, except I was so flustered by Mara, her x-ray eyes, and the falling feeling that I did what she asked. I collected my backless smock and climbed back into the hospital bed, and as I did, I glanced back up at Mara out of the corner of my eye. Hers didn't meet mine. She looked down and away from me and whatever that moment had been. She wrung her fingers around each other, like they'd squeeze out the answers. I sighed in semi-relief. She couldn't see into me anymore. The moment passed.

I looked up at the nurse looking down at me with a frown on her face. She had a facial tic next to her right eye. I could tell she just wanted the exit interview to be over, and I needed to move on to another moment so I didn't get pulled back into that one with Mara. The nurse looked like she was probably a newbie or exhausted from a long shift or a mixture of both. This would be pretty easy. I slapped on my most charismatic smile: the one I had after five drinks. It worked at the local bar and it worked on my mother. This nurse would be cake.

The nurse blushed at her temples and clutched the clipboard to her chest. I put my hand on her elbow. She smiled down at me, dumbstruck, before asking me what had happened. I turned my smile up ten more watts and told her I'd gotten drunk, fancied a midday swim in my clothes, and then decided to take a nap. When I'd awoken, I'd been in an ambulance.

A look of incredulity passed over her face. Worried she might have picked up on some of the irony in my voice, I tilted my head slightly. Though she had seen my smile, the slight change would make her see it like it was new. The blush spread to her cheeks. She smiled back and told me she would have my paperwork ready within the hour. Then she turned and walked out, her ponytail bouncing behind her like a happy, wagging tail.

I avoided looking at Mara once we were in her car. I remembered the sting on my cheek, the tears at the corners of my eyes, my stomach so high up in my throat it had felt like it'd fall out of my mouth at any moment, and I decided to avoid *it* at all costs. I was just too tired. Too. Damn. Tired. I rolled my window down. The sky was gray and steadily lightening into the day. Air rushed past like a thick wet cloud, which made my skin crawl. I tried to focus on landmarks as they sped by to distract myself.

Her name rose up from my subconscious. *Layla.* Her gold irises wrapped around her pupils, dilating at the sight of me. The right corner of her mouth pulling up into a smirk. The sweet taste of peppermint on her lips. The details started to speed by, and I felt nauseous. The gray-white sky was suddenly too bright for my eyes. I flipped my phone open, hoping to be distracted. There were no notifications, just the main menu. The generic cartoon landscape in the background mocked me; it was as real as I was.

I closed the phone and slid it back into the right pocket of my jeans. I laid my head on the headrest and closed my eyes. It would only be a matter of time before my mother found out I had checked out of the hospital. A matter of time before she created a great bitch storm. A galloping, roaring bitch storm with sideways rain, hail the size of golf balls, and winds that would blow me every which way until they landed me where she deemed fit. The thought of it made me want a drink. Southern Comfort and black coffee seemed to be the right choice. It spoke to me.

When Mara turned the car off, I opened my eyes. It was silent, save for that scream in her. I looked over, and her big brown eyes seemed to be widening by the second with the same question my mom's hands had asked: *How can I fix this?* She raised a finger and said—something. I assumed she spoke those words, but I didn't hear them over her silent scream. It was so loud, my eyes watered and blurred. *Who is she screaming for?* I blinked back the tears and answered what I assumed her question was. "Nothing. Just come find me after." Then I jumped out of the car. Ran up the stairs to my apartment before she could try to talk to me some more, before she could try to look me in the eyes with that scream behind it all. All I wanted was to feel liquor and coffee warming my chest, making all of this seem like a bad trip.

I pulled the keys down from the top of the doorframe even though I had my own in my pocket. I unlocked the door and walked in, and there she was in the bed, waiting for me. Curled up in the sheet, because blankets just *got too hot.* Her freckled back with pink undertones begged for my lips. Her strawberry-blond curls spread lazily onto my pillow, so I would have to slide them toward her to lie in the dent in the mattress right behind her. Then I'd wrap my arms around her familiar warmth, her hair against my chest, my breath slowing to fall into sync with Layla's in the dark. *Don't say you'll never find a way for us to be.*

I shook the memory away, looked away from the bed that had been cold and empty for months, and walked over to the freezer. I decided against a sweet liquor; too nostalgic. I pulled out a bottle of Johnnie Walker instead, walked over to the counter next to my sink, and put the bottle down. Then I pulled out the mug she had given me on our first anniversary. A dude teddy bear in a top hat wrote "I wuv you" with a dead man's intestines. A lady teddy bear stood to the side with her bear paws clutched to her chest. Her breath had been taken away by the dude bear's display of affection. The dead body sat to the side, contorted and torn open: the insides visible, ribs splayed and cracked.

I filled the mug with the scotch and drank down every drop. Then I walked over to the only window in my apartment, opened it, and dropped the mug out. It sounded like a flowerpot shattering when it hit the ground. I wondered what sound my body had made when I had hit the water. What sound my body would have made, had I hit the ground.

I walked back over to the cabinet in my kitchen. This time, I pulled down a glass. A dollar-store brand bought on a whim. As I wrapped my fingers around it, I had the impulse to turn and throw it at the wall behind me. Instead, I pulled it down, placed it on the counter, and filled it with scotch. Then downed half of it right then, like it was a cup of water. I barely tasted it. I felt an overall fatigue come over me, and I stumbled over to my bed and fell into it. Fully clothed, I wrapped my sheet around myself and pulled a clump of it up and shoved it into my face, hoping to find even a remnant of her.

DAICHI
1933

I WOULD DO ODD JOBS AROUND THE PROPERTY AND, ON nights when Mr. Martin was drunk and lonely, act as a silent confidante. After a while, he moved me into one of the three houses on the property. He said he liked me because I had drive. I would go far, but every driven worker had to have a bit of luck, and I was lucky to have met him. The family living in the house was relocated to the temporary camp. At the age of thirteen, I had my own home and a weekly salary.

MR. MARTIN WAS a meticulous budgeter. He kept detailed notes on all of his property, including the contracts on all of the workers he hired and how much he owed them during the entirety of the contract. He kept these contracts in the filing cabinets along the wall in his office. He never paid anyone more than the amount of money they would yield by the end of the contract, and he expected each person to yield the minimum amount outlined in each of them.

MR. MARTIN PAID his workers ten cents an hour, which was four cents less than the average hourly wage most were paying wage laborers in 1933, but because of the Depression, there were more people than there were jobs, and Mr. Martin did not have to look far to find laborers willing to take the decreased wages.

I WAS PAID thirty cents an hour. I received twenty-eight dollars and eighty cents a week, minus the fifteen dollars to rent the house I lived in and any food or supplies I needed, which was an average of about eighty cents a month. This left me with fifty-two dollars at the end of every month.

I WOULD BALL up the bills that made up my fifty-two dollars and stuff them into my pillowcase. I loved the crinkle of the paper under my head at night. The smell of my money gave me good dreams. I would walk beside a river. Huge fish swam beneath the waves, birds chirped above, the wind blew through the trees beside me, and I felt at peace because I was free. I would wake smiling.

ONE OF THE jobs I had around the property was to carry bags of harvested cotton down to the cellar and lay them out on worktables in front of the canning shelves to dry under the fans. Once they were dry, I would come back with a few other workers to separate the seeds from the cotton.

ONE DAY, COMING home after laying out the cotton down in the cellar, I found a few bills partially chewed on the floor in front of my bed. I picked them up and looked at the tiny tooth marks. I needed to find a way to protect my way off of this farm.

ANOTHER OF MY jobs was to store the peppers, vegetables, fruits, and preserves Mr. Martin's wife canned in August. The empty jars sat on the dirt floor of the fruit cellar in varying sizes. The cellar entrance sat on the right side of the smoking barn. When Mrs. Martin was ready to start canning, I would bring the empty jars up and around to the outdoor kitchen she had built behind their house.

When she finished canning, I'd carry the full jars back down to the fruit cellar. I'd place the jars on the shelves along the walls of the room, where they'd stay until it was time to bring them up for the market.

ON A MOONLESS night, I walked over to the smoke shed with an unlit lantern. I walked over to the cellar entrance and put my lantern on the ground and unfastened and pulled open one of the doors. It creaked, so I took my time opening it until I could lay it on the ground. I did the same with the other side, then descended into the cellar, pulling the doors closed behind me. I only reached for the match in my pocket once I was standing on the dirt floor. I lit the match, held it to the wick of my torch until it caught, and then blew it out.

My shadow leapt up on the wall I was facing and I nearly yelped, thinking I had been caught. Upon realizing it was my shadow, I calmed myself and walked around the tables heaped with fluffy heads of cotton to the wall under which the empty jars sat. I picked up a blue quart-sized glass canning jar and placed it under my left armpit. Then I blew out my lantern and proceeded back up the cellar stairs. I pushed the doors open as quietly as I could, then took my time closing and fastening them behind me.

I walked back to my house, my heart pounding the whole time against my chest. I jumped every time I saw movement or heard an animal noise in the dark.

Back at my house, I pulled the blanket off of my bed, and with stolen nails and a stolen hammer, I nailed my blanket up in front of my window. Since I knew it would be a loud sound, I had to get the blanket hung with as few knocks of the hammer on the nail as possible. I hesitated before each hit and clenched my eyes shut, then opened them and swung the hammer without thinking about it. I was able to hang the blanket with only four knocks.

I relit the lantern and placed it as far from the window as possible, so I could see but no one outside could see my light. I took my sheet and stuffed it in front of the door so the light could not be seen through the space at the bottom. Then I pulled my bed away from the wall. I crawled on all fours, looking for a seam between the boards big enough to stick my fingers into. I finally found one and managed to pull the board up after a bit of cajoling. Then I pulled my savings of one hundred and fifty-six dollars from the last three months from my pillowcase and stuffed it in the jar. I closed the top and secured it with the wire bail handle and placed the jar

between the joists, in the space under the board I had removed.
I put the board back, pushed the bed back against the wall,
blew out my lantern, pried out the nails holding my blanket
in front of the window, picked up my sheet from in front of
my door, hid the nails and hammer under my mattress so
I could return them in the morning, and then fell into bed
and slept the few hours I had until the sun rose, signaling the
start of my day.

I WOULD STAY up late on moonless nights, blow out my lantern,
pull my bed from the wall, pull up the floorboard, and pull
out my jar. I'd place my earnings inside, then put everything
back. Afterward, I would lie in my bed, my arms folded behind
my head, and calculate how much more money I would need
until I could leave. I figured that although my father could
not have become a citizen, I had tricked the system by being
born here, and there was nothing that could be done about
it. I would pack up my belongings when I was ready and go
buy some land out in the Midwest or even on the East Coast.

MARY
1979

AT NIGHT, I WOULD SEARCH OUT DISCO CLUBS STILL barely holding on. Holes in the wall with floors that only partially lit up, believing, despite the obvious truth, that disco would live forever. I'd sit at the bar and watch the few people still willing to stuff themselves into tight-fitting body- and pantsuits sweat out the cocaine in their systems.

I was too afraid to dance; I'd practice at home while listening to Donna Summer and Gloria Gaynor on Momma's big wooden record player. But I felt apart from them, sitting on a worn leather swivel stool with padding coming out of the bottom. I had missed this boat, as well. I would never understand the euphoria of being part of a greater whole.

MARA
2010

I STOOD NEAR THE DOOR, AGAINST THE WALL, WATCHING with my hands behind my back and clutching my upper arms, as I had been for the last fifteen minutes. When his breathing evened out, I turned to walk out, unsure of what those shoulders needed. As I turned to open the door, I saw movement out of the corner of my eye. I turned back and saw his arm extended and his palm out. A key sat in the middle of his hand, too bright and new to be in this dark and musty apartment. I picked the key up from his palm. It was still warm. I had the impulse to stick the key in my mouth, just to get a taste. I slipped it into my pocket instead.

As the weight of the key hit the inside of my dress pocket, Dai looked up at me, his eyes big and watery, his smile odd. Looking as though it might crack any second. Like it would crack and his face would follow, and behind it would be a wound: raw, hemorrhaging, and exposed.

His mouth opened, and I only heard the one sentence before the high-pitched squeal started in the middle of my forehead. The only thing I could do to escape it was run out of the apartment.

"So you can be the first to find me."

But that was not what I would remember when I lay in bed that night, thinking back on that day. It was those shoulders

I remembered. The way they had looked, once upon a time, attached to arms wrapped around another girl's hips. For those shoulders, I would go back.

PART II
Falling

DAI
2010

M^{*Y VISION IS LIMITED TO A CONTAINED PORTION OF THE*} *world...*

In the middle of my grandfather's and father's wars, I lay useless and impotent. Sometimes, when I had the dream, I lay on that hill with my eyes open, stuck for days. Other times, I closed my eyes and woke up. That day, I did neither. In my dream, I was looking at the sky, listening for even the most infinitesimal sound from my father's plane, and then I was looking at the white popcorn ceiling in my room. My left foot sat naked against the cheap plaster wall of my apartment. My sheet was wrapped around my torso and right thigh. The sweat engendered by my dream had dried from the sheet and my forehead. My back was still soaked. My hands rested under my head. My face turned toward the window. The sun's rays, too bright, snuck in through the spaces and cracks of my yellowed blinds. I opened one eye and then the other, alternating blinding each. I closed my eyes. There it was: the gold ring. The same color as her irises.

Layla. Like the song she hadn't known. She had loved Roy Buchanan and his weeping guitar, so I'd figured she would appreciate it. We had been together for a year, in this bed, when I'd sung her the song, right after she'd pulled down the mug from the cabinet. Placed it in my hand, steaming with green tea. I hadn't even looked at it, only placed it on the floor, looking her in the eyes, and the song had come out of me at the sight of her.

Layla. She had looked me in my eyes in return. Directly in them, and she'd scorched me. My hand lifting to her face, then dropped like it was paralyzed. At first, I'd thought the look was annoyance, but later, thinking back on it in my bed that night, I knew it had been more. A command. I hadn't meant to let those words dribble out of my mouth, but that look had made sure it wouldn't happen again. What was she hiding under that melody?

Layla. She had cleared her throat, said I was sweet but corny for trying that hard.

I'd chuckled and said, "Eric Clapton did the heavy lifting."

Silence on her end. She'd changed the subject.

The next day, I'd sent her the song on iTunes. We'd talked later that night, but she hadn't mentioned it, so I'd never brought it up again. She'd been a mystery.

Layla. *Turned the whole world upside-down-crazy.* I couldn't imagine her name without singing it. She'd loved music, so the only conclusion I could come up with was that she'd hated the song. The problem was, the first time she'd sent her picture to me, I'd flipped open my phone and the song had popped into my head. It had dug its claws into me, anchored itself in the folds of my brain. I hadn't even remembered where I had heard it. It had never left. How could it?

Layla. *Please.* When she'd broken up with me after four years, it had been raining. The building she'd stood in front of had smelled like fresh bread. Her lips had tasted like peppermint. The gold irises of her eyes had made a promise that had made my heart beat so quick, even in the rain, that I could feel the sweat forming under my arms and at the small of my back.

After the kiss, she'd looked up into my face and shot me full of bullets.

- We aren't going anywhere
- We live in different states
- We barely manage to see each other twice a year
- We only talk online

"It is time we move on."

It had still been raining when I'd gotten back to Virginia. I'd stumbled up the steps to my apartment, being careful not to knock the bottles of maple bourbon in the black plastic bag against the metal stairs.

In my apartment, I'd connected my phone to my speaker and turned the song all the way up. Then I'd drunk maple bourbon and sung the song over and over. I'd sung until I'd thrown up. Then sung some more, drunk some more, thrown up some more. I'd wanted to get rid of every bit of her, but in the morning, there she'd sat in my chest. Beating steadily. The song had run through my head on a loop. I'd leaned over the side of my bed, dry heaving. My eyes had watered, and a small bit of stomach bile had burned its way up. I'd leaned over the side of my bed and dangled the loogie above the floor. Down. Then up. Down. Then up. Then I'd let it go. It had seemed to fall in slow motion, then had splattered into a puddle on the floor.

What will you do when you are alone and nobody is standing next to you?

DAICHI
1933

M R. MARTIN CHOSE HIS WORKERS CAREFULLY. HE said that unlike his paranoid, yellow-bellied father, he had an eye for finding the perfect candidates. Despite this, like his father, he did not trust his workers. He was ever mindful that they outnumbered him and his family and that there were organizations of workers getting together and refusing to work until their demands were met. This had happened in Hawaii, and Mr. Martin said that when he had heard, he had not slept for a week. It was his father's fear coming to life—what would become of him and his family if his workers left? But Mr. Martin had an answer to this problem. He had always felt that his father had been too old-world, depending too heavily on others. He'd asked his friends in the League to help him get rid of all of these "Orientals" in the state and asked the mayor and chief of police to fix his "disputes" with his workers, or to clean up after he "resolved" said "disputes." Mr. Martin preferred to deal with any "disputes" and "clean-ups" himself. He believed man had a properly working brain between his ears, so instead of sitting in fear behind locked doors, he should go outside and use it.

EVERY ONCE IN a while, a few workers would disappear, breaking their contracts. In the way he heard everything—from his hired ears—Mr. Martin heard people were getting help off the farm, shorting him the money owed on the missing parties' contracts.

Mr. Martin had his answer. He had a small number of workers with no families, whom he'd hired for longer contracts to do odd jobs around the property. When someone would try to break their contract by leaving, he would send one or a few of us to collect his investment. We would escort the person to the big house, if they were alone. If it was a family, we would round up the bunch and have them stand in a line in his office. He'd choose one, and the rest would be free to go back to their camp. Mr. Martin would generally choose the member who would yield the lowest amount to him in the long run. Then he'd nod for us to escort the rest of the family back to their camp. We would never see the lone runner or chosen representative again.

MR. MARTIN WOULD then walk right outside of his property to hire someone new.

I'D DOUBLE BACK after escorting the family, or I'd simply wait until the sole runner was taken away. Mr. Martin would hand me a six-foot cord of cotton rope. Another of my jobs was to fashion it into a noose and hang it from the valley oak between the two camps.

AT THE END of the week, I would cut down the empty noose from the tree. Sometimes, families would come for the noose. Once, an older man who looked as though he had not slept for quite some time came for the noose. He looked like a dried version of a man. Like he had been dried like jerky. When I placed the six feet of rope in his hands, he brought it to his lips and kissed it, like it was a sacred thing he was mourning.

MOST TIMES, I burned the rope as instructed. The fire cracked and popped as it rendered the cotton into ashes. I would dig a hole at the base of the oak and kick the ashes into it.

MARY
1990

SITTING IN ONE OF THOSE DISCO CLUBS, MY HAND wrapped around a Shirley Temple cocktail, I'd generally wait for some coked-up idiot to strut up to me in a polyester suit. The more ridiculous the strut, the quicker I'd bed them.

Then I was thirty. It was 1990, and I was still working at the diner. My biggest form of revolt was still not wearing a bra. I had cut my fro short and started wearing bands in front of it so that it looked styled.

On a particularly slow day at the diner, I decided to buy myself a pie. I sat at the counter and dug into the pie with a spoon. Rain started to come pouring down. I turned around on the red leather diner stool to watch people run.

Then he walked in. A Black cowboy, I swear to God. He strutted in soaking wet, stood just in the doorway, and took his hat off his head. Brought it to his chest as he bowed his head to me. Then he walked right to a booth and slid in. No rush. No hurry. I put the spoon I was holding with a heaping mound of cherry pie down and took the pie pan to the back. I straightened the scarf at my neck and pulled my shirt straight. Then I ran back out and asked him what he wanted. He asked if I "didn't mind bringin' that pie back 'round." Just like that. I grinned and brought the pie back out and slid into the booth across from him.

We ate my pie. I laughed out loud at the thought and told him what I was thinking. He blushed and I realized he was a gentleman and I'd love this man for the rest of my life.

And I did. But in the meantime, I burst through the door of my house that night and hustled down the hallway and funky-chickened around the living room. My momma jumped up and, beaming, turned on KC and the Sunshine Band, and we did the bump until she had to stop. Then she turned me around and squeezed me.

"Who is it, love?"

And I smiled big. "His name is Ezekiel."

Momma smiled even bigger. "'God strengthens.' Praise God, a good Christian man!"

At that moment, I hesitated. This was nothing like the hippie commune I had dreamed of as a girl. But then my momma was grabbing my arms and doing the hustle, and I couldn't disappoint her.

MARA
2010

THE FOURTH WEEK AFTER THE FALL WE DIDN'T TALK about, I looked in the mirror and saw my father. His square chin and mud-brown eyes. The only part of my mother I saw was my cheekbones. They sat high and proud under my brown skin.

At least I gave you something of mine.

I tried to ignore my mother's voice, but it seemed to pop up whenever I glanced at myself in a mirror. Before I could counteract it, it would be there, cutting into me. I knew they were my thoughts. My insecurities. Of course they were, but it was always in my dead mother's voice.

I looked away from the mirror and started looking for my last inflexible hairband. I searched the top drawer of my bureau for it. I searched under my bed. I used one every day so that my buns stayed tight while I was at work. I was running low; most of the bands had snapped, having been pulled too tight, but I knew there was still one left. It pulled my hairline back so straight it felt like my hair would start popping right out of my scalp. It had to be here. Had to be. Variations of this thought kept churning through my head until it was so loud, I was repeating it over and over out loud to myself.

Then that tone. That pinprick of a sound—I could hear it, barely audible and growing louder, until the tone was so loud I was yelling at myself, frantic. Near tears. It had to be here.

I finally found it in my bathroom, on the counter where I had left it. Of course. Why had I been so scared? It had been here the whole time. Of course. I picked it up and, with shaking hands, pulled it onto my wrist. It snapped and clutched it. Cutting off circulation, holding me here, keeping me from slipping into whatever it was that was trying to force its way up my throat, only to swallow me whole. It made it hard to breathe, made my throat ache, and pooled tears just below the surface.

I could barely look at myself; my hair twisted and pointed in different ways, my mother's high cheekbones competing with my father's square jawline for attention on my face. I couldn't look. But really, when I looked at myself, I felt it: the fear, the feeling that some event, incipient and urgent, was galloping toward me.

I closed my eyes and swallowed it down. The fear. The sound of the galloping. I ignored the ache it left behind. I reached under the sink and pulled out the gel that sat next to the buzzer I had bought for Dai when he was finally ready to cut his hair. Though I could see through the gel, it looked like plastic, bubbles of plastic trapped in place mid-rise, and it made me wonder for a moment how it would feel to be trapped in a vat of gel. Would I suffocate quickly, or would it be agony? Would it be any more agonizing than my life now?

Make sure you use enough gel. Don't want to take that nappy rat's nest over there. You'll end up dying alone.

A gasping breath escaped my throat. The kind I would have taken rising out of that vat, except I felt it. The thing there in my throat that was rising once again. I took a few short breaths with my eyes squeezed shut. Not yet. Not yet. I breathed until it was back down. Halfway down my throat.

Stuck, but not stinging the back of my throat like acid. I took another forced breath and another until my hands stopped shaking.

I opened the gel, took a sizable portion, and smeared it on the top, sides, and bottom of my hairline. With a fine-toothed comb, I raked through my hair, spreading the gel from my hairline to my ends. I collected my hair in my right hand, pulled it tight, and fastened it into a bun with the band. I looped it three times so it was tight, then a fourth for good measure. I added gel around my hairline in the places that my curls refused to straighten and raked the comb through them so my hairline was consistent and straight. Then I smoothed my hands over my hair once again to finish it off.

Next, I went to my bureau and collected the makeup I would use for the day. I went into the bathroom and spent an hour applying it. A moisturizer to protect my skin from the makeup I was about to use. A primer to cover my pores. Foundation, then compact powder right after to keep it from looking too fake. Eyeshadow and eyeliner for my eyes. Mascara for my eyelashes. Blush to give my face back the color that I'd covered. Concealer to hide anything else I'd missed, and finally lipstick on my lips to accent the added color on my cheeks and to make my lips look bright and plump like a berry.

When I was finished, I went to the closet and pulled out an orange dress with a bright purple lilac printed across half of it. I pulled it on and stood back to look in the mirror. I smiled.

It was fake. It was always fake.

I went down to the kitchen and packed supplies for a couple of meals. Carrots, peas, potatoes, beef stock, and flour for shepherd's pie. Tomato paste, tomato sauce, yellow peppers, spinach, ground beef, lasagna noodles, and some spices. I picked out the pans, pots, and spoons I would need to cook. Then I went to the hall closet and picked out the cleaning supplies I would need. Lastly, I pulled out a few laundry baskets of Dai's clothes, now laundered and folded. When I was done packing, I lugged everything out to my car.

You know you're his maid, right?

It was true. I reasoned it was because I was afraid for him. He had tried to die, and I didn't have any control over whether he did it again, but if I went over once a week and took care of him, he would depend on that. Need that. Until he needed me. Until he needed me more than anyone. Until he needed me more than death.

But really, it was to wear him down. If my hair was straight enough, my cooking good enough, my presence felt enough, perhaps he would love me. Wrap those shoulders around me. Hold me until I could look at myself in the mirror and tell myself I was beautiful. And believe it. I needed only to wait.

ARRIVING AT THE apartment, I parked and took a deep breath. Then I grabbed a few bags of food and lugged them up the stairs. Each metal step groaned, warning me away, but I continued and tried not to imagine some long-legged girl lying half-naked in his bed.

When I got to his front door, I knocked. No answer. I knocked again. The sound of my galloping heart grew louder in my ears. I knew the high-pitched tone was next. My mouth tasted like metal. I pulled my phone out of my pocket and checked the time. It was noon. I tried to keep my hands from shaking.

I heard the high-pitched tone in the distance. I felt sure that if I leaned my ear against the cheap metal door, I would hear his life draining out of him. His shoulders would never fulfill their promise.

I dialed his number and listened to the phone ring on my side. I resumed knocking on the door. The phone went to voicemail. The high-pitched tone was so loud my eyes watered. I reached into my pocket for the key. My hand was reluctant. It took its time pulling out the dreaded harbinger. I had the urge to find a knife and cut off my arm, to run, so I never had to know.

But I heard a groan and a muffled "I'm up." It all fell away. Everything but a tremble that I felt at the bottom of my spine.

I was relieved. I wiped away the moisture that had collected at the corners of my eyes, carefully, so as not to mess up my makeup. I put the key back into my pocket and smoothed the front of my dress. Everything was okay. Yes, of course. I was just being silly. The sound of my racing heart continued in my ears, reminding me of the fear that sat within me, just under my skin.

Dai opened the door of his apartment. "Yes, darling?" He leaned against the doorframe, his arms crossed over his chest, a smirk on his face, and a bleary look in his eyes. His hair was long, greasy, and disheveled. His not-quite-beard was growing in with patches missing. I made a note to bring the buzzer with me next time I came. I didn't answer him. I stood quietly, looking at everything but his face, the bags digging into my fingers as I held them at my sides, waiting for him to give up the smile he had when he was drunk. Over the years, he'd honed this smile to deal with any number of women, including Layla, and especially his mom. I found if I ignored it, he gave it up.

"You go to work today?"

He dropped the smile, rubbed his eyes, yawned, and stepped aside, ignoring my question.

I stepped over the threshold with the bags and set them on the floor of the kitchen. "Dai, you can only borrow money from your mom for so long."

Dai walked over to his bed and fell forward onto it. I shook off the vision of his body falling from that bridge. I held my hands behind my back so he wouldn't see them tremble.

I made three more trips, getting the rest of the food, the cleaning supplies, and then his clean clothes.

I STARTED WITH the lasagna. I made two pots of red sauce so I could make two lasagnas and take one home with me. I would go home, uncover the pan, and cut a slice out for myself. Then I would sit at the table and eat my lasagna with my eyes closed. I would imagine Dai sitting on his bed, eating at the same time as me. Sitting cross-legged with the pan inevitably on his bed next to him. Eating bite after bite, and feeling the love I had for him. Knowing I would always love him.

WHENEVER I COOKED, it took me back to my father. He would sing. His bright tenor would intermingle with the smell of garlic and onion, then wrap itself around me like a warm hug. The songs usually marched to an upbeat tempo. Like he was telling me to go forward with my day, hopeful and optimistic. At night, he'd sing me ballads, reminding me to love with all of my heart. I'd sit at the table and hum along, feeling in the air the love my father had for me.

Sometimes, before breakfast or at night after dinner, I'd sit right in front of my dad's bedroom door and listen to him sing. These songs weren't for me. They had a blue, lilting quality to them. Like Billie or Etta. With my back against his door, I'd belt out the parts of the song that I knew. Songs about lost love and love that could never be. Sometimes, his voice would crack and he would stop singing altogether, like the song was too much for him. I would sing louder when he stopped. Not to drown him out, but to give him back the same love he sang to me when he cooked for me. I didn't understand then why he sang, but I knew he needed me to sing with him.

He never said a word about it. He would finish singing as though he had been singing the whole time by himself, and then he would knock lightly on the other side of his door before opening it.

DAI
2010

THE AIR WHIPPING PAST MY FACE STINGS FAMILIARLY...
I rubbed my cheek, confirming I was awake. Then I dropped my hand so I was laid out like a starfish on my bed. I felt the sweat from the dream on my back. I hummed Layla's song to myself. *Been running, been hiding, far too long.* The tune got muddled and changed. The new tune became warm like the garlic smell swirling in the air. I closed my eyes, and for a second, I could feel my mother's silk hair brushing past my face. I could feel her smiling cheek against mine. My arms remembered being tightly wrapped around my mother's neck. The air, warm and sunny and brushing against my skin. My mother's laughter, music dancing in the air. My laughter, a second away.

I opened my eyes to Mara's melody again. I stood up and walked over to her, needing to touch her. She kept humming, her hips swaying back and forth to a rhythm I wanted desperately to know. I stood behind her, unsure of how to approach her. The bones in her back moved as she stirred. Something in my chest trembled. It felt like if I didn't act, I'd fall away from her, from this, but I didn't know what to do with my hands.

Mara stopped humming. She looked over her shoulder, up at me. I saw a glimpse of her irises: the color of dark honey. There was that silent scream again, though I couldn't tell if it was her or me. The trembling in my chest intensified. My breath became shallow.

Her lips opened up like the camellia buds at my grandfather's home in Japan. Then she smiled up at me, seeming to be waiting—for something. Something I couldn't define and had no idea how to go about figuring out. And *how to reach out to a flower without tearing it to pieces?*

The moment passed and she continued stirring. This time, she was silent. Even the scream was gone. All I could hear was my blood hitting my eardrum.

I tried again to figure out how to touch her, how to sway with her, how to communicate my need for her song. I wanted to tell her *I need your song*—I wanted to come up with a one-liner that'd make her laugh. I raised my hands, but I had no idea how to reach out to her. With my hands raised, I felt as though I would strangle her and she would be lost from me forever, and all that came to mind was one of my earliest memories: *My grandmother is bent down and is scolding me in a yukata, and I look down into my hands, and there are bits of camellia petals bunched in my fists, and I want to put them up to my face to smell them, but I don't smell anything and I want to cry because my Baba is upset.* I hadn't gone near them again.

The trembling feeling in my chest spread to my hands; I put them behind my back. My stomach dropped like I was falling again. I stepped back and backtracked to my bed. Then I sat on my hands until they stopped quavering. I focused on my hands so that the falling feeling would stop.

It didn't, but my hands didn't tremble as much. I watched Mara from the bed. I watched the bones in her back move effortlessly under her skin, and I thought: *Could it be that easy?* Living. And I wanted to reach out to her, but my hands still trembled, and my stomach was still in my mouth.

She started to sing again. A high, sweet soprano. Her hips swayed along. Life was no longer terrifying; it felt like something tolerable, watching her. I wanted to kiss her skin. Thank her bones for showing me how to live. Have her melody in my chest—forever—but my hands still shook, and anyway, how did one broach the subject of keeping someone's song? Of thanking someone's bones? The something trembling in my chest started to shake, and I was falling faster. The wind cut my face as I fell toward the empty battlefield, where I would lie on a grassy hill, in a knight's armor that was too heavy for me to lift.

I turned my body so I'd roll to the edge of my bed, then I swung my legs over so I was sitting up. I got up from the bed, walked over to my freezer, and pulled out a half-bottle of maple bourbon. I pulled off the top and took a drink. It was sweet like syrup, and it burned its way down my throat. I smiled. The burning syrup settled into my chest. It drowned everything else.

I finished off the rest of the bottle, burped, and then placed the empty bottle on the counter. This time, I strode over to Mara. I threw my arms around her and locked them in place. I squeezed her body against mine. I leaned down and kissed her neck. My lips were numb. I could barely feel her skin, but I imagined it was the softest feeling in the world. I whispered in her ear, "Let it be me and you, baby."

I was serious, I swear I was, but she still tensed. She grabbed both of my hands locked in front of her and she split them, and then she spun out of my embrace. All in one quick movement. She looked up into my eyes. The honey had flecks of green. I felt sick. Mara reached up and smoothed my hair back. She put her hands on either side of my face. My heart picked up. *Ohno. Ohno. Ohno.* I could hear it in my ears. Her lips parted. "Don't joke like that." Then she dropped her hands and turned away from me. The warmth left by her hands dissipated quickly. The pleasant burn in my chest left with it. The syrup became bitter like bile and stuck to the back of my throat. I walked over to the sink and spat. A big, green loogie.

Mara turned away.

I went to the freezer and pulled out another bottle of maple bourbon, this one unopened. I opened the bottle and drank until Layla's song became muddled and the room spun. *I tried to reassure you.*

WHAT IS THE key?

Waking from the dream, I saw a badly drawn, life-sized portrait of myself sitting up. I blinked and saw a muddled reflection of myself in the door of my refrigerator. I looked at my phone—it was eleven p.m. I blinked again, hearing a loud buzzing noise. I yawned. The bathroom. I turned to get up to shut off the light, and there she was. Mara. Standing to my side. I felt her heat. It emanated from her, like tamago egg on rice, yet I wasn't sure whether she was real or whether this was another dream. Her face was naked, save for a few drops of water. Her cheeks were flushed. Her hair looked like a cloud made up of tiny ringlets sitting on her shoulders, down her back. I thought, *Is this what she needs from me?* I reached out and brushed some of the curls off her right shoulder. She trembled like a doe or some other frail, beautiful, easily broken thing, and despite this, she stood brave with her white terrycloth towel wrapped around her. A smug smile pulled at the left corner of her mouth. Though the hairs on her arms stood up, pulling the skin with them, reaching for me. Me.

What does she see? I had absolutely no idea why she was above me, exposed. Her fear, the eyes that got bigger by the second, like they were trying to take in as much as possible of this moment and the next and the one after that, seemed—misplaced. I scooted forward on the bed so I was directly in front of her. I took her hands in mine, to touch her. To soothe her.

Mara pulled her right hand from mine and brushed my shoulder as though I had the hair down my back. She tugged my right earlobe as she giggled at her own joke. A quirk I hadn't seen her do before. She lifted my chin slightly, so I was looking up at her. She said, "Let me do this for you," so I put my hands out palms-up in front of her. Between us.

I told her, "Tell me what to do." Mara circled my hands with her own. She placed her right knee on the bed between my legs. Placed my left hand on her thigh so my thumb could run up her inner softness. Soft like down, warm like a smooth, sun-warmed stone at the bottom of a creek bed. And the warmth grew wet the higher she drew my hand. I stood below her, looking up. Her eyes were fully green, and she took my right hand and placed it on her throat. She said, "Don't squeeze; I only like the pressure."

This felt like a test to me. She had always been beside me, never over me, finger pointed like my mom, telling me, *No, like this.* And my thumb was in her space, tracing the outer rim of her, and I was trying not to shake. I didn't want her to know that I was a fraud, then, though before now, it hadn't mattered. I didn't want her to push me away. I didn't want her to be closed to me. I preferred her laughter. I wanted to hear her melody, so I asked, "You trying to heal me with your cunt?" She had heard me talk this way to other girls; we had laughed about these words. Pussy. Cunt. Dick. But instead of a laugh, she kissed me, like that was the answer I was waiting for. When her lips touched mine, they felt like two marshmallows in a fire. Like her camellia lips were melding into mine. And my tongue slipped out to taste her, and I wasn't sure if her mouth would taste like camellias or marshmallows.

It was neither. Her tongue, the soft wet of her mouth, tasted like honeysuckle. My thumb slipped into her space. Her melody came from her chest and was not laughter but warmed me from my toes up. And I swear I was so hard my dick quivered. The rest of me was solid, not even a slight tremor, and I wondered *Will she really heal me?* Her tongue traced the roof of my mouth, and that honeysuckle tickling taste of her tongue made me want to moan. She tasted better than Cutty Sark, and her right palm held my face. Her nails tickled the back of my neck, sent electricity down my spine. She moaned into my mouth. And I thought, *Is this what love is like?*

I laughed, but only for a moment, because my hand was so wet it was slick. I closed my eyes, my forehead leaned on her stomach, because—I wanted to remember this moment. Her beauty was blinding. I didn't want her to see behind my eyes. I was acing this test, or whatever this was, and I didn't want to fuck it up, but there she was, smelling like peppermint. Layla. And there was the gold of her irises. Layla. And all I wanted was for her to turn back around in the rain. Not turn and walk away from me. Leaving me with the smell of fresh bread and a cold chill.

Mara bent down and whispered into my ear, "Is it working?" I heard the words but had forgotten the original question. I could only process her honeysuckle breath in my ear, which was as warm and wet as her healing space, which I needed to enter. I still had a hand rested around her throat. *How could I forget her life in my hands?* Yet she trusted me to give her this moment, so I opened my eyes, looked up at her, and flipped her over next to me.

Over her, I kissed her throat. Right in the space at the base of it. My fingers went inside her, deeper still, and were impossibly wetter. She held on to the towel but started to roll her hips on my fingers. I could feel her heartbeat in my hand. I could feel the vibrations from her moans on my lips.

I moved my hand up from her throat to her hair. Inched my fingers inside of her universe because I wanted to feel all the parts of herself she kept from me. Her head fell back as though she needed air. I pushed my fingers in deeper to keep up. She brought her head back up. Looked me in the eyes as she pulled my boxers down. Like she was waiting for my reaction. Her eyes spoke to me in that moment, in a way I had never seen. They said, *Yes, I need you.* I grabbed her hips to bring them to me, to join her rhythm. She wrapped her legs around my middle and flipped us over. I was inside of her like magic and I was nearly breathless, barely able to catch it.

I was lightheaded, but I would be valiant. Mara sat on my hips, and I sat up. To keep up, to hold on to her. The skin on the palms of my shaking hands craved the feeling of her. Wanted to memorize the curve of her. I held her hips down—squeezed them—to feel the reality of them, like if I didn't, she'd float away, because any second, she might. And it had never occurred to me that her legs might carry her away from me. Mara placed her hands on either side of the bed and brought her lips to mine. This time, the kiss pushed me back slightly, but I fell all the way back anyway, and on the way down, I grabbed Mara, afraid suddenly. I could not fall into oblivion without her.

I unwrapped her. Pulled the terrycloth towel from her body. Her nipples grazed my chest. I reached up and took one in my mouth. Her hips sped up. I held on to them as Mara tightened around me. Any moment I would be flying. I could feel it. Coming for me. I held on to her tighter, wrapped my arms around her. *Can she save me from what is coming for me? Can I stop the scream behind her eyes? Can Layla's ghost be a memory to me?*

I could feel *it*. Pulling me up toward that blue sky. I was flying. And so was Mara, above me; any moment, we would land. I grabbed her hand, interlocked our fingers so we wouldn't be separated when we landed. Her moans turned to hums, turned to my name. *Dai*. She bent over me. Her lips grazed my chin, my lips. She gave me the scent of honeysuckle, and in thanks, I licked the span of her collarbone. Nibbled at the flesh right on the bone.

I looked up at her, near the brink, tasting the salt and soap of her collarbone. Her head was thrown back, her eyes closed. Her belly exposed, taut, vulnerable, like I could reach up and tear into it. I reached up and held her waist as she started to orgasm. She hummed and moaned interchangeably. Her face was placid—I thought, *You look beautiful in death*. Her camellia lips parted, and from them sprung, "Yes," like she had cut herself open to pull out a splinter and all that was left was spilling out of her. I held on for dear life as I followed.

DAICHI
1936

WHEN HIS FAMILY WAS AT CHURCH ONE SUNDAY morning, Mr. Martin confessed, over a tumbler of Punsch, that he did not believe in God. Not truly. He felt God had simply been created for the purpose of order. God had been put at the top of the caste system to make everyone below behave. As long as a person followed the rules set in place, that person would be perceived as being closer to God in the system, meaning the better that person would be perceived in polite society. It was a trick, just like how people in this country believed there were differences between the races on the inside when really, all humans were the same. The delineations between races were fallacies that only mattered to construct the system in which the white man was at the top and everyone else placed in the system based on how similar they looked to the white man. He was just lucky enough to be at the top of this system. He could have just as easily been born at the bottom.

Mr. Martin stared, bleary-eyed, out the wall of windows behind his desk, which overlooked the valley where his workers were hunched, hands reaching out to harvest the cotton or to prune the plants, and above them the Tehachapi Mountains, peaked white, which rose above us all. He said his worst fear was one of us telling the others. Then he laughed to himself, turned, looked up at me, and winked. "But you won't be doing that, eh?"

I WAS HATED by the workers. Many times, I would come to my house and find symbols and words from other languages carved into the porch and walls. I would later learn they were versions of the word "traitor." At the time, this did not faze me. I could not read any of the languages carved onto my home. They were merely pictures and symbols.

My favorite symbols were the Japanese Kanji, as I recognized the patterns from letters that I had found among my father's belongings.

THERE ARE QUITE a few words for "traitor" in Japanese. One version's English pronunciation starts with the word "hang." Hangyakusha.

AROUND THE TIME I was sixteen, I decided I had enough money to move on. I had saved nearly two thousand dollars, which was the largest amount of money I had ever seen. The bills seemed to fill the jar, stuck flat against the sides so I couldn't see inside of it. I did not think of my contract, which Mr. Martin kept in his filing cabinet with the others—only that he liked me. I figured going off by myself was my best chance because there was no one to reveal my plan to Mr. Martin, as I would never speak it. This was my escape. I would free myself, as I had from my father's one-room cage.

All I would have to do was get off the property. I knew when Mr. Martin would be distracted. I decided that I would slip out on Saturday. I wouldn't be missed until the next day.

ON FRIDAY, I walked up to my house and found my door ajar, as though someone were waiting for me. I walked up to the door, and just inside the doorway was a noose, laid carefully on the floor. I could not help but think of my father's body prone on the ground, his hand clutching the earth below, his arm thrown across his face, my shadow casting darkness over him, my own face conveyed onto his. I was shaken to my core.

I did not know whether Mr. Martin knew of my plan to escape, if he knew about my jar hidden under this house, or if another worker was threatening me. I looked out to the fields; everyone was picking cotton, heads down, hands working, working as they always did and would until they fell dead like my father. I looked up to Mr. Martin's house, and all that I saw was a closed white door towering over me, blocking the skyline and the sky itself.

I packed what little I owned, including my jar, and I fled.

AT SIXTEEN, I towered over most men, but I hunched my back and kept my head down as I ran as fast as my legs would take me.

IT WAS NOT enough. I was found crouched in a barn three farms away. Mr. Martin's neighbors were used to runaways.

They did not come out to the barn to see who had hidden there. They did not try to negotiate a price for my freedom. Mr. Martin's men arrived, paid the neighbors, and dragged me away.

As I sat in the back of the car going back to Mr. Martin's house, I realized it did not matter where I ran within this country. I would be as trapped and as alien as I had been in my father's one-room home.

TWO MEN HELD my arms as Mr. Martin hit me in my face until I could no longer see. They led me out to the edge of the camp, beneath the oak. Mr. Martin pulled out the rope I knew had been in his pocket. He tied it into a noose. He strung the noose up in the tree and placed a log below it. He had them help me onto the log and placed the noose around my neck.

Enough of the blood on my face had dried so that I could just make out Mr. Martin's smirking face, but I knew he had no one to take from me, and if he was going to kill me, he would not have brought me back around the other workers. Full of youthful pride and convinced I had beaten him at his game, I spat at his feet, because I thought I had nothing to lose. He stepped back before my spittle could dirty his shoes, and then he motioned behind him without looking away from my eyes.

"Son, sometimes four knocks on a moonless night is all anyone needs to know your weakness."

I blinked. No. There was no way. I had taken every precaution.

One of his lackeys handed him my jar. He opened it and turned it upside down so most of the crumpled bills fell to the ground. I tried not to react. I focused on each breath I could, though my nose was broken and I had to keep my breathing through my mouth as calm as possible, as any careless move would hang me. Mr. Martin unbuttoned his jacket and pulled out a silver flask. He took his time twisting the cap off the top. He took a sip from it, then held it up toward me as though offering it. I shook my head no as much as I could. He was taunting me. He shook the flask toward me again, as though insisting. This time I did nothing. There was nothing for me to do.

Mr. Martin shrugged, squatted down, and poured the liquid in his flask all over my hope for escape from this place. He reached back into his breast pocket and pulled out a matchbox. I begged him then. Between my teeth, so I wouldn't get over-excited and fall off the log. "Please, that's all I have. I won't run again. Please." It had taken me years to collect that money. I hadn't even seen that much money before then. My life was in that jar. He struck the match. We stood on either side of the improvised pyre, watching my hope burn.

After the fire died out, he picked up the jar with a few bills still stuck to the sides, and he placed it under his right armpit. I could not tell how many of the bills were left in the jar, but I understood I had been beaten.

HE LEFT ME for three days. During those three days of starvation out in the sun, I had plenty of time to think of my father's rotting body. Of the living dead stumbling around. Of the many bodies I had brought to Mr. Martin so he could turn them into rot. Of my own body, which would be cut down and thrown in a hole to rot by another body that would have the same treatment one day. Of Mr. Martin's body, which would be placed carefully and cared for, simply because of the color it had been before it was dead.

THE SECOND NIGHT was moonless. I learned to relax the upper part of my body while keeping my legs frozen in place. It allowed me to close my eyes and rest for a few minutes at a time. Then I would wake and move my legs carefully up and down to stretch them. It was hot, which made me thirsty, but I knew I was lucky; if it had been cold, I would have had to control my shivering and try to find a way to stay warm, so I was thankful. I opened my eyes to stretch my legs, and I felt eyes on me. I looked around for Mr. Martin and instead saw the dried-up man who had kissed a noose. On seeing I was awake, he picked up a bucket he had at his feet and walked over to me. He bent down and pulled a cloth dripping with a liquid I could not see in the dark out of it. He brought it to my lips: water. I sucked on the cloth, getting as much water as I could. He repeated the process until I shook my head to show I was done. He patted me on my shoulder, nodded to me as though I had done well, turned, and walked into the dead night.

ON THE THIRD sunrise, Mr. Martin came himself to cut me down. Two men picked me up and carried me to the house Mr. Martin had rented me. They laid me on the floor just inside the door. Mr. Martin crouched down over me and smiled; the blues of his eyes were the color of the California sky. He gave me a choice. I could stay here and continue my contract or go. The noose I had found the day I had tried to leave was still on the floor near the door. I could see it out of the corner of my eye. There was no choice. Mr. Martin had invested a significant amount into me, and he expected his investment to yield what he planned it to.

Mr. Martin grabbed my chin. "Stay?"

I nodded.

He smacked my face good-naturedly, though this time, since I could barely move my jaw, it felt like a punch. "Good," he said. Then he left.

When he closed the door, I saw my jar sitting empty behind the door. He had found a way to take every last dollar out, giving me permission to save my money with the threat that if I didn't behave, he would take it away and leave me with a broken nose and a jar full of air. It didn't matter how much money I saved. I was as free as the money he had taken, as free as the bills he'd watched burn. I could be of use to him, but he could just as easily get rid of me and never think of my rotten corpse again. I wondered how much money Mr. Martin must have to burn money in a depression, how much money he paid his neighbors to return his contract workers—or were they just as concerned with maintaining the system as he was? My mind was tired. My body was exhausted. I could not move. I lay on that floor and I closed my eyes.

I WOKE TO a knock on the door. I turned my head, which was an act in itself. I tried to speak, but all that came out of me was a gasp. My throat was raw and felt sunburned on the inside. Every nerve in my body was on fire. My heartbeat and my chest struggled to rise, barely keeping me alive.

The door swung open. The elderly man who had brought me water came in with a bottle of it and a bowl of broth. He put the supplies next to my body and stood over me. *"Ni hon go ga wakarimasu ka?"*

I shook my head.

He sighed and shook his head sadly. "I will teach you."

MARY
1990

EZ MET MY MOMMA ON A TUESDAY NIGHT. SHE JUST about lost her mind when he took off his Stetson for her, as well. My daddy had been a man of the church, *But men just weren't made like EZ anymore, I was a lucky girl to have found him*, and when he asked her for my hand a month later, she said yes, and so did I.

We married at the Baptist church down by my cousin's house in Georgia, where my parents had married. He waited for me at the altar, still damp and smelling of the creek behind the church. He believed a man was only a man if he was willing to embrace every part of the woman he loved, so before the ceremony, he had been baptized.

MARA
2010

I LAY ON TOP OF DAI. HIS HANDS WERE RESTED CASUALLY on my hips. The air was so humid with the scent of us, my hair was nearly a fro. My curls were so tight my hair didn't even hit my shoulders anymore. The air smelled like coconut curry. And I was hungry for him. I could smell the maple on his breath; I was sure it was the maple liquor from earlier, but I wanted another taste. I nibbled his bottom lip. Kissed the spot I'd bitten. Slipped my tongue between those maple-flavored lips, and it was the best thing I'd ever tasted, and I had no idea if I'd ever feel that good again, lying over him, his head in my hands and him still inside of me. I wanted to replicate the taste of his tongue one day or stay there in that bed for the rest of my life. Then he brought his hands up into my hair. Inched his fingers into my tight curls. And we started again. Slowly. Patiently. His moans rumbled in his chest and he said my name, "Mara," and I was sure I could find a way to make a cake with the sweet maple-syrup taste and the slight burn of the liquor, and then out of nowhere, it bubbled up and out of my core and I was so overwhelmed I couldn't stop it. "I love you."

DAI
2010

I was—queasy. I stopped her. I didn't have a katana, and my wakizashi was useless, stuck in its saya. I wanted her song in my heart, the taste of the salt on her collarbone on my tongue, her swaying hips beneath my fingers, but love? I looked up at her still straddling me and I wondered, *How can you love a generic cartoon landscape, an incomplete thing?* I lifted her off of me; it was wet and sticky like glue. I avoided her eyes and turned over onto my side. I grabbed an old shirt or pair of boxers from the floor next to me. It was dark and I couldn't see, and anyway, I didn't want to remember the details from this part. I cleaned myself up and tossed the garment to her. Then I rolled over, afraid to meet her honey eyes and acknowledge that this was anything more than a confusing dream.

DAICHI
1942

ITO-SENSEI WAS A TEACHER AT THE LOCAL ENGLISH-language school. I could not go to it during the day like the other Japanese children, but he would come to my home at night, after his time in the fields was done and after he finished his lessons at the school, and he would teach me how to speak and write Japanese. I was sixteen and only knew a handful of words, most of which were either songs my father had sung or the prayers he'd spoken at night when he'd thought I had been asleep. Many days, Ito-sensei would get frustrated and go back to his cot on the edge of town after only a few minutes. After a few weeks, I gave him my bed and slept on a pallet on the floor.

IN THE SPRING when I was twenty-two, Mr. Martin called all of the workers together on a Monday morning, but instead of his usual Monday-morning business, he stood on a small platform and told us the "Japs" had bombed America, and, as a result, the government would no longer allow those of us among his workers who were unfortunate enough to be born as such to work freely, as we had before. We would have to sell all of our belongings, save what could fit into two suitcases.

We would then have to go to an assembly center nearby until the government decided what to do with us.

He told the owners of the homes, mine included, that he would pay them a fair price for their houses. If they left without signing over the houses, he could not promise they would be able to get them back. The families each sent a member forward to sign the houses over to Mr. Martin, and he gave them each a check right then for two months' wages.

We had a week to handle the rest of our affairs and then would need to pack up and go. Though I was Mr. Martin's confidante, had a house to myself, and was paid more than everyone else, I stood with the rest of the so-called "Japs," knowing I would be leaving as well.

IN MARCH OF 1942, fifteen of us gathered together early on a Sunday morning to go to the assembly center. We were to walk, as there was no transportation given. We were told to go to an abandoned diamond mine twenty miles away. All of us—the elderly, the children, the men, and the women—headed out along the highway with the clothes on our backs and two suitcases for each person. Many parents put bedclothes and extra supplies for the family in a second suitcase for the children, as we were not sure what we would find at our destination.

I WALKED WITH Ito-sensei, having him lean on my arm as he needed. He had started to only speak to me in Japanese. I could converse fluently but still struggled to write and understand Kanji. As we walked, Ito-sensei told me about growing up in Tokyo. About how there were only people who looked like us, and how there were so many that there was only room for the people to live in small apartments in buildings around the city. But he said he still missed it and wished he could go back before he died.

I thought of the dreams I'd used to have when I'd kept my money stuffed in my pillowcase. It had been quite some time ago. I missed the weightlessness of dreaming like a child. But I was thankful I was no longer alone. I asked Ito-sensei why he had come to me on that second night. Ito-sensei cleared his throat and was quiet. He did not speak for a while, and I thought he was not going to answer at all. Then he did.

"We are not meant to be alone." He spoke as though he was talking about the human condition, but he looked ahead as though he was speaking to the exhausted men, women, and children walking in front of us.

My jar held a little over three thousand dollars in cash that was balled up and crammed in, and it was in the bag that held my few belongings on my back. Though I did not think having this money would change anything, I could not part with it. The balled-up bills seemed to hold a promise of freedom, if not now, then one day. I could not let this hope go.

It took us most of the day to get to the meeting place, as half of us were elderly or children. When we did arrive, there was no one waiting for us. We sat down, and those who had brought food shared so we could all keep up our strength. When the sun went down, those of us who were strong enough built shelters out of the bedding we had brought and wood we found near the mine. It was cold that night; many of us put on the extra clothes we had packed so that we wore most of what we had brought with us.

THAT NIGHT, I waited until everyone seemed to be asleep, including Ito-sensei, who slept in a shelter I'd made for the two of us on a makeshift pallet of my bedding. I walked into the woods about a half-mile from the camp, broke a thick branch down from one of the trees, and dug a hole as best as I could. Then I placed my jar inside the hole and covered it with the dirt I had removed.

I walked back toward the mine and found as many large stones as I could and piled them over the fresh hole I had made. I hoped anyone who stumbled over it would assume it was an unmarked grave.

ON THE SECOND day, we rationed what little food we had left and gave the bigger portions to the children and the elderly so that they could keep their strength up. We continued to wait.

ON THE THIRD day, they arrived in trucks. They jumped out of the backs with bayonets pointed. We raised our hands, unsure of what we had done while waiting to warrant this. The elders had to get up on their own. The children did their best to do as their parents did.

They herded us into the backs of the trucks and took us to a passenger train, then loaded us into a boxcar with hundreds of other Japanese. We rode for two more days. There was no more food.

I dreamt of my jar, buried in an unmarked grave next to that abandoned diamond mine. I wondered if I would live long enough to dig it back up.

WE ARRIVED AT our destination: a large concrete building surrounded by barbed-wire fences and armed guards and hundreds of miles of sand.

Inside of the concrete building, we lived as we had been living while we had waited for the soldiers to arrive: in makeshift communal housing. They had created small sections for each family, but the walls were made of tar paper and we had no privacy.

I HAD ONLY seen the makeshift housing at Mr. Martin's farm while cutting the nooses down from his hanging tree, but seeing the shelters the U.S. government put us in, I saw that Mr. Martin was not alone in his treatment of us. At least all of Mr. Martin's workers had an equal chance at the noose. To America, we were the "yellow peril," all spies secretly scheming to bring down the American government for Japan. We were not to be trusted by Mr. Martin, his neighbors, or the guards who walked around with automatic weapons and bayonets, protecting this country from children and the elderly.

THEY ASKED ME if I swore allegiance to this country. Then they asked if I would fight for this country. The noose laid on the floor of the stolen house I had been given came to mind. It did not matter who'd laid that noose down; ultimately, I had no choice. I nodded. Yes, yes.

They told me I could have a job while I waited.

I nodded yes.

MARY
1990

I WAS PREGNANT AND WE WERE MOVING TO A TINY two-bedroom house in front of a field in Suffolk. EZ told me he wanted to grow an apple orchard. I laughed, thinking it was a joke, and I told him that, as well. I said, "I thought you were a cowboy." He lifted his hat and set it back on his head, but farther back than before. There was no mistaking the passion in his eyes.

"No, ma'am, I'm a gardener."

I asked, "Doesn't it take a few years for the trees to get big enough to bear fruit?"

He smiled. "I waited for you, love."

I sighed. Of course: more waiting.

MARA
2010

I GRABBED THE PAIR OF DIRTY BOXERS HE THREW AT ME. They had Santa heads all in a row, winking suggestively. I wiped my eyes with my free hand, quick, before he could see—the shaking hand, the moisture collected in my eyes—and then I looked over at him, and his shoulders stood between us. Stolid and square. A wall between us, too sharp to get over.

The fabric of the boxers suddenly felt like it was covered in a microscopic wriggling sickness. Like the sickness was multiplying and wriggling up my hand and soon to be up my arm. I threw the boxers away from me, and they flew lamely and landed between us. His back, still facing me, didn't even twitch. To my right was the plaster wall, pockmarked and dingy. I couldn't breathe. I scooted off the bed and nearly ran to the bag I'd left near the oven with my change of clothes. I pulled my shirt on over my head and didn't turn it around when I felt the tag scratching the bottom of my throat. I pulled on my jeans with no underwear. The denim rubbed me, and I flinched, but I didn't have time to correct the matter. I pulled my hair back, fast, so it sat as a messy bun on top of my head, no time for gel or a comb. I didn't bother with socks, just slipped my feet into my sneakers, ignored the little bit of grit and dirt I felt between my toes as best as I could, grabbed my bag, and nearly sprinted to the door.

It was only in the car that I felt what he had thrown into me like I was a meaningless target, a warm temporary holding place. They slid from between my legs to make a globular mess in my jeans. A viscous blob wriggling its way out of me, slow. I tried not to think of them swimming inside me. I tried not to cry. I tried not to feel like those boxers he used to keep his balls warm, to keep shit from staining his jeans, then threw over his shoulder when he was done.

DAI
2010

I CLOSED MY EYES AS SHE DRESSED.

When I heard the click of the door opening, I opened my eyes for a second in the dark. Mara looked back at me. Her big round honey eyes reminded me of a fawn in love, of the weight of that armor, keeping me on that hill, impotent and unable to get up. The scream sounded like a ringing this time. Like it was coming from a long tunnel. I shut my eyes again. I squeezed them shut, trying to keep her eyes, that scream, out of my head.

THERE IS A *laugh. I open my eyes. Below me and in the distance stands a rigid-backed man with a scowl on his face, and his daishō is kinetic in his left hand. He gives directions to five young men in forest-green military garb operating a Type 38 75mm field gun. I have no doubt he will pull out his wakizashi and katana without hesitation . . .*

I stumbled out into the night. It was humid outside; the air was so wet I couldn't tell if I was sweating. I walked down the sidewalk to nowhere, trying to forget the green flecks in Mara's eyes. That scream. Mara's legs bringing her to me no matter what. My stomach churned. The gold irises of Layla's eyes superimposed themselves around the green flecks, and my stomach tightened up. It felt like my body was preparing to empty itself of her.

A laugh pulled me out of myself. It rang and echoed down the street. I looked behind me, and five streetlights back, I saw a group of white people. By this, I mean they were varying shades of white, male and female, but their clothes were white, too. Like they had just come from a store that only sold clothes in varying shades of white: jeans, long flowing skirts, short skirts, shorts, T-shirts, and dresses. The only bits of color were on their heads and feet. Each had short hair colored blue. On their feet: brown sandals. They were all exactly the same, except for the figure standing in the middle of their strange white semicircle. She had orange hair and wore no shoes at all.

She wore shorts, the figure. They were tiny and blue. Her long cream-colored legs were unashamed and calling to me. She wore a white tank top. Her hair was the color of a newly started fire. And in the second I saw her, she glanced up at me. So quick I was sure I had imagined it. Because then she was laughing and falling backward as though it were as natural as breathing. A person standing in the group around her bent down on his knee and put both hands out to catch her. She fell back toward his outstretched arms, her arms thrown up in the air as though she were diving backward into space. A girl behind the guy put her hands out to catch the head covered in fire. The rest of the group looked at her as though their lives depended on this firestarter's pleasure. Her lips were the color of strawberries.

I turned around and walked toward her.

The guy set the firestarter back on her feet. Then, as though she had expected all of this and had planned accordingly, she looked right at me as her bare feet touched the ground once again. She watched me walk toward her. Her creamy legs waited until I was within a few feet of her, and only then did they come toward me.

The group followed, in unison, as though they were merely personified extensions of the firestarter. When she stopped in front of me, they stopped, as well.

She grabbed my hands as though we were long-lost lovers, finally reunited. She kissed the palm of each of my hands. Then she looked up into my eyes with a playful grin on her face. She stood on her toes, and I thought she was gonna kiss me, but she wrapped her arms around my neck and whispered in my ear, "Good tidings, Beloved. What can I do for you tonight?"

I was confused by her language, and her nipples under the thin material of her white tank top sent thrills through my chest. I cleared my throat and put my hands behind my back, afraid this was some kind of trap.

She pulled back from the hug, her arms still around my neck. Her strawberry lips inches from mine. She looked into my eyes. Into them, as though she was looking for something. Her eyes were big and green. Her nipples were definitely gonna be pink. She smiled at me then, a quick movement with the left side of her mouth, as though she had found what she was looking for or knew what I was thinking.

I cleared my throat and scratched my head. She grabbed my upper arms and pulled me forward, her pelvis just barely brushing mine. "Beloved, there is nothing to fear. Come, join us tonight." Then she stood on her tiptoes, pecked me on the cheek, turned, and walked away. As she turned away, I saw Layla's strawberry-blond hair soaked by rain, turning away from me. I saw Mara's pleading honey eyes in the dark. *What will you do when you are alone?*

As the firestarter turned away, she reached up to the bottom of her tiny blue shorts and pulled them down. Without hesitation, they slid right back up, revealing the bottom of her cream-colored cheeks. Then, there was the tattoo. Right in the middle of the back of her left thigh was a broadsword with a rose on the hilt and a vine, covered in thorns, rising from it and wrapping around the blade, and though I knew it was simply a picture, I wondered if it would prick me when I touched it. I wanted to reach out and brush it. I wanted to run my hands through her hair, have it burn my hands to ashes.

Hands pushed me forward, and a voice in my ear said, "Her name is Kit." A hand slipped into mine, and I didn't look because it didn't matter. All that mattered was her newly kindled hair and her name.

I stepped forward. It was half a beat before Kit did, a full beat before her extensions followed. Then there it was again. The scream. The scream inside of me. Starting in the middle of my forehead, spreading. Taking over. Could they hear it?

She stopped. Kit. She stopped, and, without looking at me or at anyone, she reached up to the back of her shorts and pulled them down. They slid back up, and then she walked forward. The group followed. Another step. The group followed. Then she stopped once again and pulled the bottom of her shorts down, and they slid back up. Over and over—the pattern was simple. The scream faded as I watched my north star, her tattoo, always guiding me forward to the rhythm she walked. Soon, I was walking in time with everyone else.

As we walked, Kit made a sign with her hand and then pointed up. We followed suit. Up above, I saw all of the stars seemingly scattered, but really placed specifically into patterns that made up pictures and stories. I did not need to know what sign she made to understand this message. I knew all of our hearts beat to the same rhythm: Kit's. Our goddess. She stepped forward and we followed again. As she walked, her newly kindled hair shook, and my heart trembled offbeat.

KIT STOPPED IN the parking lot of a warehouse. The group stopped as well. Kit made a motion with her left hand at her hip. At this movement, the ground shook as though the earth itself were part of her, too. There was a jostling. Everyone fell into place around Kit. I was pushed to one end of the semicircle.

Kit stood in her place, in front of the semicircle, waiting. She held an orange pill bottle in her left hand and a bottle of Wild Turkey in her right. These seemed to appear in her hands as though by her force of will. Once everyone was settled, Kit placed the bottle of Wild Turkey on the ground. She opened the pill bottle, walked up, and slipped a tablet into each of her followers' mouths, then handed them the bottle of Wild Turkey. There were twelve of them, I realized. Twelve disciples that trusted her absolutely. Each of them closed their eyes and opened their mouth for her. After she placed the tablet on their tongue, each person took a swig from the bottle without hesitation. I couldn't help wondering if this was her love she gave them. Pills and bourbon to the blood of her blood, the flesh of her flesh, her children, the extensions of herself.

When she got to me, she took the tablet out of the bottle and placed it on her own tongue. Then she put her arms around my neck. Her green eyes looked into me. I couldn't look away. Her strawberry lips parted as they came toward me. The small white tablet sat on her tongue, dissolving. Then she reached up with two fingers in the shape of a "V" and closed my eyes. I could feel the ground beneath my feet, pounding, pounding. It had never stopped moving. Then, the kiss. It was bitter. Her strawberry lips tasted like bourbon. Her tongue flicked the inside of my left cheek. She bit my bottom lip. My lips went numb, and a spark of electricity ran from my tongue to the bottom of my heels. Kit pulled back from the kiss; I was breathless and lightheaded. I opened my eyes. The bottle of Wild Turkey appeared, almost emptied, in front of my face. I drank the rest of it. Someone patted me on my back. "Come, brother."

Gunfire goes off around me. The world shakes under my feet.

I stumbled into the warehouse. A warzone of lights and pounding music. My spine tingled. I looked around me, and there were people of all varying shades and shapes all dressed in white. Bodies gyrated as though possessed. Sweat streamed down faces.

Then, Kit. She danced by herself. Everyone gave her room, even in that warzone. She threw her hands in the air as though celebrating. She moved her hips front to back, side to side, as though she were a drunken snake. Her eyes were closed. A look of sweet abandon was painted on her face. I felt there was something just below that smile, but at that moment, it didn't matter. There were colors raining down from the sky. Blues and yellows. Oranges and pinks. I raised my arms to the ceiling because I could feel it, too. The absolute futility of fear.

My legs moved apart from me. The tingle in my spine spread, and I felt as though I was made up of little bugs all working together as one consciousness. Me. Was this what Kit felt like? Had I become a god, as well? I closed my eyes. I felt the heat within me, burning hotter and hotter. I felt the sweat pouring down my face, hot but immaterial.

There was a cool respite. I opened my eyes, and rain fell from the ceiling. I twirled around in it, my palms up. I opened my mouth and took in the baptismal rain. White-clothed warriors started to take off their fear. I joined the warriors, stripping off every last stitch. When I was naked, I felt as though I could shake off my skin next. The warehouse door slid open with a bang like thunder. Then we ran through the industrial streets, reborn as deer.

. . . IN THE MIDDLE of a battlefield . . .

Deer are we.

Running and jumping. Galloping are we.

The moon our compass. The stars our map.

We run across it.

Hooves staccato.

We glance at each other. Buck our heads, playful.

We run and jump over curbs, around parked cars. We dance and snort and play.

Our leader is glorious. An impossible whirlwind of orange flies behind her. Her eyes are green and shine brighter than our compass.

We follow her into a forest, between trees. Through thickets. Sweat gleams on her body and it is beautiful.

I break from the we. Run alongside her graceful nudity.

I have made myself human to run alongside the goddess. She smiles and twirls. I follow, turning in the moonlight, hoping to be half as graceful as she.

Before I have finished turning, she has disappeared into the distance, our leader, galloping and prancing, guiding us across the map, showing us what it looks like to be beautiful.

And I, a deer once again, join the herd.

. . . WITH NO WEAPON to hold on to . . .

I opened my eyes. Above me, I saw one of the sprinkler heads on the ceiling that had provided me with much-needed respite the previous night. It seemed to stare down at me, mute and immobile. A person with hair cut boy-short and colored blue appeared above me. The person wore a generic white shirt and bright orange shorts, and it took me a second to recognize whether the person was male or female. Which may have been the point of the hair. She handed me a water bottle. I took it before she got annoyed holding it out to me. Her left arm extended, revealing a vine covered in thorns wrapped around her shoulder, down her upper arm and forearm, and fastened with a rose right at the pressure point on the underside of her wrist. After I took the water bottle, she bowed her head and said, "Peace be with you," and then she turned and offered the person next to me a bottle of water, as well. I stood as naked as all of the bodies strewn around me. Dried rainbow puddles decorated the concrete floor. Another person with short blue hair handed me a T-shirt and a pair of shorts. I thought he was the same person as before, but, looking up, I could see the girl still offering bottles of water and bowing her head in the distance, "Peace be with you" following the bow shortly after. The man also had a rose vine tattooed on his left arm.

I felt a pang in my bladder. I opened a small door next to the garage-style door that had been opened last night. The sun was bright. I shaded my eyes and stumbled out back behind the warehouse. I pissed on the wall, leaning on it for support.

When I walked back around the warehouse, most of the bodies were up and wandering around in generic white T-shirts and bright orange shorts. The bodies started to form lines. The smell of bacon and eggs drifted through the room.

Bodies walked around with plates that had steam wafting from them. The bodies started to sit in large concentric circles. They ate silently.

I stood at the back of the line. When it was my turn, a girl with shorn blue hair and a big smile asked me if I wanted a banana with my breakfast. I tried to think of a joke. I couldn't, so I nodded yes. She handed me a paper plate with a banana sitting on the rim. I saw the rose vine tattooed and spiraling up from her right forearm, the tell-tale rose blooming red on her wrist. I looked back up at her face, and her smile grew brighter.

"Brother, you will understand when the time comes."

I smiled wide. "A sex cult, then?"

The smile got bigger, but she didn't laugh. I took the bowl from her and found a place at the back of the circles to sit.

Kit was nowhere to be found.

After breakfast had been eaten, everyone dispersed. I stood in a corner and waited until everyone but the twelve disciples who had passed out supplies had left.

The girl with the smile looked up at me. I approached her and asked if Judas needed help betraying Jesus. This made her laugh. She smiled bigger than she had before, then turned to the boy next to her and signed to him. She did it at her hip, as Kit had done. If I hadn't been so close, I would have missed it. She signed quickly, as though she was signing a secret. The boy she signed to also had shorn blue hair and a vine spiraling up and around his left arm. I recognized him as the one who had knelt to catch Kit when she'd fallen into space. He signed back to the girl. Then the girl turned and nodded at me.

"Sure, you can help, Beloved."

AFTER WE FINISHED, the disciples piled into a beaten-up van and drove away. I waved, missing the feeling of running through the streets with my herd.

. . . I LOOK UP to the sky above me.

Once a year, my mother would buy me a new suit. We'd go to my father's tailor, and the suit would be custom fitted. Then I would go to my mother's hair salon and get my hair cut.

My mom would wake me at 11:30 p.m. on Christmas Eve. My custom-fitted suit, my tie, and my dress shoes would be laid neatly at the foot of my bed. I'd put on everything but the tie, which my mom would tie herself, then give a quick tug. Then she'd lean down, kiss my forehead, put her hand out to me, and say, "Come, little one: it's time."

In the car, we'd sing songs, some in English, some in Japanese, and when my dad could remember the words his grandparents had taught him long ago, in German, too. As we sang, I'd look up into the sky, searching for the constellations my dad would point out to me with his telescope, which I pretended I could see so as not to disappoint him.

When we arrived at the Catholic church down the street from our house, a man waited at the door for us to approach. He would open the door with a big smile and crouch down to my level to give me a high five. As a kid, I'd thought the man lived in the church and came out once a year to open the door for our family.

Inevitably, I'd fall asleep during the Mass, and my dad would lay me on the bench between him and my mother and cover me with his suit jacket. He would be seated by my head, my mother at my feet.

After Mass, my dad would pick me up and carry me to the car. I'd always wake up in his arms, but I would keep my eyes shut so he wouldn't put me down. I would close my eyes lightly, trying not to move them enough to alert my mom. My chest would feel warm. Like my dad was not just carrying me but hugging me. He'd fasten me into my seat. Then my mother would start to sing in Japanese. She was the only one who sang on the way home. The warmth from my father carrying me would not dissipate. It would seem to spread through my body as my mother filled the car with her songs, and though I could not understand the words, it didn't matter. My mother's melody told me secrets. I needed only to listen long enough.

If she stopped singing, I would call out, "Mama, again," and she would. Even after my father had laid me in bed early on Christmas morning, I'd hear her songs in my dreams.

Walking home after meeting my fellow warriors, after meeting my goddess, my chest felt warm like driving home after Christmas Mass.

My right hand closes, expecting the metal hilt of my broadsword, but instead, it clasps empty air.

As I climbed up the metal stairs to my apartment, my chest grew cooler. By the time I stood in front of my door, there was no warmth left. I opened the door. The smell of garlic and pasta sauce hit me. I tried to sigh away the queasiness, thinking of the green flecks in Mara's honey-colored "I love you" eyes, which I felt I had seen a lifetime ago, but the flecks stuck to the wall of my stomach and collected at the back of my throat. And despite this, my chest ached for her food. I walked over to the fridge and pulled out the glass pan she had left me. I pulled out a clean fork, plunked down on my bed, and started to eat, mouthful after mouthful, until I couldn't eat any more. Then I fell back and slept.

ON MONDAY, I woke. I rolled out of bed. I got a garbage bag from under the sink. I put any half-eaten or rotten food in the bag. I collected plates and cups and put them in the sink. Then I pulled my sheet and blanket off of my bed and put them in another bag. I pulled shirts and boxers from under my bed. Then I vacuumed the floor using the handheld cordless Mara had left.

I went into the bathroom and pulled a buzzer my mother had gotten me when I'd moved in from under the sink. I shaved the stubble off of my face. I brought the buzzer to my hairline and decided against it. I tried to picture my hair cut short and dyed blue. I thought, *I'd rather jump off of a bridge.*

I combed my hands through my hair, and the memory of Mara's hands running through it made the bottom of my spine tremble. I shivered. It was violent, and I missed her. At that moment, my hands wanted to reach out to her soft, swaying hips. I shook away the memory, stripped down, and stepped into the shower.

When I was done with my shower, I stepped out and went into my room. Lying splayed, naked, arms behind her head, was Kit. Her whole mouth pulled up into a smile as though she had imagined this moment over and over in her mind and it was finally coming to pass.

When I did not move, Kit sat up on her haunches, grabbed my hands, and pulled me down. She nipped my neck and made noises like an animal.

I was not sure what sounds a buck made, so I stayed silent.

She reached between my legs, but her cool hands and her animal noises scared me, and I couldn't get an erection. She looked up at me with those wild eyes. Then she lowered herself down the length of my body until her butt was high in the air and her strawberry lips were right above me. I felt at that moment that Kit would give me great pleasure or great pain. Pleasure or pain. I breathed in slow motion, looking into her eyes. She curled her nose as though she was about to snarl at me. Tear me to pieces. A growl came from my chest and flew from my mouth. Kit smiled and lowered her mouth onto me.

WHEN I FINISHED, Kit crept up from her downward-dog position so that she was on all four limbs above me. She kissed me. It was thick and salty. I tried to move away, but Kit held my chin down. Then she sat on her haunches, looking at me, waiting. My throat felt thick, I was sick to my stomach, and I was not sure what she was waiting for.

The door opened. Mara stood looking at us, for a moment. Then she stepped out and closed the door.

DAICHI
1942-1945

TIME IN THE CAMP RAN SIMILARLY TO THE TIME I'D lived with Mr. Martin. I did as I was told. I was employed as a sanitation worker. They paid me four and a half cents an hour. I would buy supplies for Ito-sensei and me at the store they'd set up for us, when or if they had supplies in stock.

WE DID WHAT we could to keep our tar-paper prison clean, but there were too many of us and too little space. Many of us became sick with a rattling bloody cough that brought fever and turned the person into a skeleton.

I made sure Ito-sensei did not have to contaminate himself looking for resources. I helped him get up and get dressed. I made sure he had food to eat and got to the bathroom in the middle of the night as he needed. I saved my money to buy him books so he would have something to do while we waited.

MANY YEARS LATER, when I inquired about Ito-sensei, I would be told he'd died on his cot in the next camp they'd sent him to. They did not tell me what had happened to his body, after, but I imagined it was dragged outside the camp and buried in an unmarked grave in the middle of the desert, like my jar of money but worth less.

A YEAR AFTER arriving at the camp, I was asked to join the all-"Jap" regiment. The guard who asked me smiled wide as he said "all-'Jap,'" like it was a joke. His eyes were as blue as Mr. Martin's, the California sky, and what I imagined Uncle Sam's eyes looked like in the minds of so-called true Americans. I answered the questionnaire anyway.

OUR PLATOON WAS sent to Italy first. Though we were all Japanese, our commanding officer was white. Lieutenant Watson was competent, and he was kind, but he did not have time to speak to us or to learn our names, so he designated one of us to act as a go-between.

Ueno Daichi was a good-natured man. He was quick-thinking and fluent in both Japanese and English. He could joke with the rest of us but knew when and how to get the group to quiet down so that we could listen to Lieutenant Watson. If we had a problem with the directions Watson gave us, Ueno Daichi knew how to appeal to him to get him to change his mind while making him think it was his decision. We knew we could depend on Ueno Daichi. Throughout Italy, we lost very few men. Rumors spread that we could hold our own against the enemy.

THINGS CHANGED WHEN we marched into Germany. Our squad's mission would be simple. We had gotten word that the major factories were closing up shop and cleaning out their inventory as fast as they could. Our job was to go and confirm entrances and exits, the number of guards, and the major weapons outside the buildings and to prevent anyone from leaving. We were all excited. We joked and laughed. We were restless; many of us stopped sleeping. It was the end of the second Great War, and we would be able to go back to America having proven we were heroes and not the enemy our faces made us out to be. All we had to do was this last operation, and we would get our papers.

Then we arrived. We looked out from a distance to the large concrete building and thought, *Are we back in America?* The inventory they had sent us to free was bodies. People that were, like us, gathered from their homes and held behind concrete walls surrounded by barbed wire. And now they were killing them. There was no mistaking the black smoke rising from the chimneys on the building and the smell of burning flesh in the air. There was no mistaking the piles of bodies stacked and waiting to be burned. This was the next step. We had come to Germany to free a people enslaved, like us, only to return home to America and await our fate in the camps.

I WAS SOBER that night, though I drank whiskey and celebrated the end of the war with everyone else. We all knew what everyone was thinking, though none of us would say it: we all knew there was still a job to be done. We were split into two squads. One squad would go out into the forest and create a distraction, and the other squad would run around the building—look at and record the layout of it. Since our regiment as a whole had been established as a support for the *real* Americans, we were only here to collect information.

In the morning, Lieutenant Watson separated us into the two fireteams. As always, the men were ready. They cleaned their weapons and packed their supplies. They joked: we would make our regiment famous, the most decorated in history. They joked: we would have legends about us. America would finally learn yellow doesn't crack under pressure.

I laughed with everyone to show my support, but I was glad to be on the team going into the woods. I did not want to put myself in danger any more than I already had. I did not want to risk being thrown into the German camp myself. I did not want to die for a country that would leave my body to rot.

Before we all packed up to go to our separate duties, Ueno Daichi stopped me and put a folded piece of paper into my hand. It was folded so many times I thought it was a piece of carved wood. He told me to unfold it six times and to deliver the letter to his wife, whose address would be written there. She was to unfold it the rest of the way to get the letter he'd written for her.

I nodded.

He nodded in return and then slapped me on the back in a companionable way, bowed, and walked away. He was more American than I and more Japanese than I, yet I knew in that moment that he would die. His body would fall and no one would come to claim it.

MY TEAM WAITED until nightfall. We had the Divine Twins Saito, Kobayashi, Nakamura, and me. The Divine Twins were not actually related to each other, but they shared a last name and an intuition for each other so strong that we wondered whether they were actually divine twins. Riku Saito was our forward observer. He traveled light: binoculars and his .30-caliber Browning. He had the steadiest hand, was the best and quickest at cleaning his weapon, and was the best with the map. We figured if we were in trouble, he would be our best bet and therefore should see the enemy coming first. Haru Saito set the range. Many times, he seemed to know exactly where we needed to be positioned even before Riku could run back and tell us.

Nakamura and I loaded the shells. Nakamura was the middle child of three and had worked as a librarian before being forced into the camps like the rest of us. He was often in a bad mood but was a good team player. I would load while Nakamura stood watch with his M1 Garand and a scowl on his face, and I'd confirm where to fire, then fire. We'd switch and I'd keep watch. Kobayashi would sleep with his Thompson on his chest and his legs propped up on his mule's behind. We'd poke fun at him, but he always seemed to be alert the moment Riku told us we had to move.

We used high explosive rounds and shot above the compound to confuse the guards. They came running outside to see what was happening, and they either got hit with an explosive round or Riku got them with his Browning. Then we moved to another part of the forest and Riku gave us the new coordinates. He killed twelve guards, and we got the rest. We killed thirty guards in total. We lost no men.

EARLY THE NEXT morning, everyone met at the agreed-upon safe zone in the forest. My team's mission was a success, and we had lost no one. On Ueno Daichi's team, only Lieutenant Watson and one other teammate, Sora, had survived. We retreated farther back and waited. By that night, the battalion sent to save the camp arrived with tanks, machine guns, and a howitzer. They took the camp in a matter of hours.

Many of us joined the battalion in freeing those in the camp. I did not. I could not find a reason to put my life at risk any more than I already had. I had done the job I had signed on to do. I was still alive. I was done.

MARY
1991-1995

WHILE WE WAITED, MY COWBOY HUSBAND WORKED as a short-order cook at three diners. EZ would come home around midnight with leftovers from his last job of the day and pass out until four a.m. Then he'd get up and sit at the table while I made him breakfast. He'd tease me, saying my face was too serious for no reason. I'd exaggerate the face and he'd kiss me on the side of my neck. "Your face will get stuck like that, wife."

Our daughter Mara, whom we called Little Ma, teethed, lost her baby teeth, got chicken pox, recovered, and started singing in the kids' choir at church.

My momma sold her house, moved down to Georgia, moved back up to Virginia, and shared a room with Little Ma, then moved to a retirement home because she thought our tiny two-bedroom was *a bit tight*.

MARA
2010

I WALKED IN. AND THERE WAS MY FEAR: A PALE, LONG-
legged girl sat on her knees, naked, next to Dai, her hands
resting calm on her thighs. Calm even as I opened the
door and her green eyes raised to meet mine. She smiled at
me, welcomed me into this space she'd made her own for the
time being. The space was hers.

Embarrassed, I stepped out, like I'd accidentally walked into
the wrong apartment. I even said, "I'm sorry," like it'd been my
mistake. My bad. After closing the door, I wanted to spit. Who
was she to take what was mine? Those shoulders did not belong
to her. It was my food in his belly, my love. It was my hips he
was supposed to have naked in his bed, my mouth gleaming
and pink from his body. No, I would not let her take what was
mine. I stepped back inside the apartment and walked with
purpose toward the bed. Stood my ground at the foot, offered
her hospitality by my hand. Food. Drink. "What can I bring
you?" It was my hospitality to offer because he was under *my*
care. Not under her nonchalant care, as she sat next to his body
like it did not matter whether either of us was there.

She did not respond to my offer of food or drink; she
turned her head, looking at me as though she were a curious animal figuring out an even stranger animal. Then she
stood. Naked, her breasts barely moved—they hung high,

pink, and unconcerned. She strode toward me, and I feared at that moment that she was the harbinger of my death, or his. She walked toward me like she could move unbothered even by the uneven terrain of the tousled bed; her hands were raised, palms up and to the side like the Virgin Mary. This being—she—strode toward me until she reached the foot of the bed. Then she hopped off and landed in front of me. She reached out for my hands. I threw them behind my back and held them, tried to take a step back, but those green eyes held me in place.

She smirked with the left side of her mouth. She smirked and then dropped her hands, turned, picked up her shirt off the floor, and snapped it in the air like she was about to hang it on a line to dry. Then she slipped it over her head, picked up and put on her tiny blue shorts, no panties, and slipped her feet into the leather flip-flops by the door. She turned to me, not Dai, kissed her hand, and blew it to me. Like I was her lover. She raised a hand and waved, again just to me, then turned, opened the door, walked out, and closed it. No hesitation. She didn't look back.

I was not ready to look at Dai after the door closed. My hands fidgeted and wrung around each other; I felt the need to crack my knuckles but was afraid of what would happen if I introduced sound into the air. I couldn't meet his eyes. And he didn't say a word. Didn't look my way. He fell back onto his pillow, pulled the sheet over himself, and threw his arm over his eyes, indifferent. I looked to my right and saw black garbage bags slouched on the wall next to me. I peeked inside one of the bags and saw clothes. I looked around the room and saw there were no clothes on the floor. I gave a grateful look to the bags. I grabbed as many as I could carry and took them outside to my car so I could wash them and bring them back next week on my day off.

At least he tried. You'd be a bitch not to forgive him.

My hands shook, and when I got to my car, I had to drop everything and take a series of breaths so I could hold my car keys long enough to press the button on the fob to open the door.

When I went back into the apartment, Dai was dressed in jogging pants and a hoodie. He looked up at me and smiled as though he had been working on his laptop and I had come in unexpectedly, only instead of a laptop, he had a bottle of whiskey in his hands. I nodded at him. A quick acknowledgment of his presence. Then I hurried into the kitchen to start cooking his meals for the week.

DAI
2010

MARA WALKED A WIDE ARC AROUND MY BED AS though she was afraid it would contaminate her. I fell back on my bed with my bottle of Johnnie Walker. I drank and tried not to think about it. About any of it. The apartment warmed with the smell of food, and soon, Mara started to sing. I sat up and watched her hips sway, and I drank a gulp of whiskey every so often.

WHEN KIT CAME back on a Sunday night six days later, I was dressed and waiting for her. On the refrigerator, I wrote in black Sharpie: "*Gone traveling, will return.*" I thought about writing *XO*, or *Love*, or *I'm sorry*. Instead, I put a period at the end of the fragment. Then closed and locked the apartment door.

After the door was closed, I took Kit's outstretched hand. It pulled me down the stairs, trying to keep up with her cream-colored legs, anxious to dance with abandon under flashing colored lights.

DAICHI
1945

I DECIDED I WOULD GO DIG UP MY JAR, THEN TAKE UENO
Daichi's letter to his wife in Japan and find a tiny little
apartment of my own there. I would look like everyone there and I had money saved up; it would be easy. I had
nothing left waiting for me in America. Ito-sensei was dead,
which left nothing for me but the camps or the house I had
rented from Mr. Martin.

ON THE TRAIN to the airport back to America, I opened the
folded piece of paper six times. An address in Osaka was written in Ueno Daichi's neat handwriting. I unfolded the letter
all the way, as I was curious. Inside was a letter written in
Kanji, with the exception of an American address at the bottom of the page. The city happened to be a few miles from
Mr. Martin's farm.

WHEN I GOT off of the bus from the airport, along the gate
surrounding the base, protesters stood with signs: "No Japs
wanted." Nothing had changed.

AT MY DUTY station, I received my discharge papers, but I did not look at them until I was on the bus to Mr. Martin's farm. When I looked at them, I wanted to laugh out loud, as the American government had confused me with Ueno Daichi, giving me his discharge papers. Now, looking back, I can only see it as Fate reaching out its hand. American racism might have made it so that I could not go into many restaurants or stores, but it also made me look like Ueno Daichi, though I was a foot taller than him, broader in the shoulders, and a year younger.

WHEN I GOT to the farm, I looked out over Mr. Martin's couple hundred acres and saw the same sight I had seen when I had been thirteen and had laid eyes on this farm for the first time: a couple dozen workers bent down, picking and pruning the crops, as they would be until their contracts were up and they moved on to the next farm. Or until they dropped dead.

I turned and walked the path I had walked with Ito-sensei leaning on my arm and telling me what he could remember about living in Japan. Since I was by myself, I made the trip to the diamond mine in a matter of hours. The memorial looked the same. I pulled the stones away from the spot, then dug at the hole with my military-issued E-tool. This took me quite a while, but I finally uncovered it. I pulled up the blue glass jar stuffed with the crumpled bills and gave it a loud kiss.

I UNPACKED MY sleeping bag and camped out there with my jar in the bag next to my feet.

THE NEXT MORNING, I walked to the address Ueno Daichi had written in the letter to his wife. It was a half-day from the diamond mine.

When I arrived, I stomped off the dirt from the road on the porch, then knocked on the screen door. Mr. Wilson opened his screen door while wiping his hands with a white rag soiled to a dark gray. He put it in the back pocket of his coveralls, then immediately put his hand out to me. He was a mechanic and apologized for the grease on his hands. He told me to call him Rich.

Richard Wilson had eyes the color of the ocean I had just flown across to get here from Germany. I showed him the letter, then explained I was here for Mr. Ueno's things. Rich could not read Kanji either, so he assumed the letter was written for me. He went to the back of the house and came back out with a suitcase. It was filled with carved wooden birds and some articles of clothing. Rich explained that Mr. Ueno had carved them and then given them to him to sell, and they had split the money for them. "These, he carved for his family back in Japan." He handed me a coffee tin with about a thousand dollars inside and then handed me a hundred-dollar bill. "Please give these to his family. He loved them and talked about them often. This farm would not have been able to survive if not for how hard he worked to grow the fruits and carve the birds we sold in our store."

I looked into Rich's face. He was an older man. Any day now, he would die, and his family would buy a wooden coffin to place his body in. They would weep over him and ask why it had to be his time just then. This man looked me in the eyes, and I saw in his eyes that I was a human, as human as anybody with a face like his.

I shook his hand and lied to him. I told him Mr. Ueno had been a close friend, that he'd talked of him often, and how appreciative he'd been that he had met such a kind American to work for. Then I took the suitcase, the coffee can, and the hundred-dollar bill, which I folded into my wallet as I left.

MARY
1996

Then Little Ma was getting ready to start the first grade. I was excited. I'd finally get time to figure myself out. I hadn't dreamed of anything but apple trees, the church, my mom, and Little Ma in a while. Things would be good.

I sat at my kitchen table, drinking instant coffee and eating bacon, when I saw a flash of light outside the window. I walked outside, barefoot and curious, and there on a tree hung a bright, juicy red apple. I reached up and pulled it down. I looked all around it, and there were no blemishes or holes where a hungry worm might have eaten its way through. I didn't take it in to wash it—I simply bit into it, trusting nature. The juice from the apple ran down the sides of my mouth, sweet and a bit tart, and I got it. My cowboy's patience.

I decided I would go back to college and get my teaching certificate, like I had planned to do eighteen years before. I signed up for classes. I bought my books, a backpack, notebooks, and pens. EZ chuckled deep and rumbling as he watched me flit around, getting everything ready. He said he had never seen me so excited. He sat at the kitchen table comfortably. He had quit his morning job so he could tend to his trees now that they were bearing fruit.

He put a cigarette in his mouth and lit it up and pulled on it. Then he balanced it in his mouth as he drank his black coffee. He reached into his back pocket and pulled out his wallet, handed me two hundred dollars, and told me he had saved this money so I could buy some new clothes and shoes. Little Ma came into the kitchen, ready for me to walk her to school, but I was too excited. I jumped up and picked her up and swung her around. Then I put her down and taught her the moves to the hustle, and EZ sat back in his chair with the cigarette still in his mouth and he laughed and laughed.

Little Ma ran outside to the orchard, and I chased after her. She stopped, breathless, in the middle of the trees and started doing the hustle to no music at all. I sang and did an exaggerated version of the dance, and Little Ma did the same, only stopping to hold her sides as she laughed. EZ came out the back door with the kitchen table, and then I started to laugh, too. He carried the table out to the middle of the trees, where we were. Me and Little Ma ran for the chairs. Then we sat outside mid-morning, in the middle of our orchard, smiling crazy at each other because we had all decided to skip out on everything we had planned to do that day. Then Little Ma jumped up and started singing "Hot Stuff" while hustling around the orchard. I got up to join her but found myself winded, so I sat back down and watched our little girl twirl and sing and dream.

MARA
2010

ON THE MONDAY AFTER I MET KIT, I LUGGED THE cloth grocery bags up the metal stairs to Dai's apartment. I was determined to stay in his line of vision even with his arms wrapped around another girl. I had survived Layla and I would survive Kit. Despite how—*unsettled* she made me feel. I dropped the bag at the top of the stairs to rest my arms. Then I took a deep breath, picked up the bags, and walked the rest of the way to Dai's apartment door.

I didn't knock; we were past that. I had faced my worst fear in his apartment. I could handle her. I took out the key Dai had given me.

So you can be the first to find me. I hadn't thought about that day since. We didn't talk about the fall. About Layla. He drank and I cooked. No mention of anything else.

My right hand wrapped around the key and extended, started to shake. It was a tremor, I reasoned. I was just tired from climbing the stairs. Yet the timpani beat of my heart grew louder. This time—this time he was gone. All I would find would be his cold—

My breath sped up. Shallow. Both of my hands shook so bad, I couldn't get the key in the lock. My hands were thick with sweat. I wiped my hands on the front of my dress, which I realized at that moment was the yellow one I'd worn the day I'd picked him up from the hospital, where he'd cared so little about his life he could joke about it. *So you can be the first to find me.* The key was suddenly hot and heating up in my hand. I put the key in the lock and turned it quick, so as not to burn myself. I turned the doorknob. It clicked, and I pushed the door in.

I didn't realize I had been holding my breath until the door swung all the way open. The stale air hit me in my chest. His bed was empty. Not even a cold body for me to mourn over. Nothing. My legs shook, but they took me into the apartment anyway. It was a vacuum devoid of sound or air. Then, something inside me was forcing its way out. Crawling up the back of my throat. The piercing high-pitched sound was distant but coming, accompanied by the rhythmic hooved sound of my heart. I stumbled into the bathroom and opened the toilet. My stomach emptied itself. I vomited, then spat bits of food left sitting and swimming in my mouth into the toilet. Left over. I put my hands up to my face, covering it.

You are a coward. You should have said something last time you saw him.

I stood up from the toilet in the half-dark and walked over to the mirror. I stared into my eyes. I gripped the sides of the porcelain sink. I willed myself to breathe, but the sound, the tone, was louder. It was so loud I could barely keep my eyes open and my head felt as though it might crack open like Dai's face had looked that first Monday. Did I have a wound ready to hemorrhage, as well?

I had to focus. I concentrated on my eyes in the mirror. There was nothing, at first. Then, the funnel. I saw it in my left pupil. It was coming for me now that it had been born into the air. It was coming for me and getting bigger and bigger. It was coming to kill me. I could feel it. My hands gripped the sides of the sink. The tone was so loud I could barely keep my eyes open, and my face was tight, as though it were starting to tear in half.

I succumbed. I squeezed my eyes shut, felt the cool porcelain under my palms and fingers. I took quick, shallow breaths, but they made me lightheaded. I held on harder. It would not take me. I would not fall.

I took another breath. Deeper this time. I swallowed. I let the air out slowly and opened my eyes. I blinked. I looked around, unsure for a moment where I had been for the last few minutes. I avoided the mirror. I turned the bathroom lights on. Then I walked out, watching my feet with each step, fearing otherwise, they would take me back to the dreaded mirror.

I crouched next to one of the bags I had left on the floor next to the door. I rocked on the balls of my feet. I hugged my knees and tried to wipe away the quick, silent tears as they fell.

He needed you once. If you keep yourself around, he will need you again.

I gave in. I nodded to myself and wiped my face with the back of my right arm. Then I stood up and walked over to the kitchen sink to wash my hands. That was when I saw the message scrawled on the refrigerator: *"Gone traveling, will return."* The period at the end of the fragment looked as though the Sharpie had been thrown like a dart at the refrigerator.

I washed my hands, then grabbed the bag off of the floor and put it on the counter. I reached up to the cabinet above the bag and pulled down the spices I had bought, which Dai had also left behind. Garlic, cayenne pepper, and minced onion. Then I reached into the bag and pulled out the ground turkey and placed it on the counter. I put the ground turkey in a bowl, also left behind, and added the spices in varying measurements. Then I plunged my hands into the bowl. The chilling cold of the ground turkey kept my mind present and away from the careless message or the mirror in the bathroom.

Soon, I was calm. I put the meatballs in the oven and pulled out the ingredients for baked mac and cheese, one of my dad's favorite meals. Then I was singing with the memory of my daddy's easy tenor.

DAI
2011

OR THE FINISH, THEY ALL LAUGH ONCE IN UNISON, OR, rather, they all audibly push air from their diaphragms as one unit. One harmony.

We burst into the apartment. Legs and arms and lips and feet.

Kit, our base, hands raised, hips swinging.

We were. All of us. Naked.

A hand grabbed mine and we were twirling. It let me go. I fell back into a chest. Hands around my waist. We were swinging side to side. My face in front of the girl with the big smile. Then another pair of arms around my waist. A head on my shoulder. Fire hair brushing my clavicle. Kit's green eyes, catlike, magnetic, inches in front of mine. Strawberry lips. Breath smelling like Jim Beam. A hand stroking my chest. Then music, and we were bodies. Rubbing and turning and sweating.

And Kit again. Only Kit. Her body on mine, silk and velvet. Bodies turning and swirling and grinding around us. But Kit, her eyes refused to let mine stray. Then there was a drink in my hand. Cold to the touch, fire down my throat. But her eyes refused to let me go. The cup was taken, and her cat eyes said, "Do it." So, I put my hands on her hips. I pulled them to me. Her fire hair shook as she continued to dance. But on me.

More silk and velvet, and my body hard and sweat-covered and ready. Green eyes locking me in. I wouldn't—couldn't—look away.

Her smile pulled up. Slowly, all of her mouth pulled up into a smile, and for a second, I was afraid to lose myself, but then her strawberry lips, tasting like Jim Beam, were on mine, and *I* was nowhere to be found.

. . . BUT I KNOW my war is still coming. I feel it in my chest . . .

I opened my eyes and blinked a few times until the world was no longer a blur. I rolled over on the living-room floor, groaned, and sat up. I rubbed the broadsword now tattooed on my chest.

I had not wanted a thorned vine like the others. Nor did I want to be a faceless extension of her: one of the twelve silent blue *ands* to her *Kit*. In fact, in my head, I had started to call them "Kitand." When I'd told her this, she'd turned her head and looked at me for a few minutes as though she were observing a curious oddity. Though she was a full foot shorter than I was, I'd had the same feeling that I'd had as a child when my mother would stand over me, looking down, so tall it had looked like she was the same height as our ceiling.

A realization had occurred to Kit. I'd known this because her right eye had twitched and she'd nodded definitively. She'd walked up to me, thrown her arms around my neck, and kissed me in the ear. I'd flinched, thinking the smacking of her lips would be too loud for my eardrum, but it hadn't made a sound. She'd turned away and pulled down the bottom of her shorts. They'd slid back up, and she'd walked out. Leaving me alone. No comment on my differentiating myself from the others or on the status of our relationship. If we even had one.

When Kit had seen the finished tattoo over my heart, she had brought her fingers right above it. I'd expected a sting, to have her fingers dance lightly on my newly burned skin. There had been nothing. Her fingers had come within inches of touching the sword, and then her hand had fluttered away. Quick. As though an intense heat had been emanating from it.

WHEN SHE AND I and the others stripped down and ran under the full moon, she would run next to me at first, her eyes lingering on my chest. Then she would look up to my face and away, like the first time our eyes had met. She would make no comment about the tattoo or anything she might have seen in her quick glance. She would run ahead of me, stretching her arms to the stars, and she'd open her mouth wide as though she were getting ready to scream, except nothing would come out. I would only hear the sound of her naked feet slapping the pavement.

KIT WAS LAID out naked and chaotic on the carpet in front of me. Her arms were sprawled and bent at odd angles above her head. Her legs were intertwined with mine. Her hair was fanned out and looked like a ray of sunshine. She had a tan line at the top of her thighs where her shorts stopped. The skin of her pelvis looked delicate in the early-morning light. I wanted to get up and lay my lips on skin untouched by the sun. I wanted to be the only lips to touch her body. Kit's eyes fluttered in her sleep. My breath caught in my throat. A body lying behind Kit stirred and pulled her closer to its chest. I let out the breath. I fell back on the floor. *And there is no one standing next to you.*

My phone vibrated. I sat up and reached over to pull it out of my jeans that lay in a heap by my head. I flipped it open. The text was an invitation to my own birthday party. Mara. It came with an attachment, but my phone was too cheap to be able to open it. I closed it and tossed it to the side. I put my right arm behind my head and let my mind wander. I thought of the last time I had seen her big honey eyes, looking at me as though I were a semi speeding at a hundred miles an hour toward her. Had it been six months already? I counted again. No, it had been eight months. I closed my eyes and hummed Mara's heart song to myself.

I REACH DOWN for my wakizashi, but it will not be unsheathed . . .

A week later, I was nervously standing outside with Kitand, in front of Mara's door, before the party. I unbuttoned my shirt and scratched my tattoo, which itched for the first time in eight months. My heart beat quick. I tasted Kentucky Bourbon in the back of my throat, but, mixed with the tablet slipped into my mouth on the drive over, it tasted metallic. I swallowed, but my mouth was dry, and I coughed, having swallowed air. The grains in the wood of the door formed patterns. Constellations. I wondered why I couldn't see the ones in the sky. I looked up to confirm my problem, and I saw a swirling mess. The stars looked like streetlights in a haze. Like mini suns but not as bright. As I watched, their rays grew bigger, and soon, it was a sky full of dandelions so big they filled the sky with light, and there was room for nothing else. I looked away and back at the wood constellations. They started to merge together and move, like a connect-the-dots that comes alive. But those started to smear, and the lines blurred, and I had to look away to keep from feeling sick. Colors outside of the wood constellations started to take on an odd quality. They didn't change per se, but they were slightly brighter. I thought, *Will she remember the night she looked back at me, her eyes filled with love? Will I be able to be everything I need to be?*

The door opened. Mara stood wrapped in gold. The patterns of her dress swirled. The honey color of her eyes gleamed amber. Her skin was the color of dark brown sugar, and I wanted to melt her down and swim in her juices. My mouth watered. Her arms were opened wide for me, waiting for me to walk into them. For me to enter into her atmosphere and join our galaxies. Her sugar skin and gold-swirling dress and amber eyes, but her hair—it hung like my mother's. Silk sitting matter-of-factly on her shoulders and down her back.

I had wanted to walk into her arms, to be overwhelmed by her, but I was pulled back in time.

I AM SIX and it is my birthday, and the arms outstretched belong to my mom, who is wearing my dad's favorite yellow dress. Which is my favorite dress, too, because it is the color of the sun and tamago, and I can see on the counter that my mom has made some tamago. It's fluffy and sweet, and I am excited. I can't stop dancing and jumping around my stool. My mother is standing above me, but she isn't far away, and up in the sky, she is a Mongolian oak, smiling down at me. Bits of starlight escape from between her lips, and her hair is framing her moon face, and she squats down to my level and watches as I dance a circle around her. I reach out to run my hands through her hair. I run so fast that she and the room are a whirl of sun and tree, soft laughter, silk hair, and cool tile, smelling of green tea and egg.

But finally, I must calm my legs enough to climb onto the stool. I pick up two of the tamago and stuff them in my mouth. My mom stands, still within reach, turns, and hands me a cup of tea. I chew once, twice. Then throw some warm tea into the delicious mixture in my mouth and swallow. My mom holds her hands out in the shape of a cup. I place my hands in the cup of her hands, and she encloses my hands in hers. A warm, comforting blanket without the excess heat. My mom smiles, then—big as the sky and as beautiful as the stars is what my dad calls it.

A version of myself, not six, wonders if this is why my father spends so much time staring at the stars. Is he deciphering my mom? Are the constellations my mom's story broken into pieces?

My mom starts singing the birthday song, and the six-year-old version of me is back. She sings in Japanese, which I do not understand, but I know it is the birthday song because the tune is the same. The words are just different. It is the most beautiful song I have ever heard, but the song finishes quickly, and the sky-star smile is back, and I am sad because my mom has stopped singing the beautiful mystery. The code that will help me understand what it means to be a man, like my father, like my grandfather. If my mom would sing the song one more time, I could learn how to become a man a woman could love. That could stand tall and protect the people he loves. I open my mouth to call out, "Mama, again." But before I can, she bends down and picks me up and twirls me into a hug. She holds on to me tight, and I feel dizzy and happy and loved.

I was not six.

There were the voices of Kitand laughing and the amber eyes of Mara in front of me, framed by my mother's hair. Kitand grabbed my arms and rushed forward, pulling me past and away from Mara. I felt dizzy assimilating back into and-hood, but I got my bearings and turned back, only to be swept into and-hood again. I was trapped. I could only look back at Mara standing alone, holding her arm up, as though it might fall off at any second.

A glass appeared in my hand. It turned out to be a magical, refilling glass. Cold ice clinking. Burn down my throat. I looked down and my glass was filled again. I nodded appreciatively at the glass. The colors were getting brighter. I'd need sunglasses any second. Mara announced dinner would be ready in fifteen minutes. Layla's song was playing so loud in my head, I wasn't sure it wasn't playing in the room. *When your old man failed you.*

I drank what was in my bottomless glass, and when I looked down at it, the glass was refilled once again. I looked up and across the room, and Kit's smiling mouth was wide as though she was laughing or about to, but no sound escaped, and her audience leaned in close, waiting. Any second, it would fall from that gaping miracle. Mara was stirring the pot on the stove and staring into it, looking, I assumed, for constellations. What answers they gave her, I had no idea. The gold of her dress swirled so fast I started to feel dizzy, and I looked away. *Like an idiot, I fell for you.*

I looked down at my glass, and it was empty. I could see through the bottom of the glass and onto the floor. I thought, *What is real?* I looked around for the keeper of my drinks. All

I saw were feet and arms and mouths all separated into pieces and coming together with other pieces. Swirling and whirling around with each other. Leaving me a solitary I, with nothing. *Turned the world upside-down-crazy.*

I saw the liquor. There were about five bottles sitting on a cheap table in the corner of the apartment. There was a bottle of Johnnie Walker sitting up front. As I approached it, I saw it was almost empty. I poured the last finger of scotch into my cup and drank it down. Above the table sat a reproduction of Klimt's "The Kiss." A faceless man held up a woman. She was beautiful. He didn't need a face—he had her—but it was a cheap reprint. There was no gold. They simply held each other in washed-out colors. I thought to myself, *The faceless man did not make the right choice and that is why there is no gold. Please.*

But how to know the right choice? I looked over at Kit as she tugged down her shorts. Mara announced dinner would be ready in another ten minutes. Layla was a mystery down in Georgia. *Calm my worries.*

I saw one of the bottles was Cutty Sark. I had told Mara it was my favorite because it was my grandfather's favorite drink. It made me feel closer to him. Around the bottle, a gold bow was wrapped, the same shade as Mara's dress and the gold cascading from the couple in the Klimt painting above my parents' fireplace, like a flag waving to me. Sending me a message. But I didn't know the language and the message was meaningless to me. *Let's do what we can.*

I finished my drink and poured another. Kit laughed at one of her appendages' jokes. Her own, then? I drank from my glass. A playful fire made its way down my throat, and I didn't remember tasting the first glass. *Before I go crazy.*

Kit lifted her shirt to show off the freckles on her stomach. The disciples and I came to gather around her. What we were looking for, who knew? Only Kit, our base. Mara stayed in the kitchen, glancing up to watch us through the kitchen doorway every once in a while. When Kit released us, I made my way back to the table and poured myself another glass. *Don't say never.*

I walked over to the window next to the table, looking for the ineffable. *Don't say my love is useless.*

A HAND ON my elbow. Warm. It smelled like cocoa butter. It was a faint smell, and when I turned, it smelled like chocolate. Kit laughed loudly. I breathed in the smell. I wanted this to be us. Standing next to each other, like this. But when I looked down to tell her, Mara was gone and my elbow was cold. *Please.*

Kit laughed again; her appendages were hilarious. I drank what was in my glass and refilled it. I took a gulp. Out of the corner of my eye, I saw headlights. I rushed back to the window, and though I had no idea how she would have known about the party, my heart sped up, knocking on my chest so hard it drowned out the song. For a second.

The headlights passed. *I am on my knees.*

I could feel my smile threatening to rip my face in half, and my stomach dropped as I fell, and the wind whipped past my face so hard my eyes started to water. *Please.* I needed her. I would tear open a body and write my love in their blood on a wall, if that was what she wanted. Anything. I'd go back in time and be anything she wanted me to be. Then, cocoa butter. I breathed it in. This time—this time she would not turn away from me in the rain. She would kiss me and tell me she loved me.

My mind seemed to be working seconds behind time. I could barely remember who Mara was supposed to be. *I am pleading with you*. I could feel that my smile was so tight, my face would start ripping apart at any second. It felt like if I drank from the glass in my hand, it would all spill onto the floor. I'd melt with it and Mara would cry over the puddle in her gold dress. Kitand would laugh and dance and forget about me because I'd succumbed. *Calm my worries*. Mara stood between me and the window. She put her hand on my chest. Her newly straight hair made me want to curl up in her arms while she spun me around and around, hugging me tight to her chest. *Please.*

"You okay? You look kind of crazy." Mara's round amber eyes were back to honey. My heart sped up. She reached up and touched the palm of her hand to my face. I turned into it, then leaned toward her, anticipating the tickle of her tongue on the roof of my mouth, looking into her eyes the second after the kiss, her lips a breath away, a movement, really. The softness of her lips a memory on mine. The taste of honeysuckle. Mara's eyes got big and looked behind me. I heard hushed laughter.

A weight hit my back. Thighs wrapped around my torso. Mara jumped back and away. I grabbed Kit's legs and spun her around. I walked over to the liquor table and left my glass. With Kit on my back, I jumped around and growled and neighed and roared. Kit laughed, clinging to me, digging her nails into my shoulders. I welcomed the pain. It felt real and easy to understand. Her breath was short and excited on my neck. Her thighs squeezed my torso. My ribs ached and I laughed. Enjoying the feeling of reality. I danced, pranced, and spun until she patted my shoulder. I got down on the ground. Kit climbed off. An appendage wrapped itself around her. She threw her arm around a second appendage that appeared at her side. They picked her up in unison, and she was lifted away. She leaned back and mouthed something as she floated away, lifted by her appendages. Her too-bright lips seemed to move at different speeds, and I had no idea what they were trying to convey. *What will you do when you are alone?*

I turned back to the table and poured another glass. The room vibrated. The song went silent.

Then she stood in front of me. Layla. Everything was swimming. Any minute, everything would spin. I wondered if I still looked crazy. Her mouth moved. Layla. I couldn't decipher what she was saying. With the room so quiet, I wondered if I had become deaf. I took another gulp of my scotch; finished it. I turned to refill it, took another gulp, turned, and she was gone. Layla.

Distant laughter. Any second, the room would spin. Cocoa butter. A warm hand on my elbow. Mara's lips were moving, too. Another one. All I could hear were noises in the distance. Then a whooshing in my ears, and all the sound came back at once. Full volume. Laughter and music and Mara's eyes looking up at me, waiting, waiting for something from me. *And there is no one standing next to you.* I shook her arm off. She walked away, chocolate. The room started to spin as a shoulder appeared under me.

In the distance, before my mind gave up trying to keep the room from turning, I saw Mara and Kit locked in a kiss. Kit held Mara in her arms, dipping her, embracing Mara like her dearest lover. Their eyes were both closed. Mara's arms dangled like a life-sized doll. I was too tired to process all the information spinning around me, standing right in front of me, holding me up. All the rooms were playing movies I wanted to understand and could not. I closed my eyes and took another gulp from my glass. The room spun even with my eyes closed. *You've been away too long.*

DAICHI
1945

I ARRIVED IN OSAKA. IT SMELLED LIKE BITTER DEATH. IT was humid, too. I was drenched in sweat and trying to swallow the smell of smoke and rotten meat before it stuck to the back of my throat. I was not successful, but I coughed, and it settled low enough in my throat so that I could only taste it when I swallowed. I breathed through my nose and took off the just-too-small dress coat I had found in Ueno Daichi's luggage and rolled up the sleeves of his shirt, the back of which was glued onto me with sweat. Looking around at the airport that had been acquired by the U.S. government, I saw a familiar sight: defeated Japanese faces. Menacing American faces with rifles.

I pulled out the letter from my breast pocket and looked at the address. I sighed looking at Ueno Daichi's neat kanji characters. I had no idea what message they were trying to convey. I had no idea what message I was bringing to Ueno Daichi's wife. I had no idea where to go, but I had money. I went out front and watched Japanese hands hail a cab, and then I did the same. A cab stopped, and I gave the driver the letter. He looked at the address printed on it, then handed it back and spoke in Japanese. He spoke quickly, unlike Ito-sensei, who I then realized had spoken slowly so that I could take the time I needed to understand what he'd been telling me. I stayed silent, nodded, and handed the driver some of the money from Ueno Daichi's tin.

THE DRIVE TOOK an hour. We sat in silence. Out the window, I saw an expanse of burnt rubble and piled bodies. I did not have to ask what had happened. I remembered America. It did not take a leap of the imagination to think of the hate America had to have to round up its own people and put them in camps and how that hate might look if there were no kinship.

STANDING IN FRONT of the door to the address I had been given, I thought, *Will she know I am not him?* Then I laughed at myself. Of course she would know. This was not America, where we all looked the same.

She opened the door, and I did not know her name then, but later I would learn she was named Akira, which means "bright" or "clear." Sometimes the kanji is written to mean sunlight and moonlight; bright, intelligent, wisdom, and truth. But I did not know any of these things at the moment that I met the woman whose husband I would pretend to be. I only saw her face, clear of makeup, puffed up and red with sadness. I saw quickly that she knew I was not her husband and that her husband was probably dead. I bowed as I had seen the Japanese here bow, and she came outside because there was only one room in the apartment and in it sat a sightless old woman, weeping. I would learn this was Ueno Daichi's mother—meaning she was now my mother—and I remembered warm hands touching my face and singing to me in Japanese, and I realized I had once had a mother of my own.

At the moment I saw that woman on the floor, her opaque eyes pointed toward the door, weeping, I mourned the death of the mother I had forgotten I had had.

Akira did not waste time. She asked how it had happened. I told her he had been brave. She was strong, stronger than any of the soldiers I had fought next to, because she nodded practically. Unafraid. No crying. Just a nod. I showed her the discharge papers I had been given. She looked them over briefly and handed them back. I handed her the letter to read, and she turned from me to read it. Her crying was soft, so soft I did not hear it, and she raised her hands and the letter to her face once she was done reading.

I told her an American lie to comfort her. "He is in Heaven looking down at you." She turned and looked up at me with disgust, and I thought she might slap me for opening my mouth without thinking, for letting something so stupid fall from it. She shook her head. At that moment, I felt a violent buzzing underneath my skin. I knew I had to do something to make the old woman in that apartment smile. I had to do something to lighten the gray bags under Akira's eyes, and though I did not know her name just yet, I had to make her smile. I needed to protect her.

I pulled out the tin with the money that Ueno Daichi had spent years saving, the one-hundred-dollar bill Mr. Wilson had given me, and my jar with nearly four thousand dollars. Akira smiled, threw her arms around my neck, and kissed me, and I realized it would happen. I really would be Ueno Daichi, Akira would be my wife, and the old woman inside would be my mother; I would get them a home with more than one room, and we would be happy.

MARY
1996

THE NEXT DAY, I COULDN'T GET OUT OF BED. I FELT like I had the flu. I blamed it on the shoeless outdoor dancing the night before, but after two weeks, EZ drove me to the hospital. After a biopsy and more waiting, they told me I had stage-four breast cancer that had spread to my lymph nodes and my lungs. There was nothing they could do but give me painkillers and the contact information for the local hospice. I went home.

MARA
2011-2014

Kit's lips were slippery. Like I had kissed the outside of a wriggling eel. She had asked me if I'd wanted to dance with her. I had said, "No, I have to finish up in the kitchen." She'd stood back and smiled at me like I was a kid that had said the funniest thing and didn't know it.

Then she'd stepped forward and whispered in my ear. "What can I do for you, Beloved?"

Before I'd had time to answer, she'd dipped me and those wriggling eels had pried my lips open. Her tongue grazed the inside of my right cheek. I felt the burn at the bottom of my spine. I opened my eyes and watched Dai close his and crumple into the arms of a blue-haired boy, wrong side up. Dai's shirt flapped open for a second during his fall up, and there was a flash of a sword tattooed on his chest. No one had to tell me he had branded himself for her.

You're too late. He wanted a real woman, with straight hair and no shame.

Then Kit was lifting me back up, so the world made sense again. She held my hands. They sat between us. She stroked the backs of my hands with her thumbs. It was gentle, like she was calming a scared animal. She told me I was beautiful. She had this look in her eyes as though she were proposing to me. As though she were down on one knee, promising to love me for the rest of my days. I saw it then. What he saw.

Kit made a motion with her right hand, and all of her followers got up and walked out the front door as though they had all been watching and waiting for her signal.

I stood to the side and watched them stumble out.

Once they left, I fell to the floor as though she had been holding me up with her presence.

I STARED AT a stranger in my full-length mirror. I wanted to put my hands around her throat and squeeze the life out of her. I wanted to tell her she was pathetic. I wanted to tell her she deserved to have that storm come and get her. She deserved to die. I grabbed a facial wipe from its package sitting on the bureau behind me. I pulled it across my face. The high-pitched squeal was distant but coming for me. I reached back for another wipe. My stomach started to drop. After three wipes, my face was naked. I felt the wind ripping past it. Next, I unzipped and released my dress. Any second, I would hit the ground. The dress fell to the floor next to the wipes. My hair had started to curl back to its natural form, but, denatured, it simply pulled back and hung at odd angles, creating the illusion that I had been shaken.

Maybe you need to be shaken.

The high-pitched squall was so loud I had to put my hands over my ears and squeeze my eyes shut. But it was inside me. The tone. I might have vomited up the storm that was coming to get me, but this tone might tear me in half. I walked to the bathroom. I bent down in front of the sink, opened its cabinet doors, and pulled out the buzzer. I plugged it in and looked down at it. My hands shook so hard it looked as though it was already on. But it wasn't. I clicked the button. It whirred alive, and I couldn't tell if my hand was still shaking. I smiled. I took the buzzer to my head. The buzzing was so loud it drowned out everything else. I could hear nothing but the buzzer, and it tickled my scalp as my hair fell away.

The hairs floated down like feathers. I was molting.

When I was sure I had finished, I ran my hand over my naked scalp. My hand was cool, and I shivered. I walked back into my room. There, in the full-length mirror, I saw myself. My big eyes had finally settled into my face and were now the focus. My cheekbones sat quiet and high. My forehead spoke of the intelligence within, and my smile was small but genuine.

I climbed into my bed. The fibers of the sheet tickled the tips of my nipples and excited the skin across my stomach. Something inside of my chest shifted, and I breathed into it. I let my hand fall down the side of my stomach, sending tremors down my spine. My hands ran down my pelvis until I was there. The place I should have been, the way I should have done it, instead of waiting for Dai to do it for me. I closed my eyes and felt that shifting in my chest turn into a click. A lock inside of myself came undone. As I orgasmed, I lifted my hips up and down with the waves of pleasure. I had no shame.

After, I lay with my arms thrown freely onto my pillow, the sheet pitched off of my body, and I cried at the rebirth of myself.

THE NEXT MORNING, I looked at myself in my bathroom mirror. I ran my hand over the stubble on my head, and my mud-brown eyes sparkled. I smiled. I walked over to my closet and picked out a navy-blue dress I had kept in the back because it was too simple. Not bright enough. I slipped it on. My brown skin gleamed. I had not seen its beauty until then. I picked out a pair of small gold hoops and slipped them into my ears. I ran my hand over my naked, stubbled scalp. It was time for something new.

SITTING IN THE grocery-store parking lot, I was not sure what I wanted to make myself for dinner, but my hands were restless and I did not want to be who I had been the day before. I walked quickly from my car to the store. I kept my head down. The door dinged as it slid open. A few people looked absentmindedly in my direction, then away.

One pair of eyes stayed with me. I felt them dancing over and around me. I blushed and hurried over to the produce aisle. The eyes followed me; they felt like the sun on a warm summer's day. I forgot about them, though, once I was surrounded by inspiration. I decided to make ratatouille. I had never made it, but now was the time for something new.

I picked up a butternut squash and knocked on it. Then, I smelled pickles. I looked down at the squash, accusatory, and then saw movement in the corner of my eye. A tall brown woman dressed in black with dreads down to her butt stood beside me. She smiled and then pointed to the butternut squash.

"You're gonna wanna use zucchini for ratatouille." Then she smiled at my look of surprise. "You talk to yourself, love." Then she put her hand out to me and said, "My name is Sailor, and I think you are beautiful."

SAILOR SMELLED LIKE pickles because she grew her own cucumbers in her backyard, then set them in homemade barrels she kept open all year round. "The open air makes them taste better" was her reason why. She sold homemade pickles to mom-and-pop shops and restaurants. She had even started to sell them to a few corner stores.

After a month, I helped her lug her barrels of pickles over to my backyard. I helped transplant a good number of cucumber plants over from her backyard to mine, as well. Once we'd moved what we could, we went out for two seasons in a row to harvest the remainders. Sailor said they were her babies and she couldn't abandon them, but she couldn't be away from her Rosebud. The last part would always follow quickly behind the first, as did her sun-warmed love eyes.

SAILOR TAUGHT ME how to love the earth. She told me to take off my gloves before planting. To plunge my hand deep into the soil, so that it dug itself under my fingernails and became a part of my person.

She taught me how spongy black soil could grow almost any plant. How red-caked clay had to be mixed with better soil to grow anything.

How it was important to put a bit of soil on your tongue to taste the acidity of it.

I balked at the practice.

Sailor laughed at me. "You'll eat a dead cow, but you can't taste a little dirt?" She was vegan and believed it was a human being's prerogative to care for all creatures.

I enjoyed a rare steak. We didn't talk about it. I simply waited to eat my meat on late nights when Sailor was on overnight business trips, trying to convince owners of various businesses to sell her homegrown, sun-warmed pickles.

During these secret nights, I would bite into my bloody steak. I would close my eyes and imagine walking up to a black-and-white Holstein and biting into the side of it. The surprise on its face and the sound of its cry followed me into my dreams. I'd have nightmares of the same scene every night until Sailor came back through the door, her smile lighting up my condo and chasing the nightmares away.

WHEN SAILOR WOULD return, she'd ask me to help her pull her hair down. I would quickly unknot the piece of hemp she tied her hair up with, and then I would wash my hands and get back to whatever recipe I had been cooking beforehand.

Sailor would come up behind me, put her hands in my hair, and kiss the side of my neck. Then she'd hold me from behind and rock us side to side, her head nestled between my shoulder blades.

"WHEN YOU WANT to see if something is ready for pickin'—" That was how Sailor said it every time, and soon, I started to look forward to the absence of the small hanging "g." "—you bend over and let its smell drift into your body."

I was skeptical of this, as I was of all of Sailor's aphorisms—another Sailorism—but the first time we made love next to her pickle barrels and my newly planted herb garden, I smelled coriander. I thought perhaps it was the herbs next to us, but the tender green shoots barely peeked out of the black spongy soil, and besides, I bent over to smell them, my right nipple grazing a shoot of rosemary, yet smelled nothing but earth.

Sailor chuckled at me, lying on her back, raised up on her elbows. She lifted her throat to me again. I got on top of her, my knees sinking into the soil on either side of her and sticking into the red clay underneath. I grazed my nose on the inside of her throat, and there was the smell again. Coriander. I smiled. I leaned in and took in the smell, deeper this time. I let it sit in my chest and create a memory that would float up every time I made lamb chops. We made love again next to those barrels. I closed my eyes and nipped Sailor in the hollow of her neck a few times.

After, I made a curry. I put in potatoes, carrots, and onions from my garden. Then I took a whole chicken and slathered it in butter, salt, pepper, and coriander.

Sailor watched me silently.

I baked the chicken, then cut a few pieces of it up and threw them into the curry. I looked up into Sailor's eyes as I did this, so there was no mistaking what I was doing. The rest of the chicken, I served up as a side for the curry.

Sailor refused the pieces of chicken on the side, but she ate a whole bowl of curry and then another.

Later that night, I woke to Sailor vomiting both bowls into the toilet and crying. *Weeping for a chicken.* I snorted to myself, then closed my eyes as Sailor stumbled into the room and fell into bed.

We didn't talk about the curry incident ever again.

AFTER THE NIGHT of the incident, I started wearing a sprig of rosemary behind my ear, or a sprig of it braided into the side of my fro. When I washed my hair, pieces of rosemary fell down into the shower.

Sailor would smile. "It's like seeing mother nature cleaning herself in a waterfall." She would say this and sit back on the toilet seat, watching me with a sad look on her face.

I closed my eyes and turned around.

SAILOR WAS AN older woman. In the morning, when she sat in my kitchen drinking black tea and reading her morning paper, I would see this. It wasn't the way she wore her glasses at the tip of her nose, but the way she didn't push them up on her nose self-consciously when I walked into the room. How she licked her finger once then twice when turning the pages of her morning paper. How she would look at me over her reading glasses just like my grandmother telling me to finish my plate of food.

SAILOR'S SMILE WAS youth: her mouth raised her cheeks; the laugh lines at her eyes smoothed out her forehead. But I loved Sailor's wisdom. Her hair spoke of timelessness. I found myself reaching out to run my hands through her dreads, but then I would hesitate, and the taste of maple bourbon would collect at the back of my throat. My hands would flutter up to smooth my own hair or rub the back of my neck instead.

Sailor's youth would dry up from her face.

HER BREASTS SAT comfortably on her chest. Even when her head was thrown back while she was coming. Her breasts sat heavy and calm on her chest like they knew life was not as serious as my high, anxious breasts suggested. I envied the way Sailor approached the world. Sailor laughed off so-called pickle days as days that happened and would come again. Pickles had their usefulness in the grand scheme of things.

I laughed and said she thought of pickles a lot for a lesbian. Sailor said nothing. She walked out back and didn't come back until dinner.

WHEN I HAD bad days, Sailor would listen thoughtfully to everything I said. Even on the phone, I could hear her dreads brushing her shirt as they followed the rhythm of her head moving understandingly up and down. Then she would go upstairs and run a bath for me. I'd come home and climb in. She'd climb in after me and sit behind me, massaging tea-tree oil into my scalp with the tips of her fingers.

I went along with this for the first year we were together. It was . . . nice. But afterward, I still felt unresolved, and the way Sailor smiled at me then, as though I were a child throwing a temper tantrum about a toy getting stolen on the playground—it made me angry.

The second year we were together, the anger I felt after the bath would bubble up as soon as Sailor's left foot touched the bottom stair.

I would scream at her:

"Why can't you take things seriously? How does nothing bother you? Why do you think a neck massage and sex will fix everything?"

Then I would storm out of the condo and walk, feeling the acute anger vibrating throughout my arms and legs.

When I would return from my walks, Sailor would be practicing tai chi in the backyard. She would be moving slow, but her dreads would be lively and shaking at her waist. I would sit on the ground in front of her and watch until she was done. She would not look at me until the end of her routine, when she would look down at me with the kind of smile that hid a frown. I would jump up, and Sailor would bend down and pick me up. I would wrap my legs around her middle and kiss her hard with my hands clasped tight around her neck.

These times, we'd make love on the kitchen floor. I would have friction burns on my knees and elbows. Sailor would have hickeys and bite marks on her neck, her breasts, and her hips. These were the apologies we gave each other.

TWO WEEKS BEFORE our third anniversary, we fought about my dad. Sailor asked why she had never met him, why I was ashamed. She had broached this topic before, and each time I had not given an answer, she had simply left the subject alone. But this day—this day was different.

Sailor gave reasons why she should meet my dad. "It is what couples do." "Besides, we love each other, right?" "It's time." Reasons why she felt I had not introduced them. "I get it—your dad is a traditional carnivore; he never expected you to bring home a vegan twice your age." "But you know this is not something to procrastinate with, right?" "You don't see how this hurts me?" And an ultimatum. "Rosebud, I don't know how much longer *this* can wait."

After the ultimatum, Sailor stood silent behind me, waiting.

I turned off the stove, moved the pan of spinach ravioli to a cold eye, and then stomped outside and angrily pulled weeds from my garden.

Sailor walked to the other side of the yard. Though she didn't stomp, I heard the angry swish of her dreads.

After I finished weeding, I walked inside and called my dad. He told me he looked forward to finally meeting this elusive Sailor that I refused to bring to our steak lunches. I explained *she* was vegan. My father gave a smoker's cough in return and said that was fine; his doctor had been trying to get him off of red meat and smoking for years. He could accommodate. I thought, *I love you more than anyone, for loving me.*

I said I loved him and would see him Tuesday. My dad pulled on his cigarette over the phone, and I could see him scratching the back of his neck and flicking the cigarette away. "See you then, M&M." Then he hung up.

My middle name is Maybelle, and my father was the only person who knew. Sailor did not know. I liked it that way.

I WALKED BACK outside and watered my plants. Sailor started her routine from the beginning. Neither of us said a word.

She finished and walked past me. I finished and walked back inside to continue the spinach ravioli for dinner.

Twenty minutes later, Sailor came back with a small tree and dug a small hole for it. Then she picked up the tree with both hands, raised it above her head, and shoved it into the ground. Then she picked up chunks of bright red clay and dropped them into the hole. She crumbled the clumps between her fingers while facing the kitchen window, smearing the clay soil onto her palm and between her fingers. Her dreads jumped up as she dumped every handful into the hole.

I stood back behind the kitchen window, watching her, unsure of how to approach this situation.

When Sailor finished, she walked back to the other end of the yard and started another routine. Her face was scrunched up and her breathing was heavy. Her breasts seemed to jump up with every movement. Her dreads danced behind her back.

I went over to the tree and removed the clay. I removed the tree. I dug a deeper hole because it was too shallow. Then I mixed some spongy black soil from my front yard with a bit of the clay and some plant food. Then I tucked the tree's roots into the soil. I put a bit of the soil mixture into my mouth just to make sure it wasn't too acidic, and then I sat back on my feet. I felt Sailor standing behind me.

She felt menacing for the first time in our almost three-year relationship.

I continued looking at the young fruit tree, but I said, "Tuesday at noon." I heard Sailor's dreads hit her back as she turned away and walked to the other side of the yard to do another set.

I REMEMBER SAILOR would massage sandalwood-scented conditioner through my fro. We'd talk, her hands busy in my hair and me with my eyes closed and waiting for her to finish and slide her hands into the water.

On one such occasion, we were talking about the soil out in San Luis Obispo. How where she'd lived as a girl near the beach, the soil had been salty. The cucumbers she'd grown there with her mother had been naturally salty as a result, and she'd used a small amount of brine from that sun-warmed ocean to pickle them. Her mom would pick one up with her hands, gnarled by arthritis, and eat them straight out of the barrel while Sailor watched and smiled. Her mom had smiled every time and told her they were the best batch of pickles she had ever made.

Sailor grew quiet. She leaned down and kissed the back of my neck. She reached around and held me against her chest like she was trying to find the comfort she needed. She whispered in my ear, "Rosie, I wish I could mark the back of your neck so that your next lover would know I existed and that I loved you."

I turned around, mentally shutting away the feeling of *his* shiver underneath my hand. I said, "I hate that name."

Sailor laughed, wide-mouthed and silent. "Well, Rosebud, when you open up to me, then I'll stop."

I stood up, turned around, leaned over her, and kissed her smiling mouth.

SAILOR'S DREADS HUNG limp on her shoulders. Her eyes were red-rimmed, though she had not cried yet. "Whose hair are your hands itchin' to run through? You wrap your arms around me. You sleep with your face next to mine. But you never run your hands through my hair. You raise them to me like you want to, genuinely, but your hands always drop limp at your sides, like there's no point." Her voice quieted to a pleading whisper. "Whose hair are your hands itchin' to run through?"

I felt the outcome of this last conversation before it could come from Sailor's mouth. I stepped into her atmosphere and put my hand up to her cheek. She leaned into my palm. Her tears seemed to appear and fall at the same time. I didn't disturb them. I moved my hand to the back of Sailor's neck and spread the tips of my fingers into her hair. Then I brought her trembling lips to mine.

WHEN SAILOR WANTED to love me, she would come into the kitchen swaying her hips. Most of the time, there was no music playing. I would look up and smile at her. Sailor would offer me her hand. I would turn off the stove and place my hands in hers. Sailor would spin me in a small, tight circle, then bring me to her chest and hold my hips as we swayed.

I would lay my hands on Sailor's chest and lay my head between my hands. I would hum one of my daddy's songs, which Sailor would never know belonged to both my daddy and me. She would close her eyes and rest her chin on the top of my head. I could hear her eyes close because her breathing would get heavy. Sailor would run her hands up to my lower back and rub it while kissing the side of my throat. She always knew how to make me moan.

When I would open my eyes, there Sailor would be, looking at me with her "I love you" eyes. Big and hopeful and needing. For a full minute, this would go on. I couldn't stop it. I could only look past Sailor's eyes. Into them but not connecting with anything. Just staring at her pupils until they became the funnel: black, spiraling, and coming for me. Death would always be coming. I would see this in her eyes. Always to the rhythm that Sailor swung our hips. Then, she would kiss me. Hard and sudden. Taking my breath away and making me dizzy.

I hated the look. I asked Sailor why we couldn't just have sex and look at each other any other time.

She asked how two people could connect if they didn't look at each other.

I laughed and said I looked at her plenty. It didn't mean that much.

Sailor replied, "We create meaning, Rosebud."

I looked her in her eyes and asked, "Then why is this so important to you?"

Sailor went out back, and I heard the sound of her dreads dancing even from the kitchen.

AFTER THE KISSES that left me breathless, we would make love on the floor of the kitchen, just like after our fights, except after this, I would get up stark naked and cook Sailor fried okra and plantains. The oil popped toward my naked body, making my heart beat quick.

After I was finished cooking, Sailor would pull me down to the floor and we would make love again. The kind with bites and friction burns, though we weren't angry with each other. Then I would lie on the kitchen floor, breathing heavily with my legs spread wide, while Sailor ate fried okra with the hot sauce I made from jalapeños I grew in my backyard. She would slurp and hum as she ate. I would lie on the floor and feel the vibrations from my orgasm still rippling through me.

After Sailor moved out and 3,000 miles away, I would lie on the floor of my kitchen, the smell of newly made fried okra and plantains collected in the air, and I would touch myself to the smell. After, I would cry a few tears, get up, and throw it all away. These were the only times I allowed myself to miss her.

DAI
2015

*I*STRUGGLE WITH IT, PLEADING, BEGGING, BUT *I* KNOW IT IS *stuck because I am not yet worthy.*

We stumbled and rumbled and danced. Then she grabbed my hand. Kit. She grabbed my hand and she ran ahead. I was dragged behind, my hand sweating and slipping, but she grasped it tight. She was fully naked, and the tattoo right under her left butt cheek, right on the back of her upper left thigh, spoke to me. Told me to reach out. Her skin would be velvet. The thorns on the tattoo would be sharp and they would prick me and I would enjoy every second. That was what it told me.

Then she pushed me, and I was falling, and I reached out for her hand but she moved it, quick, like her eyes the first time I'd seen them. I am sure of it. I hit the bed, and above me was Kitand. And I was apart from them.

A pair of handcuffs appeared in Kit's hand and she locked me in, attached me to her metal headboard. Only then did she climb onto the bed and sit on my hips. Pinned my pelvis down with her legs. She looked down into my eyes as though she were smiling to a child she loved. "Beloved, everything will happen in time. You must simply go along with it." A hand, on cue, appeared and slid up Kit's thigh. A tongue appeared, licked Kit's hip and up her side. A hand lifted her fire hair. A mouth kissed her throat. Kit moaned. It came from her core and out of her throat. She fell back, and arms held her up. She swayed her hips up and back to a rhythm everyone in the room seemed to hear but me.

The hip movements became harder, and my body reacted. Kit's whole body swayed from side to side. Her body and the others were one movement. Kitand. I was apart from them and falling onto that hill alone. My body was trapped, immobile.

But I could still blink, so I closed my eyes. A gold ring floated into view. The song played. *Layla. Calm my worries.* I heard rain. It sounded like a shower curtain being moved back and forth. I shivered, waiting for the cold air and the rain to soak me. Layla stood in front of me and moved back from the kiss. *Like an idiot, I fell for you.* I couldn't remember what the kiss felt like. Layla looked at me with her big golden eyes for what felt like hours. Then, she blinked. The gold rings turned to honey. Layla's strawberry-blond lashes turned to cherry wood. Her hair phased to brown curls that floated down past her shoulders. Mara grabbed my face and kissed me. Her tongue tickled the roof of my mouth. I smiled. Mara leaned forward and stood on her tiptoes until her forehead touched mine. She smiled back. Our lips were breaths away from each other. I could lean forward and taste her honey-suckle breath. Mara brought her camellia lips together, and she started to hum.

A voice cut into my dream: "Look at me."

I opened my eyes. Kit's green eyes were hypnotic, and I was coming to the end of my rope. Not stretched thin, but my body saw respite coming any moment, like reaching out to that soft darkness at the bottom of that lake. She gyrated around me, Kit. Writhed around me. My body tightened up, waiting for pain, the impact of my body hitting the earth. Wet fear dripped from my head, under my arms—any second, the impact, and I did not know if I would be able to pull myself out of this black lake or if I would drown. And in that moment of panic beforehand, I reached toward her throat. Kit. I wanted to tear her throat out before I shattered into pieces any second, before I was lost from Mara forever, but the cuffs kept my hands tethered above my head. And Kit's eyes were the moon, I realized—the moon I was trying to swim away from. My body once again acted against me; it moved to her rhythm until the only thing I could do was break through the surface. Relief. It spread through my body so fast it felt like death, yet I was still here. Still whole.

Kit smiled, patted me on my chest, released me, and got up. Hands with a damp washcloth cleaned her. Arms offered a bathrobe. A hand fastened it. Kit put her arms around two different shoulders. They turned and walked away.

I lay back on the bed, my right arm behind my head, Mara's honey eyes in my mind's eye. I smiled and rubbed my chest, which felt liquor-warm. I hummed her song. I could feel the pressure and warmth of her forehead against mine. I could almost feel the breath from her mouth in front of mine. Something clicked then started to shift in my chest. Green flecks floated up from the honey. I felt queasy, jumped up from the bed, and followed Kit's path.

Her laughter, bright and high, led me down the hallway. I found Kit splayed on a lap, still naked. Fingers combed through her fire hair. Hands kneaded her feet. Her head was, as always, thrown back in laughter. All eyes focused on her. When she was ready, she released those standing around her with a flourish. Then she stood up and walked back to her bedroom with a few hands and mouths. She didn't look back.

I poured myself a drink. Johnnie Walker on ice. Then I stepped over bodies lying sprawled on the floor and plopped onto the couch Kitand had just deserted. The couch was warm and smelled like Kit's lips looked. Like strawberries. Mara's song flew out of me like a bird's high trill. It took me a second to realize what it was. And there it was again: the feeling of her forehead against mine. Her honey-scented breath escaping past her smile. My body's need to bring her lips to mine. My chest lost its liquor-warmth. I finished my drink and walked back to the room to join Kitand.

I reach my hand out as far as I can, so I can grasp my sword. I reach until my arm aches and it feels as though my muscles will snap.

It is not enough.

The tiles that had been cool when I had first stepped into place were warm. The wood of the doorframe dug into the side of my right arm, as I had been standing for a while, leaning with all of my body weight on the frame of the door, trying to look nonchalant, though I was not sure what the information in front of my eyes meant.

Kit let out a breath. It was a small release. A puff of air that quickly left her mouth. The sound of it at that moment let me know it was something substantial made to sound as though it wasn't.

Kit spoke: "I have this dream. I leave my house. Everything looks like an allergy commercial before the meds kick in. When anyone speaks, it's muted. There are words coming from the gaping mouths of these people, but it comes out as a low gibberish. At this point in the dream, I know I am the only real person. The dream used to scare me. I'd wake crying, then climb into my parents' bed, so if I woke up again, I'd know it was just a dream. And that's what would happen. I'd wake up, and my dad would smile at me and kiss my forehead. My mom would comb her hands through my bedhead and sing me a good morning. It took them years to get me to sleep alone again."

Kit's right hand clutched a positive pregnancy test.

"People are safe. I know no matter what, I will never be alone. Teddy will always catch me, Cassie will always hand me a plate of food with a big smile on her face, and any number of my people will always be there. And when I am afraid that I am the only real person left, they will look at me with their smiles, speak, and I will always hear them."

Kit's eyes flicked up to my chest.

"I can't always hear you, Dai. You go in and out. Sometimes you love this life, but other times, you want to be in control, and that's not how this works." Kit swept her arm in a wide arc as though she were talking about the bathroom itself, or the world around her, but she looked down at the tiles as though she were referring to them. Then she looked up into my face. "I cannot be alone again. In a group of two, there are always alone times. This is the only time in my life that I have been happy. I think that's true of everyone h—" In the middle of the word "here," Kit stopped, as though she had stumbled over a topic we had both agreed not to talk about. Her eyes moved back to the broadsword on my chest. "Dai, some people do better not thinking about things. Others have to control everything in their lives. There is no in between."

Kit sat back on her feet with her hands placed on her legs, staring at the toilet in front of her. Her right hand was clutching the pregnancy test so hard her knuckles were bone-white. Her whole body shuddered, then. One fluid movement, as though for a second, her body turned liquid.

I didn't offer her help off of those blue porcelain tiles that fit perfectly next to each other, providing no gaps, simply a place for me to step over and on to take a piss. I looked at Kit:

her hair was less orange today—dingy. Where was the fire? It dawned on me that we were strangely alone.

"Where are your appendages?"

Kit took a moment to look into my eyes. She didn't return the same joking tone. "They'll return when it's time. It'll be me and you for today."

I blinked, thinking back on the loneliness of two. I stepped over the tiles and put my hand out to Kit. She put her hand in mine, and her face relaxed into a smile.

THIS WAS A test. I could feel it. I stood over the cold stovetop, realizing the only thing I knew how to make was a box of Kraft macaroni and cheese.

Kit approached, looked up into my face, and laughed. "Beloved, I can do this. Go sit at the counter."

I looked down at Kit, thinking of Mara facing away from me and singing to herself, of Layla moving back from the kiss. I grabbed Kit's hands in both of mine. "Do you like macaroni and cheese?"

Kit looked up at me with a smirk she hid away with the back of her hand. "Sure."

WE ATE AND laughed. Kit told me she'd grown up in Indiana, that she loved Elvis, and that pears were her favorite food.

I told Kit about Layla. Kit got up and played the song, and we danced. Then she asked me about the other song. The one she would catch me singing in the shower or early in the morning when I woke. As a means of distraction, I kissed her. Deep and long. We were dancing when she asked. I stopped mid-turn and grabbed her by the waist, dipped her, and kissed her. Hard. Kit dug her fingernails into my shoulders and pulled me down to the floor. This time, I growled loudly in her ear and pinned her to the ground like we were animals, even as I was inside her. She gave me an appreciative smile.

We lay exhausted, our legs intertwined, after. I looked down at her eyelashes. They were platinum, nearly white, and they quivered. The strips of fire in her hair looked like orange Cheetos cheese powder; there was a layer of chestnut behind it, and at her roots, that platinum again, like it was slowly washing away layer by layer. I wondered who colored her hair. Could I, layer by layer, cover her secrets? Protect that which she found sacred? Be an appendage to her godhood?

I couldn't keep the question in me, so I asked, "Are you gonna let your hair grow out while you're pregnant?" Then I couldn't stop myself—I was throwing facts and questions at her about pregnancy. I didn't even know where they came from, but I couldn't stop. After I was done, I was out of breath and I had no idea how long I had been talking.

Kit waited to look up at me as though she were on a delay and had to process the information—or as though she were trying to swallow something she didn't want me to see. She sat up with her back to me. Then, there it was again: the fluid shiver.

I sat up next to her. She was hot. Hotter than she had ever felt. I wondered if it was a part of pregnancy. Another language I would have to learn. She turned to me, and there it was. What was hidden beneath her smile when she danced. Naked contempt. I couldn't look for long. It was hotter than the heat radiating from her body. I felt colder than the ice I put in my drinks. Another one gone, and another one, too. I fell back onto the floor and looked up at the ceiling.

Kit spoke.

I didn't hear any of it. I had failed, and now, bullets.

Kit stood up and walked into the bathroom. When she came back, her face was back to the way I had always known it to be. She got down on her knees over me, and she kissed me. I tried to keep all of the details for later, when she was gone, but all I could remember was the taste of peppermint, which I knew had been the same taste after Layla's kiss, and I wondered, had I made that up, too? Had I come up with details from the kisses because they had left me so quickly I hadn't had time to keep track of them?

AFTER SHE WAS gone, I was at a loss. I woke from a dreamless sleep on the floor of Kitand's living room. Next to my hand was an unopened bottle of Jim Beam and a note I didn't read. At the bottom of the note, Kit had chosen to write "XO." She'd given that to me to soften the blow of her absence.

I got up. I looked down and saw that I was naked. I crumpled the note in my left hand, picked up the bottle of Jim Beam with my right, and stumbled back to the bedroom. I struggled to think about what I had left Mara when I had followed Kit. Had it been a note? How had I signed it?

In the bedroom, I opened the bottle of bourbon and put it to my lips. I fell back. I got two gulps in before my body hit the mattress. Two gulps. What the fuck did that mean, and where were Kit and my—? I opened my hand with the yellow piece of paper crumpled in it. A Post-it? A Post-it was enough to tell me I wasn't enough for her? That she needed a baseball team to keep her happy? I tore the note into pieces and poured liquor on top of it. This shit wouldn't haunt my dreams. *And there is no one standing next to you.*

I threw the bottle of bourbon against the wall before the song broke me. Then I got up and went into the kitchen, opened the cabinet, and started throwing glasses and plates to the ground. Plates splintered at my feet, glasses shattered, and the shards sprang up and rained down on my toes. When I was done, I was surrounded by a sea of glass, naked, with a jagged piece of porcelain in my hand. I was even less prepared than in my dream. Even more vulnerable. I squeezed the splintered piece in my hand, and blood seeped from my fingers. I barely felt it. I crouched on the floor. There was no place to go. Tears had started pouring down my face before the bottle of Jim Beam had hit the wall. It didn't matter how hard I fought. I screamed as I pulled the jagged piece across my throat. Blood seeped over my fingers. The darkness took me.

... AND I HAVE *déjà vu, and there it is again: this is death.*

The first thing I saw when I woke was the blue tiles. I blinked. They were white tiles, and I was in a hospital bed once again. My neck felt raw. I put my hand up to it and flinched, as my body was sore, as well. I was sweating everywhere, and sounds went in and out as though someone were bringing everything near and then pulling it away too quickly for me to process. I brought my hand to my neck and felt the thick bar of gauze laid across it, fastened with surgical tape.

A doctor walked in. His steps were quick, but he walked from heel to toe as though he was trying not to walk too loudly. Instead of standing over me, he purposefully pulled a chair up next to me. He smiled at me, trying to look kind.

Inwardly, I groaned.

He asked me questions. Many questions. The only two I remember were: "Did you do this to yourself?" and "Have you tried to hurt yourself before?" I replied yes, yes. He asked me about my drinking, and I told him. Then I was too tired, so I closed my eyes and separated from my body. I felt nothing in that moment. Not a thing. I thought: *How hard would it be to climb to the top of this building and jump?*

The doctor came back. I turned away and closed my eyes so he'd leave.

The doctor brought someone new when he came again. The new doctor was dressed in jeans and a white-collared shirt with a yellow sweater on top. He had white hair that sat wrong on his head no matter how he combed his hands through it, though he did this often. His name was Jerry. He said this and put his hand out for me. I stared at him. I had nothing to say.

He came back the next day whistling "Hey Joe," and I couldn't help but laugh at the irony of his whistling a song about a homicidal man to a suicidal patient. He chuckled with me. "You like Hendrix?"

I nodded. "Yeah, and dark humor."

He laughed. "Yeah, you seem like the type." And he pointed to my throat.

I snorted. "Something like that."

"You ready to talk about it?"

I shook my head.

He pulled out his phone. "Have you heard the cover by Roy Buchanan?"

I lied. "No." I got thirty seconds in before I told him I had made a mistake. I had heard the song and hated it.

He came on the third day with more music, and we listened and talked about it. He handed me his card. "I'm going to give you the therapist spiel, because I have to, and I like to let everyone I'm working with know exactly what they are getting into with me."

I nodded.

He said, "Depression and alcoholism are battles you are going to have to fight for the rest of your life. Some days you'll win and you will feel great, and some days are going to feel like it's an impossible fight. The thing to remember is you can't do this alone. No one can. We all have bad days, and having that shoulder to lean on can be the difference between wearing battle armor and running naked into the fight."

I looked at his face. He was kind—weird, but kind. He wasn't trying to be kind. He believed all of this.

He laughed. "Corny, I know, but I warned you."

I nodded; he had warned me. I didn't have to think about my answer. "No." It was an easy answer and slipped through my lips like Cutty Sark with a single cube of ice. If this was my war, I would fight it myself.

After he left, they brought the paperwork so I could sign myself out. They handed me the belongings they had found with me, sans shirt, which was probably in a garbage can soaked in blood, so I kept the paper gown on over my jeans. Among my belongings, I found my car keys with two new keys. One was gold and one was silver. The gold key was the bigger of the two and had a label on it: "51 North Lily Drive Indianapolis, IN." The silver key did not have a label on it, but I didn't need a label to tell me I could choose Kitand in Indiana or I could go home.

I took an Uber to Kit's old apartment building and got into my gray Impala. It had been a long time since I had claimed something, called it mine, but the familiarity of the worn leather and the faint smell of the royal-pine-scented car freshener were comforting. I pulled down my visor and looked at my throat in the mirror. The thick white gauze hid it: proof of my mortality. I pulled the gauze away from my throat. The cut was puckered and yellow at the edges. A clear substance leaked from it. I put the bandage back, closed my eyes, and leaned against the headrest. I thought back to myself naked, crouched, and surrounded by a sea of broken porcelain and glass, the jagged piece pressed against my throat and nothing stopping my hand. I thought of that song I couldn't listen to for thirty seconds without seeing the sun shine through her strawberry-blond hair. I reached into my pocket and took out the card the doctor had given me, then started the car. Before I could think about it, I drove to the address listed on the card and checked myself in.

Jerry patted me on the back and showed me to my room.

EIGHT WEEKS LATER, I left the clinic with a two-month chip, a smoking habit, and a referral to an outpatient therapist. I pocketed the cigarettes and the chip. I put the referral card on the dashboard of my car. I pulled down the visor and looked at my throat. The scar was barely visible now. I closed the visor and started the car.

In the clinic, I hadn't been able to drink, so once I'd detoxed, I'd spent most nights lying in bed, thinking of how I had gotten to the top of that bridge.

Layla. I had to go see her. I was convinced seeing her would fix everything.

MY HELMET IS ripped off. I see the full world around me for the first time. It is a bright blur of colors.

Arriving in Macon, Georgia, I opened my car door and stepped out to look at the bakery in daylight. It was a small brick building with a bright blue door. A bay window barely fit on the right side of it. I closed my car door and walked in. The bell above the door jingled. A whirlwind of brunette blurred past the porthole door in the back. It flew past again, and then the door opened. A smile lit up her face in a way I did not recognize, and for a moment, I was worried I had come to the wrong place.

LAYLA
2015

I SAW HIM FOR THE FIRST TIME IN ALMOST FIVE YEARS AND thought, *Shit*. I didn't need to recognize his face to feel the pressure change in the room. It pushed my smile back to the one I had worn when I had been a cold fish next to him.

I turned and popped open the kitchen door to let Theo know I was going out for a smoke. Maybe he heard the change in my voice, or maybe he felt the pressure change in the air, too. He questioned me with his eyes. I shook my head no; I'd have to tell him about it later. He nodded and whistled my soul song, like that first time he'd strode in to cheer me up. He hadn't just happened to be there, but had come to his aunt's restaurant to see me. Said he'd woken up and I had been all he could think about. A shadow of my happiness returned.

But it waned sitting outside with Dai, while I patted myself down for my emergency pack of Pall Malls. Life had come easier to me once I'd stopped pretending. I didn't need to be with him just because he felt I should. Fuck that. It made me twitchy to think about. Thankfully, I found my cigarettes in my apron pocket. Sherry was trying to get me to quit, but she'd forgive me for this relapse.

I caved on being the badass I needed to be to get him to leave. I could have told him that stalking was illegal or that Sherry was just waiting for me to give the word so she could pull out her Remington from behind the counter. Instead, I offered him one of my Pall Malls.

He hesitated, then took one. The way he stopped right before grabbing one screamed that he wasn't a smoker. So why take one? As always, he had to pretend we were the same. He liked all the music I liked, the same movies and food. He might've jumped sooner if I'd jumped first.

That was how it always was with him. He didn't know what he really wanted. He *thought* he knew what he wanted, and that vague thing existed somewhere out there. So, he went around trying to find a woman to fit this general outline he was pretty sure he wanted, and he'd somehow decided Layla Lee Thompson was the perfect fit. Which pissed me off. Why waste time forcing me into a mold you're not even sure you want? You think you're a fucking god that can hypnotize someone into loving you—just got to be similar enough to the person to trick them?

The last time he'd fumbled around in the dark, I'd asked him why he didn't turn on the light so we could see each other. He'd shrugged. "I can see you."

All he could see was his damn outline. Not me. Never me.

DAI
2015

I SAT ACROSS FROM LAYLA WITH MY PALMS DOWN ON THE table and tapped my fingers to her song. I didn't look at her. Every time my eyes met hers, I thought of rain. Then, through the smoke, I saw Layla's eyes were blue, and, remembering the blur of her chocolate-colored hair through the porthole, I could not remember if she had been strawberry blond or if I had made that up, too. I had no idea what to say.

Layla finished her cigarette and flicked the filter away. She sat on her hands. I pulled the cigarette out of my mouth. I didn't want to smoke it in front of her. It felt like something secret that she shouldn't see me do. Like this was my first time and I didn't want to embarrass myself. Like I was the kid before the fall pretending to be me. But I had it in my hands, so I watched it burn down between my fingers. Then I flicked it away. Ash and all.

Layla lit another cigarette. "How have you been?"

I shrugged. The straight brown hair emphasized the lack of gold in her eyes. I had nothing to say.

Layla jumped up out of her seat and turned to go.

I kept tapping. My eyes were glued to my fingers as though they moved of their own volition. Layla knew it was the song. What else did I have after seeing her eyes were blue?

She turned back, walked over, and stood over me, her palms on the table.

"Dai, you do not want me. You didn't want me then, either. I was always alone next to you. When we were together, you'd look at me in the eyes, but not at me. You'd look into your future. You had this future for yourself where you had everything you wanted, except you had no idea what that meant. I was just a prop for your future. A means to an end you couldn't even define."

The song was gone. My mind reached out for it and clutched empty air. I couldn't look at her. My body spasmed then froze at that moment with her. Her blue eyes waited.

I looked up and met them. Time continued, and my body reacted.

I laughed. She was right. So right, it was hilarious.

Layla was so thrown by my reaction, she laughed, too.

We laughed so hard our sides hurt and tears fell from our eyes.

LAYLA
The Break-Up
2010

I SIT LISTENING TO THE RAIN HITTING THE PAVEMENT outside, hitting the gutter of Reginello's next door. The garbage can out front is silver and a quarter of the size of the dumpsters behind the other shops next door and down the street. I can just make out the sound of the rain hitting the dumpsters, but that tiny can *tinks* so loud that it overpowers the sound of the rain on those dumpsters. The dumpsters don't seem to mind; they continue on the beat. *Bom. Bom.* The *tink* of the rain on the smaller can continues as a bright harmony on top. *Tink. Tink. Tink.* Then the whack of the rain hitting the worn paving stones of the road, running down the street. The gutters gurgle along. The gentle knocking of the rain on the roof rounds it all out. Then, to accent the ensemble, the smell of warm, fresh bread to bring a smile to my face. The yeasty smell of the bread is joined by the warm smell of cinnamon. My favorite.

A bell clangs.

I cringe.

I look up and see it's the bell above the door that hasn't made a sound in years. Below it, Dai. His eyes are big and watery like a fish's, but because he is not a fish, he is soaked. His hair sticks to his face and his forehead. Water drips out of his hair and down the sides of his face. His shirt looks like he took it out of the washer mid-cycle and slapped it on. He's slumped forward like he is being weighed down. He throws his hands through his hair, and water gets everywhere. Sherry's going to be furious. I jump up and grab him by the arm and pull him out of the bakery. The bell is silent as I swing the door open.

Once outside, we start to walk. I try to listen to the rain and realize I can't hear the differences anymore. It all sounds like *whoosh*. I look up at Dai. His hands are stuffed in his pockets, and he doesn't look like a fish, he looks like a wet dog. I smile over at him but remind myself I have a specific message to convey. He puts his hand through his hair again. It looks greasy, not even wet. I feel myself frowning. I put my hand out to see how much rain will collect in it. It's barely any, so how is he soaked?

Dai sighs deeply, like a balloon full of air that never runs out.

No. I stop walking. That inaudible *no* in my head is seconds from bursting through my lips at full volume, but the southern belle in me refuses to let it out. Dai keeps walking. His back is still slouched. His hands are shoved into his pockets. I watch him continue to walk like it doesn't matter: the rain, the place, or who is beside him.

When he gets to the four-way intersection, Dai seems to come alive. He looks around, and when he sees me, he looks down at his feet while he runs back. I wonder if he has to watch his feet to make sure he comes back to me. Does he have to repeat my name over and over to remind himself whom he is running back to?

Dai reaches his hand out when he arrives, standing in front of me. I want to say, "Sir, I don't know you." I wonder if he'd keep running? I look up into his eyes—they are puppy-dog eyes, wet and big. His nose is red. I put my hands on either side of his face. His cheeks are frigid. Dai gives me a mechanical smile. The rain in his hair keeps dripping down like he has a damn faucet on the top of his head. What's crazier is he doesn't acknowledge it. The water pours down into his eyes and into his mouth. He doesn't blink or spit out the water.

I still kiss him, though. Against my better judgment, I stand on my toes and put my hand on the back of his neck. I touch his lips with mine. "Touch" is the best word to use. I feel nothing from it, and his lips are cold. He could be a statue. I sigh deeply afterward—a fellow balloon. Dai runs his hand through his hair once again and smiles at me. It's the same ventriloquist-dummy smile he gave earlier.

We walk back to the bakery. I grab both of his hands. I look him in his puppy-dog eyes and say, "Dai. This is it. Don't come here again. I won't be coming up, either." He hums a few bars of *the* song. I can barely hear the words, but I know he's humming "Layla." He hums the song every time I try to end this.

I turn to open the door. As I lean into it, the bell tings. Dai grabs my elbow. "Don't forget, I'll be down to celebrate your birthday in a few months." Then he drops his hand and runs to his car out front. The rain picks up, and half of me is soaked and cold. I stand, watching Dai drive off, leaving me cold, wet, and regretting him.

I push the door open and walk in. Sherry rushes over with a towel. "You need to tell that boy to stay his ass in Virginia and to leave you alone."

I sigh, but it feels like a continuance from the start of my earlier sigh. It comes out low, infinite, and unproductive. He will keep coming down, cold as a fish on ice, and turn me into one, as well.

Sherry brings me a cup of what looks like hot tea and lemon. I drink it and grimace.

"Sherry, what's in here?"

She smiles at me. "Dove, just drink it, and you'll feel warmer after."

I drink the whole cup before I realize it's brandy. I take out my phone and dial his number. It rings once, and I hang up. I pull up our text chain and type: "*We aren't going anywhere. We live in different states. We barely manage to see each other twice a year. We only talk online. It is time we move on.*"

Sherry brings out two slices of her cinnamon bread, fresh from the oven and toasted. She puts a small dish of homemade strawberry preserves next to it. I smile up at her, appreciative. Then I pick up the knife at the table and spread the preserves on the toast. As I spread, I close my eyes and listen to the soft scrape of the knife against the toasted bread. I take a bite.

Sherry's nephew Theodore walks in. Everyone in town calls him T. I call him Theo, and he lets me. He doesn't have a drop of rain on his white T-shirt. He whistles my song like the happiest bird, with trills and improvisations. It sounds alive, fluid, warm. His hips seem to move like a cat's. My heart picks up. I can hear it in my ears. He slides into the other side of the booth. He lays his brown arms across the table, palms up, looking into my eyes, and sings my soul song.

I put the toast down, put my hands in his, and he slides out of the booth, holding on to me. He makes this awkward movement as smooth as though we have done this a thousand times before. He spins me around and then brings me to his chest. He rocks me and whistles my song. I rest my chin on his shoulder and close my eyes. On cue, he starts to sing the words softly into my ear. I wrap my arms around his neck. I rock with him. His voice sounds like a promise I want him to keep.

MARY
1996

I HAD MISSED MY CHANCE AGAIN. I SAT AT THE BREAKFAST table alone; EZ had decided to go back to his morning job so he could pay for my medical bills. He had also decided to move the breakfast table back inside so I wouldn't catch a chill, and I'd laughed at that.

Sitting inside at the table, looking out at those apples, I decided I still had a choice. I took the money EZ had saved for me and bought the cheapest cruise I could find. It was a '70s revival two-night cruise on Chesapeake Bay.

That night, I told EZ I didn't want Little Ma to remember me shriveled and bald. He held his forehead against mine, his hands holding tight to my hands. He didn't say a word. He breathed in and out four times, and then he let me go, turned, walked into our bedroom, and closed the door.

I didn't say goodbye to Little Ma.

Momma insisted on coming on the cruise with me. I told her, "Mom, come collect my body after." She asked how I knew God was ready to take me. I told her, "God had nothing to do with this. This is *finally* about me."

She looked up at me, getting my meaning. It made her an old woman, the realization. She seemed to cave in on herself. Her face sagged and wrinkled. Her roots grayed. She fingered the cross at her neck. Then she sighed. It was never-ending.

I stood with her, allowing her *her* time. Then I reached out for her hands, the way she'd used to do when I'd fallen and needed comfort. I leaned down and kissed my momma's forehead. I told her, "I love you." She nodded like a child consoling herself. Then she grasped my hands tight, squeezing tighter and tighter, trying to convince my body to live. Pleading. I stood quietly. Patiently. Resolved. She released me. I turned and walked away, quickly, so she wouldn't think I had changed my mind.

When I reached the end of the hallway, I turned around for one last wave. She stood watching me walk away, her hand raised. Her other arm supported the raised arm, as though it were taking all of her to do this one simple action. I waved, turned away, and walked out the door.

MARA
2015

THE DAY *WE* WOULD HAVE GONE TO MEET MY FATHER, I
went alone. I wore a white lace sundress that flowed
with me as I walked, and I didn't realize I looked like
a bride until I was sitting in the car in my father's driveway.
I didn't cry. Not then. I got out of the car and walked around
back to the small cherrywood table sitting in the middle of the
orchard of apple trees my father had planted many years before.

After I sat, he looked up into my face and smiled gently. I
couldn't say it. My father reached his hand out to mine and
squeezed it. Still holding my hand, he sang Etta James's version
of "How Deep Is the Ocean." I had never seen him sing one of
his melancholy songs. I had only heard it through his bedroom
door. His tenor started low, like he didn't want to be too loud
and startle me. Then it soared big and loud, covering me like a
blanket. On the high notes, he would return to a hush, so that
I would have to strain to hear the vibrato, which brought the
tears, and then I was singing melancholy with him. And when
we got to Etta's telltale finishing note, we looked at each other. I
saw it in his eyes, then. This was what happened behind the door.
He mourned my mother and I sang with him to cheer him up.

We sang another song, and when we were finished, he
brought out the steaks to grill. He had bought them "just in
case." He didn't say anything more about it.

I started another melancholy song, and when I stopped in the middle to sob, he picked up the melody and sang it loudly until the end.

I HADN'T KNOWN my mom. She'd died when I was six. I had memories of her. Glimpses. The feeling of her hand patting my back to calm me, the smell of Isoplus in her hair, but I couldn't remember seeing my mother with a smile on her face. I could only recall the frown she'd worn to her own funeral, her skin the color of gray wax, and the look of irritation she'd worn at having died so young. These things had made it hard to know how to react. I'd looked up at my dad, and his head had been in his hands, tears streaming down his neck.

I remember my dad had joked with my mom when she'd been alive; he would tell her that the pissed-off look on her face would get frozen into place. She would give him an exaggerated version of the look and wave him away. She'd never smiled.

One day in Sunday school, my cousin had whispered to me that my mom had had a look meaner than anyone alive or dead, lying in that coffin. I'd slapped her and run into the service to be held by my father. He'd taken me outside. He'd held me and sung me a ballad until I calmed down. I'd never told him why I had cried, and neither had my cousin. Twenty-three years later, I sat thinking of my mother's face, which I had started seeing in my mirror. I sat at my breakfast table, two years and a month after Sailor had moved out, and I wept.

I told myself I was sad because Sailor's absence reminded me of my mother's absence, or in some twisted way, I missed the companionship of my mother's voice snarling and snapping at me, but it was the silence. The feeling of being absolutely alone.

LONELINESS WAS NOT always a rabid dog at my heels; six days a week, I worked eight-hour shifts as an in-home aid. I would change bedpans, clean homes, and help with rehabilitation, but my favorite chore was cooking meals for my clients, and in my free time at home, I would cook even more. Each morning before work, I'd pick out a recipe to make when I got home. On my way home from work, I would stop by the grocery store and pick up the ingredients, and when I got home, I would start cooking.

On Sundays, I would work all day in my garden. It was heaven to be surrounded by inspiration. Many Sundays, I would rush inside with an idea and throw a recipe of my own together. When the recipe turned out well, I would take it to the food bank. When the food turned out terribly, I would throw away the failed meal, make a recipe that worked, and take that to the food bank. Soon, I had a whole book of my own recipes that were successes. Oliver, who ran the local food bank near my condo, started to look forward to my tiny little blue Beetle chugging up the hill to the church. He'd come outside and wave to me. I'd roll down my window and wave back.

OLLIE TOOK ME on a walk through the park at midnight. He said it was the best time to see the stars. When he had asked me, I had been standing in the doorway of his office, handing him a pan of fresh lumpia. His ring finger, naked, had been barely touching my pinky finger. I'd decided, why not?

Standing in the dark across from Ollie, a bedsheet spread out between us, our eyes connected. His eyes were hazel and sparkling behind the wire-rimmed glasses that took up half of his face. We threw up the Caribbean-Sea-colored sheet at the same time, and it rippled in the air like water. It felt like the parachute game I'd used to play in kindergarten. I giggled, feeling playful and ready for an adventure. We lay side by side, on that Caribbean Sea on the hill in the middle of the park, at midnight, our pinky fingers side by side, brushing each other on occasion. He turned over and shut off the lantern by his head, then pointed out constellations to me. I didn't see them, but I listened to his stories. His voice rose and fell like water, like music, and when he turned toward me on our isolated sea to kiss me, I kissed him back and grabbed his shirt to pull him to me. He shifted toward me so our hips were parallel to each other and so close, but needing to be closer. He put his hand under my skirt, and in the dark, I didn't have to close my eyes to pretend I was with *him*, I needed only believe. I pretended this was *our* first date under the stars, but then Ollie bit my earlobe and pinned me to the ground. I wrapped my legs around him and flipped him over, triumphant, and then we were animals in the night, watched by the constellations. We howled, throbbed, moaned, and pounded.

TARA WAS SWEET. She worked at the coffee shop I stopped at on my way home from my bakery-in-progress. She had a small smile on her face at all times, her bottom lip was the same color as toffee, and when I asked her out, she blushed. When she came, her moans sounded like singing. I would kiss her collarbone and nip the inside of her neck, which smelled like ginger. She loved to pinch and suck my nipples, which seemed strange to me—a woman loving breasts as much as a newborn—but I would come, and then, so would she. It was joy.

I DECIDED TO install the wood paneling of the floors in my bakery myself. I watched a few YouTube videos, then went to the hardware store and decided on redwood because it was warm and bright. It wasn't in the hardware store that the memory surfaced or driving over to my shop in my borrowed pickup. It was the moment I laid the second board down and connected it to the first that I remembered the muggy heat of Dai's tiny apartment kitchen: the smell of simmering garlic, the sound of my knife chopping bell peppers for lasagna, and the summer-sun feeling of his eyes on me, reminding me I wasn't alone.

It was on the sixth board that I remembered the dark brown of his eyes looking up at me at the hospital, as I'd always wanted, but asking for answers, too, to questions I could not answer.

When I fit the final board into place, I stood and looked at my handiwork. The boards fit well. I walked across the ten-by-ten room that would serve as my dining area. Mine. I walked across it again, and then I sat down cross-legged against the wall and closed my eyes.

AND THERE HE is, waiting just outside the doorway of my tenth-grade English classroom. Waiting for Layla. His hands are stuffed in his jean pockets; his hair is long enough to cover his ears and sits right over his eyes, which seem to be attached to his shoes, and his shoulders are squared and full of the potential to hold anything. Layla walks toward Dai, her hips swinging, chestnut hair gathered over her right shoulder. A slight space on the left side of her neck is exposed, showing a few strands of hair at the nape. As she approaches him, Dai leans into the classroom, his hands still shoved into his pockets, his body still leaning against the wall, but right before he meets her eyes, he meets mine, and in his dark-brown eyes, I see a world—for me.

I STOOD UP, picked up my wallet and keys, and slipped them into their respective pockets. I grabbed the borrowed tools and put them back into my dad's toolbox. I locked up my bakery-in-progress and placed the tools on the floor of the pickup, locking it up, as well. I decided I would walk home and return the truck the next day.

Walking down the sidewalk, I looked up at the gray and clouded sky. I had everything I wanted and needed, and yet his memory still haunted me. I crossed my arms over my chest. I hated him. Which made me laugh, because somehow, after all these years, I was still that girl, mooning after him, dancing around in my daddy's orchard, daydreaming about the boy who'd sat at my empty lunch table on my first day back, and instead of saying "I'm sorry your mom died" or sitting awkwardly silent because his mom had told him to be nice, he'd stuck a straw in either nostril and snorted them out, and I'd laughed and laughed. We both had. And there it was: the gift he had given me so long ago. My laughter had been the start, though I wouldn't understand that butterfly-wing, heart-pounding, dancing-in-my-daddy's-apple-orchard feeling until the day in tenth grade when he'd met my eyes at the moment before his eyes had met Layla's.

I put my hands back into my pockets and continued to walk. Then I heard a sweet soprano that danced into my ear. I looked back toward the voice, and Tara leaned out the front door of her coffee shop. Her right hand waved me in; the bright pink polish on her nails called to me. I turned around and walked back toward her, because all I wanted was to hear her sing so I could forget about Dai and my loneliness.

LYING BESIDE HER the next morning, seeing her pink fingernails on my hip, twitching when I moved, as though she might dig her nails into me to keep me planted here in this bed with her, I knew I loved Dai. Of course I did. When I closed my eyes, I saw visions of him; when I kissed anyone else, the taste of maple bourbon collected in the back of my throat, and I could not explain it. Nor did I want to. I turned my head and settled back next to Tara. She turned around, and I wrapped my arms around her and kissed the middle of her upper back, right on her spine. I left my lips on her skin and took in the ginger scent, then closed my eyes, hoping to dream of the sound she made when I kissed her inner thigh, though I knew that what I would really dream about was the taste of maple bourbon and that moment in tenth-grade English when he'd first looked up at me with those "I love you" eyes and I couldn't help but feel the same.

ON THE DAY I turned 31, I had a quiet dinner at my condo with my father. We made gumbo. I pulled out a battered stock pot that I had bought for fifty cents at a yard sale. It was blue with white flecks scattered across the outside like the stars I had seen with Ollie about a year before. My father chopped up vegetables, and I cleaned the shrimp. We stood side by side and hummed. Quick, upbeat gospels that made us look at each other and smile. As he made the bacon, it started to pop and snap, and he closed his eyes and started to sing a ballad. It was a deeper bass than I remembered; or, perhaps, he had changed, too. My alto lifted and accented his bass.

Once dinner was ready, my father and I sat down to eat. He asked me how my maple cake recipe was going. I told him I was still trying to perfect it. He told me about a new book he was reading. I mentally noted the title so I could add it to my reading list. We talked about a Netflix special we both had seen and enjoyed.

A guilty pang hit me. I let go of my father's hand. I cleared my throat. My father asked me what was wrong. I pulled back the collar of my shirt and showed him the bouquet of baby's-breath I had just gotten tattooed on the nape of my neck.

My father stood up and looked at it and then sat slowly in his chair. He pulled out a heavily creased and wrinkled picture from his wallet. In the picture, a young woman stood with a sly smile on her face. She had a white lace scarf tied around her head, her fro standing out behind it. In her hands, she clutched a bouquet of baby's-breath above her stomach, which was so swollen that her belly button could be seen sticking out through her flower-print summer dress.

My father folded the picture of my mother back up, and before slipping it back into his wallet, he brought it to his lips and kissed it. The kiss was loud, and I couldn't help but smile at them. Even death could not separate the love my father had for my mother.

After putting his wallet back into his back pocket, he grabbed my hand and squeezed it. "You're as beautiful as her, you know."

DAI
Paths Converge
2018

*I*F I'M FIGHTING A WAR, ONE I BELIEVE IN, EVEN IN THIS SUIT, *I will be valiant.*

I rolled out of bed and sat on the edge; the carpet tickled the bottoms of my feet. I coughed. It was too shallow, so I coughed a few more times until the phlegm came up. It sat like a liquid slime pearl in the middle of my tongue. I stood up. My knees cracked. I stretched my arms in front of me and fell into a squat. Then I stood up and danced to the bathroom. I slid my feet on the carpet. Pointed finger-guns to no one with a Hollywood smile. Swung my hips salsa-style. I jumped into the bathroom and felt the satisfying sting—followed by the cool relief—of the tiles. Mara's song buzzed between my lips. It sounded like honey and tasted like garlic simmered in olive oil. I spat the phlegm into the sink. It went straight down the hole. I gave myself a couple of golf claps. *Why not celebrate the victories?* as Jerry would say. I picked up my pack of Lucky Strikes from the sink counter, pulled one out, and stuck it into my mouth. I patted myself down for my lighter, then laughed, because I was in my boxers. I opened the medicine cabinet and pulled my lucky yellow lighter off the shelf. I licked the tip of the cigarette propped between my teeth, just to get a taste. I lit it while it sat in my mouth, covering the tip of the cigarette with my hand out of habit. I pulled, deep and slow, until the smoke hit the bottom of my lungs. I blew it out. Smoke escaped through my nose and mouth like I might be on fire on the inside.

I thought back to the conversation I had had with Layla three years back, when we had finally stopped laughing. "You're different, Dai," she'd said. "I thought you hadn't changed, but now you seem—maybe not happy to, but willing to go with the flow." I'd sat back in my metal lawn chair across from Layla, and Kit had come to mind, kneeling on her blue-tiled floor with the pregnancy test in hand: *Sometimes you love this life, but other times, you want to be in control, and that's not how this works.* Then the bones in Mara's back moving underneath her brown skin, unconcerned. Alive. Beautiful. "You found her, then?" Layla had leaned back in her seat, looking amused while yanking out another cigarette. I'd known what she'd meant. I hadn't wanted to give her the satisfaction, though, so I'd shrugged. Layla had shrugged back. "Well, I'm happy for you. Hope you guys have your happily ever after."

I had almost been upset with her, at that moment. All the time we'd known each other, and she had been patronizing me. I had looked up at her. "There's no such thing. People don't find one another, then the story ends. If that were true, love would mean more suicide pacts."

Layla had laughed. "Suit yourself." Then she'd gotten up and walked away. Hadn't looked back at me once.

I hadn't come back for Mara. It had seemed like setting myself up for failure—or that suicide pact—so I hadn't. My parents had sent some money, I'd gotten a nine-to-five that'd take me, and life had kept going. Simple. Easy.

I took another drag on my cigarette. This time, as long as my lungs would let me. I watched half the cigarette turn to ash in front of my eyes, and then I let the smoke out before I could begin coughing. I started coughing anyway, spat the offending phlegm into the sink, and looked in the mirror. "Fucker, you gotta quit this." I flipped off my reflection and ran my hands through my hair, and a twinge of electricity ran up my back. I smiled to myself and continued humming Mara's song.

DAICHI
1945-1975

SUDDENLY, I HAD A FAMILY. A WIFE, A MOTHER, AND A family name with a future that I needed to protect. I finally understood why my father had silently worked the same piece of land for thirty years, why Ueno Daichi had run valiantly to his death, why I could not help but offer my precious jar of freedom to Akira. Because family was not just a word. These people were now bound to my fate. What I did rippled out to them.

UENO DAICHI'S GRANDFATHER, now my grandfather, had been a smart man. When Japan had opened its borders for the first time in 200 years, Ueno Giichi had started a company that had researched new technology abroad. His parents had been dead, and his wife's parents had died, as well, so it had been just he, his wife Sachiko, and eventually, their son Ueno Tadashi. Ueno Giichi had been good-natured and quick like his grandson would be, so people had liked him, and he had had no problems keeping his partners happy. By 1870, the company had been doing exceptionally well.

But by 1890, the company had started to lose money, as farmers could no longer afford to live in Japan and had started to move overseas for more money. Ueno Tadashi had been impatient. He had been trained his whole life to take over his father's company, yet it had been failing even before he could take it over. In 1910, he'd decided to go to America with everyone else, so he could make a fortune and bring it back to save his father's company.

WHILE HE WAS away, his father, Ueno Giichi, had died.

UENO SACHIKO, HIS mother, had taken over the company.

UENO SACHIKO HAD learned well from her husband. She had run the business for quite some time, but, after a few years, had missed her son and had written that he should come home to run the business himself. Ueno Tadashi had not had the same business sense that his parents had. Within a year, he had nearly bankrupted the company and used up most of the savings. Though she'd loved her son, Ueno Sachiko could not watch him squander the work she and her husband had put into their company or watch their workers become homeless because her son was careless. Ueno Sachiko had given her son as much money as she could, and then she'd sent her son and his new wife, Sayuri, back to America to protect him from the embarrassment of stepping down.

Ueno Tadashi had been bitter. He had failed to make a fortune his first time in America, he had failed to run his father's business, and then he'd been back in America at the same place he had started the first time he had arrived. In despair, he'd gambled and drunk his way into legend. One day, he'd gotten up and spoken a rhetorical phrase along the lines of "Going to get cigarettes" or "I'm going out," and then he'd pushed open the screen door, which had squeaked awfully with rust, gripped his late father's briefcase packed with a few clothes, and stumbled down the stairs into oblivion.

Sayuri had been relieved. Which had horrified her for an hour, sitting at her dinner table. She'd had no idea how she would feed young Daichi. Undeterred, she'd written to her mother-in-law, Sachiko, then had gone to the local Buddhist church for guidance. At Walnut Grove Buddhist Church, Sayuri had found a community. She'd found a job as a typesetter for the *Nichibei Shimbun* from a fellow temple-goer, and she'd rented a space for her and her son's pallets in a house with a few other families through another typesetter.

Daichi had played and grown up surrounded by other Nisei kids whose parents had gone to the same Buddhist temple as his mom and the Japanese/English-language United Methodist church nearby. He'd gone to a school where he'd learned Japanese and English with the rest of the Nisei kids in his neighborhood.

Over the years, Ueno Sachiko had pleaded with her daughter-in-law to bring her grandson home, so that he could be raised Japanese. Sayuri had missed Japan, but she'd had a job, friends, and a church community, and her son had been thriving, so she'd stayed.

WHEN DAICHI HAD been old enough, he'd moved his mom and his wife Akira into his employer's home with him, where he would grow oranges and carve wooden birds.

SOMETHING HAD BEEN coming. There had been a change in the air. Sayuri had seen it in the number of shops with new "No Japs Wanted" signs and in the pamphlet she'd seen on the ground outside of the local grocer that had shown the differences between a Chinese face and a Japanese face. In May 1940, Sayuri had received a letter from Sachiko. As had always been the case, Sachiko had been concise: "I am sick and do not want to die alone." Sayuri had told her son she was leaving to care for his grandmother. Daichi had insisted Akira go along, as Sayuri had been losing her eyesight and had been getting too old to travel alone.

BEFORE THEY HAD boarded the boat, Akira had felt the urge to show an uncommon amount of emotion toward her husband. Daichi had been a patient and kind partner. Akira had known Daichi had been a great match for her impatient—and what her mom called her "wandering"—mind when she had met him at a Nisei mixer at Walnut Grove. He had smiled at her across the banquet room, then had brought her a cup of punch. Even after five years, Daichi had still made her a cup of tea every morning, in the chipped green mug he had given her on their wedding day. She'd wished she had packed it in her things, but she just couldn't stand the thought of breaking it. She'd feared it would have been a bad omen, so she had left it on the kitchen table for her return. Akira was not a tall woman, nor did she enjoy bringing attention to her height, but something in her core had told her this would be the last time she would see her husband, so she had stood on her tiptoes and leaned in to kiss Daichi, which had put her slightly off-balance. Daichi, though unsure of his wife's behavior, had still reached out for her hands and locked his with hers, wrists up, to anchor her. And at the moment before their noses would brush, he'd seen her eyes were not all brown but had gold dots like molten bits of sunshine. Their noses had bumped, he'd laughed, and she'd blushed and put her hand in front of her mouth in embarrassment. Daichi would dream about this moment for many years. How could he not?

On overcast days, muggy, wet, and heavy, I imagine Ueno Daichi dying on the ground in Germany, feeling his heart counting down to the end of his life, struggling to pull in enough breath to remember Akira's eyes one last time.

MOST NISEI WERE treated as outcasts in Japan. Many of us did not speak Japanese. Though I was surrounded by people who looked like me, I would have been jobless and homeless, as I was seen as an American since I had been born there, dressed like them, and knew very little about Japan. I was finally seen as an American, and I was hated for it. But of course, I had my Akira. I was thankful to Ito-sensei for teaching me what he had been able to, but Akira ensured my survival in Japan.

Though she was also Nisei, her predecessors, Ueno Sachiko and Ueno Sayuri, had taught her as much as they could in the four years she had lived in Japan, caring for the dying Sachiko. Luckily, Akira, like many of the women in the Ueno family were, and as our daughter, Nozomi, would be, was quite an intelligent woman and had a natural talent for business.

We decided Akira was the natural choice for the new face of the company, as Sayuri's eyesight had been taken by a degenerative disorder and I knew very little about Japan or running a business. I would only be associated with the company in name as "Ueno Daichi." I would sign forms, but Akira would head meetings, talk to investors, and for all intents and purposes run the company. Over time, she taught me what I needed to know to be a publicly respected businessman in Japan, but for twenty years, I would be her silent partner. I worked hard to be worthy enough to stand by Akira's side, to hold up the Ueno name.

THE COUNTRY WAS in chaos. Everyone was working to rebuild after years of bombings, raids, and the atomic bombs dropped on Hiroshima and Nagasaki. The country was devastated. Few had time to question who I was. Everyone was focused on rebuilding their lives and the nation as a whole.

WHILE AKIRA WAS building the company in Japan, I wrote to Nisei I had served with overseas. I invited college-educated Nisei to come and work for me, as I did not care if they spoke Japanese, only that they could work hard. Then I traveled and invited educated persons from other countries to come to work for me, as well. If Mr. Martin could create a system in which he forced non-white persons to build him an empire, I could work with people from all over the world to help rebuild my father's homeland.

Soon, we were keeping up with the technology of America.

Soon, the government took notice and contracted us to help rebuild Osaka and Tokyo.

WHEN AKIRA GAVE me our daughter, for the first time in my life, I understood what patriotism would have felt like, had I been born in Japan or had I been white in America. I took her around my company proudly, showing her to everyone. I told everyone how proud I was to give Japan such a beautiful gift. No one would truly understand how meaningful she was to me. The only family I had by blood. I would give her the world.

I MOVED MY family out to Karuizawa, where my mother, Sayuri, could bathe in the springs to soothe her aches and the temperate weather and mountain air would allow her to breathe easy. I would often take her on walks down the path near our house so she could listen to the narcissus flycatchers sing their mating calls as they flew over Kumoba Pond. I would describe the many birds flying around and the wildflowers blooming along the paths.

On these walks, I would wonder whether she hated me for taking her son's place beside her. I would take the breath in to apologize, and she would turn her sightless eyes toward me, smile up at me, and pat my hand as though to tell me everything would be okay. Then she would start to hum, and I could not help but hum along with her. Sometimes I would sing the songs I could remember my father singing in our sugar-beet fields, and Sayuri would walk silently next to me, patting my hand every once in a while, to encourage me to continue.

SAYURI DIED PEACEFULLY. Akira found her in her bed with a smile on her face. She would go to her son in the next life with pride. We packed dry ice around her and covered her with a sheet. Then I sat next to her bed and begged her forgiveness for my lie. I told her where and how her son had died. I thanked her for my place in this family and for my daughter's place. I asked that she show kindness and protection to my daughter. I bought Sayuri a new silk kimono for her funeral. I place an inverted screen in her casket so she could be forever young in the afterlife. There were so many white envelopes brought to her funeral that it would have covered the cost twice over.

After we cremated her body, my daughter picked out a piece of bone from her grandmother's head to foster intelligence and a finger to protect her hands. We hung a picture of Sayuri in the alcove near the door to the house so that she could watch over us and prevent anyone from entering that might want to harm her family. I gave my daughter prayer beads and taught her to pay her respects to her grandmother and her other ancestors every day. For the first Obon after her passing and for many years after, we spent the day at Sayuri's gravesite, cleaning her grave, talking with her, and eating our meals with her.

AKIRA AND I named our daughter Nozomi. "Nozo" meaning "hope," "Mi" meaning "beautiful." It used the kanji for wish, hope, and desire. I hoped all of the wishes of my beautiful daughter would come true.

MY DAUGHTER WAS a gifted pianist. Her grandmother protected her hands and kept her mind from becoming distracted. She was obedient and every bit the perfect daughter.

THE DAY BEFORE I met my daughter's future husband, Sayuri came to me in a dream. She told me I would lose my daughter as payment for my lie, but I would have my place as an ancestor in this family, and my daughter would prosper in this life and join the ancestors when her time came to cross, but only if I let her go.

When my daughter stood fidgeting like a young child before me and refused to meet my eyes, my heart sank. I only asked that she return every year for Obon, that she move back to Japan once I died to care for her mother, and that she keep the family name. Her grandmother had not asked this and it was against tradition, but I hoped it would cause the ancestors to smile kindly on us.

It was also the only way I could tell my daughter my secret. Who I truly was.

MARY
1996

I CHOSE A RENTED GOLD BODYSUIT TO DIE IN. TIGHT LIKE liquid gold poured straight onto my body. Kinetic, with rainbows swirled in, and if I looked close enough, I could see my daughter's dreams and that blind childlike happiness she still had, that she would always have for me, because I wouldn't know her outside of it. But it wasn't the time for nostalgia. I didn't have time for it. No one does, but me especially. I didn't. So, I stopped looking. Liquid gold and rainbows were enough. Are enough. Have to be.

I opened the orange prescription bottle and dumped out three pills. Tossed them back. I barely tasted the chalk, but the bitterness in the back of my throat stayed. I took time with my hair, massaged castor oil into my roots to soften them and into my ends to make them resilient. Then I put olive oil into my hand and laid a light layer of it throughout so I wouldn't scorch the hair my mother had tended to until I had been twelve—that I had tended since then, until my death. And would my momma be the one to fix my hair the last time? Would she forgive my body its cold-wax indifference? And who would do Little Ma's hair, tell her it was normal to fear-hate-love your hair, that her struggle was a microcosm of life, that the second you fell in love with your hair, you realized death wasn't something to be frightened about; life could be fun once you stopped struggling with it, when you stopped trying to make it something it wasn't. And there I went again, forgetting about the time.

I shook out three more pills and didn't feel nauseous, so I took a fourth. It was gonna go down anyway. The chalk taste made me shiver a bit. The bitter taste didn't change. I put the comb attachment onto my blow dryer and pulled it through my hair. Stopped at my curly ends, because sometimes there's a time to fight and sometimes a time to let things go. Timing is what's important, what should be emphasized, not the fight. The loud dryer covered my silent tears. Normal reaction. Like the trembling at the bottom of your spine when you see lightning. You know the thunder is coming. Has to; it's nature. I just hoped when my daughter looked in the mirror at her own face, which would one day look like my face, she saw my love for her. Felt it in the marrow of her bones. Flowing through her veins. In the melanin of her skin. I stared at my reflection, willing my love to travel to the future version of her that needed me most. The love I knew weighed more than anyone's she would ever meet, because it had to—to make up for my absence. I hoped in that mirror one day that my love would come up and out of her and into the air and give her peace when she needed it most. Fuck prayers; a mother's love, *my* love, would—will—cross time and space.

My fro was perfect, but because I was—am—human, I picked it out one more time. And that word again, that curse word that tortures you whether you have too much or too little. This time, I shook out three or four pills, but I couldn't stomach more than one in my mouth and down my throat. I patted my hair, felt that crisp cloud of half-cooked hair that'd be smashed in the back, permanently crushed on satin. I pulled out a white lace strip of cloth I'd last worn two days from bursting with my Little Ma, that my EZ had tugged the end of and looked up into my face and said: "Until the end of my days, I will love you." And I hadn't worn that scarf again. I hadn't wanted to jinx it, hadn't wanted to remember being angry in it, or sad in it. I'd only wanted to remember that moment before he'd spoken, that slight tug of the material around my head making me think, *Will he pull it off? Will it come away and will he disappear, or will this moment mean everything to me, to us? Will he let me keep this little bit of happiness that exists exponentially in this moment?*

I looked at myself, but really at the future version of my daughter, and sent her that moment, too, because if I couldn't give her all the prayers and food and dancing and the love my mother had given me, I could at least give her what I and EZ had shared.

Three more went back. I opened my bottle of water and only then realized my throat felt like cotton because I'd swallowed those pills dry. I drank half the bottle of water.

I wiped the tears. Timing is important, and mine was running out. Is running out. I need to focus. I put gold eyeshadow on my eyelids, gold lipstick on my lips, and blush on my cheeks that'd sparkle in the light. I slipped on rented gold platform shoes, which, like the bodysuit, I assumed they wouldn't take back after. I stood in them and looked in the mirror.

I saw my daughter all dressed up and ready to dance, and I smiled because I knew my music would always be in her, and she'd give it to her daughter, too. And I knew that tonight, I had to be the Queen and there would be no one to dethrone me, to take my daughter's birthright from her.

I took three more pills before I went out. Then put the last seven in my bra. I wasn't going to wait around in my room to die. I was tired of waiting.

I strutted down the forest-green-carpeted hallway to a big crimson room with gold chandeliers and accents. The waiter made the joke that I should be sitting up in that chandelier. I told him I was too alive to sit for too long, then I laughed at my joke. I didn't explain it to him, because who has the time for that?

My last meal was lobster. I asked for two extra bowls of butter, soaked each bite of lobster I took, and followed each bite with a spoonful of butter. I imagined the slick salty liquid was gold, too. I let it coat my fingers, run down my chin and onto my breasts, because I am Queen and woman and I would be keeping none of these calories. And I drank a bottle of Italian wine on the side, which was so sweet it made my lips pucker. After two glasses, I was lightheaded and my face was warm and I was ready to dance, but I wanted apple pie for dessert. I ordered three pieces. I ate each bite of apple pie on a silver fork and followed each bite with a sip of wine. I followed it with three more pills, and when I was ready, I got up and walked away from my table.

I strutted my way down that hall again. Green as the apple orchard my EZ would have. And I closed my eyes hustling down that hall, so I could be selfish one last time and think of him, but all I could see was that apple. So, I opened my eyes, and in front of me were two big mahogany doors. I grabbed both gold-plated handles and swung them open. It was a small, dingy room with colored lights hanging from the ceiling. But it didn't matter—this was my kingdom. I didn't look at a single person, because they didn't matter. I mattered. This was my time. I would be Queen until I dropped dead. I walked onto that floor with all eyes on me, and I started to hustle. I twirled and gyrated. Stomped my feet. Swung my fro. Then it didn't matter what I did. My body moved to no discernable pattern at all. Sweat cascaded down. I couldn't feel my lips; they were numb. My arms flailed. My feet stamped. My hips moved side to side.

This is my moment. The wind plays with my thin summer dress that can no longer sit at my knees and flutters mid-thigh instead. The bluebells tickle my calves and my swollen ankles. EZ's hand, warm and emanating love, hands me the bouquet of baby's-breath that he went to two different flower shops to find. Then the anticipation for his lips on mine, though his bottom lip is always a bit dry, and right after our kiss, I will lick his bottom lip, which always makes him smile but only in the dimple on his right cheek. And he will carefully place his hands on the swell of my stomach, which is like dough pulled tight over a pie crust, and my Little Ma will reach out to the world, to her daddy, so soon. And her tiny reaching fist or big toe feels like knuckles gently stretching out dough, and in my chest, that kid-Christmas-feeling as I wonder what she will look like. I can't wait to love her. Nothing else matters.

MARA
2018

I *FAILED HER* IS THE THOUGHT IN MY HEAD AS I FALL TOWARD the lake below me. Sailor's hands cover her face, her dreads are limp, and her tears are falling down her neck into the lake I am going to drown in. I am falling fast. The wind burns my cheeks on the way down. I know she will not save me. Sailor does not look up, but she wades into the middle of the lake. Her dress doesn't balloon, it sinks, pulls tight so I can see the drooping, melting outline of her body, and I can taste Kentucky bourbon in the back of my throat, but I know those tears in that lake will cover it. I will drown tasting Sailor's pain.

I WOKE WITH tears on my face. I put both palms over it and wiped them away. I sat up and yawned, rolled over, and jumped out of bed. Exhaled, bent over at the waist, and put my palms on my hardwood floor. I sat back on my feet. Stretched my arms out and back in child's pose. I took a deep breath in, feeling the potential for the day. I let it out, releasing yesterday, though I could still feel an aching pain in the back of my throat. I swallowed it down, then I sat on the ground and swung my legs around. I stretched my hips on either side. Once I was done, I stood up, went to my stove, and started some tea. I opened the tea canister for mint, let the scent of peppermint soothe my mind.

When I got back to my room, I went to the bathroom and started the shower. Then I took off the giant Garfield T-shirt I'd slept in and stood naked in front of the full-sized bathroom mirror. I looked myself up and down. I said, "You are beautiful." I spoke this mantra two more times before absentmindedly rubbing the baby's-breath tattooed on the back of my neck for my mom, but really for Sailor. I frowned, thinking of her tears. For a moment, I felt the warm friction of her breasts against mine. The familiarity of her hair tickling my hair, my face. I shook her off and stepped into the shower.

I CHOSE AN orange sundress to wear. It was long—hugged my hips tight, then brushed playfully at my ankles as I walked. I decided against a bra and combed my hands through my hair. I figured I would wear it down. The kettle whistled. I walked into my kitchen, pulled the kettle off the eye, and prepared my tea. I left it to steep in my favorite blue mug and, in the meantime, pulled down a piece of not-quite-dried rosemary from above my stove. I braided it into my hair, then looked at myself in my full-length mirror. And I smiled.

ON THE WAY to my bakery, I made my usual stop at the store near my house. I stood in my favorite section, the produce aisle, looking for inspiration. There was none that day. I wandered into the condiment aisle and picked up a jar of sweet pickles. Though it broke my rule, holding those pickles, I felt it: the gaping loss of her.

I heard one of my daddy's songs as a bird's trill. I looked up and to my right.

Dai stood next to me, pretending to look at a jar of maraschino cherries, whistling my daddy's song like this was a coincidence. I put the jar of pickles I had been about to cry over down. Then I turned to face him.

Dai put the jar in his hands back on the shelf and half-smiled, half-smirked, but he looked at me and then away. On and off.

"You're nervous?" I asked his on-and-off eyes. They stopped and looked at me then. His eyes. I felt my smile stretching back to the place it had sat when we'd known each other before.

I dropped it. Lest it get stuck in place.

I said the first thing that came to mind. "Let's get some coffee." I offered my hand in my usual way. Open and confident. Dai put his shopping basket on the ground, took my hand, and followed me out.

DAI
2018

WE SAT AT A TABLE IN THE BACK OF THE COFFEE shop. The seats we chose were upright, like we were afraid of being too relaxed. We settled. I looked around the shop, and my eyes landed on two baristas in red aprons flitting from table to table, asking customers if they needed anything else. The male barista looked up at Mara and gave her a charming smile. I could tell he had seen Mara before and liked her. He looked at her for a few moments, like he was touching her with his smile, kissing her. She looked up and waved back.

The female barista walked over with a smile and bright pink lipstick on her lips. She kissed Mara on her cheek and laid a hand on her shoulder. They talked for a time. I watched back and forth as they talked and gesticulated. I couldn't help wondering where this version of Mara had come from. The girl took Mara's hands in hers and kissed Mara on her cheek again. This was how I knew she loved Mara: as the girl walked away, she looked behind herself like she was trying to keep all of the details of that moment in her mind. I smiled to myself. *Cute.*

Mara simply stirred milk into her tea. She took her time swirling it. Not looking at me. At them. Her tea was the most important thing to her at that moment, or else she just wanted to make me wait. I gripped the underside of the table, trying to hide my anxiety.

Mara brought the mug to her lips, drank, and then placed the cup down on the table. Only then did she meet my eyes. I cleared my throat and gave her my best Hollywood smile, sans finger-guns.

Mara smiled back. "A friend of mine from a while back."

I let her keep her secrets. I wasn't gonna pry. "Kit was pregnant."

Mara looked nonplussed for a moment. She picked up her mug and took a few sips before putting it back down again. "Oh, that's why you're back—running?"

I squirmed in my chair. I was already management at my company, made decisions with a cool head, yet there I was in front of Mara three years later, and I was still that kid. "No. Uh. I mean, she left. I came back here three years ago."

Mara sat forward. Her elbows were razor sharp; they sat on the table in the same way they might if she were preparing to smash me in the face with them. I wondered where she had gotten this power from. She had not raised her voice, yet I feared her. She focused her honey eyes on me until I couldn't stand it and looked away. Ashamed.

I saw movement in the corner of my eye, and I looked back at her; she had put her arms on the table, palms up. Her elbows were hidden. I let out the air I had been holding and rested my arms on top of hers. I traced the veins on the insides of her arms until a laugh fell through her lips, making me smile, which was why I had taken her outstretched hand in the pickle aisle, why I had sat at her empty lunch table in first grade: to see her smile. She looked back at my face. Her eyes turned gentle. She lifted her arms easily. Not in a scared way or in an aggressive way. She simply moved them and stood up. I stood up, too, unsure of the protocol.

Mara walked around the table and into my atmosphere. She held me. Her arms around my neck. Her chest on mine. My arms wrapped around her waist. I realized she was bra-less and her hips fit perfectly on mine. Her nipples brushed against my chest, or perhaps I just wanted to remember her hug like this.

I rocked her side to side as though we were about to waltz. The song played, or she was humming it, and then we were dancing in place. I leaned down and whispered into her ear, "I want to listen to this song forever."

Mara leaned her head back to look me in my face. She wanted to gauge the meaning behind my words. She let go. At that moment, I felt the lake water hitting my chest, dry-ice cold. She kissed my cheek without touching any other part of my body. I smelled rosemary so strong my eyes watered. Then she was walking away, not turning back once to tell me, with her eyes, she still loved me.

I shouted out, "Mara."

She turned around. It happened so slow I feared I was dreaming the whole day, but I asked her to dinner anyway, and when she accepted, I was so thankful I had to excuse myself to wipe tears from my eyes in the bathroom.

AT THE RESTAURANT, we sat over candlelight; it danced back and forth between us, and I had no idea what to say. Mara spoke first. "After Layla broke up with you, why did you jump off of that bridge?"

I couldn't remember at that moment what my mouth had been doing the moment before the question had been asked. Smiling? Frowning? I suddenly had no idea what to do with my face.

I AM BACK on that bridge. Layla's name is shooting out of my mouth like it is vomit. Her song is playing on repeat in my head. There is that incessant crawling, itching underneath my skin like something needs to be done—to get her, or to get away from her. I step up onto the metal railing with my right foot, grab the railing with both hands, and bring my whole body up so I am standing on it. My hands are out to either side, wobbling to keep me balanced. It's late spring, but I can't feel anything anyway, I'm so drunk, except for that buzzing. It feels like a million hornets stinging underneath my skin. I take off my jacket and almost fall trying to get it off my left arm. I drop my jacket, and it floats through the air, a giant black-and-red-striped leaf showing me the way down. *What will you do when you are alone?* I say her name out loud once more, before. I want to feel how my tongue flicks the roof of my mouth, how it tickles a bit, making me grin, even as numb-drunk as I am. It makes me giggle. I open my mouth wide, spread my hands to either side, and fall forward.

BACK AT OUR table. My hands shook as I reached for the glass of bourbon I'd ordered for appearances, as I always did when out with coworkers these days, so I didn't have to go into my story. Took too much energy. But that day, I took two gulps. The taste of Kit's bitter kiss floated up in the back of my throat. It tasted like iron. Which I knew was the memory of the pill mixed with bourbon, neither of which I had swallowed in years, but I still thought, *Could I be bleeding?*

I cleared my throat and answered Mara's question with the first thing that came to mind. "I was a boy with a broken heart."

Mara picked up her drink and sipped it. "You think that's all there was to it?"

I rubbed my chest, which was suddenly itching. I drank some more bourbon but needed some nicotine. "You care if we go outside while I smoke?"

Mara stood and walked out. I got up so quick I bumped the table forward a bit. I cleared my throat and followed her. Outside, I lit a Lucky Strike, then offered her one. She declined. She waited for me to take a few drags before turning her eyes on me again. I took another drag.

"I was a kid and didn't know life was gonna keep going."

Mara reached out and took the cigarette from my lips, sucked on it, and handed it back to me. I was stunned. She blew the smoke to her side and laughed at me. A laughing dragon. My complement.

Mara turned those eyes on me again. "I think you wanted to rush to the end. You wanted to be where you are now but weren't sure how to get there, so you panicked."

I took a long drag on my cigarette this time. I swore I could taste rosemary on it. I blew out the smoke, thinking of Mara's lips. I smiled to myself and looked at her. "Did you love the waitress in the coffee shop earlier?"

Mara took my cigarette once again. "No. Not her."

I stood, watching her finish my Lucky Strike. I wanted to get on my knees and offer her the whole pack, anything to get to happily ever after. Instead, I leaned against the brick facade of a chain restaurant and asked her about the last person she'd loved.

"Her name was Sailor" was all she was able to get out before the tears came. I grabbed her hand and started to pull her into my arms. Mara put her hand up in front of my chest, and I knew this was a private pain. Something she wanted to feel on her own. Though I would have burned down that restaurant to make her feel better, I stood in front of her instead and held her hand while she cried. It was quiet. The tears fell quickly, as though her body was used to keeping that pain inside. When Mara finished, she wiped her eyes and squeezed my hand in return.

We walked back inside and paid for two more drinks at the bar. Then we sat back at our table. Mara hunched forward with her hands wrapped around her tumbler. She looked small, like when she'd been a sad six-year-old, alone at her lunch table, trying not to cry. I reached out for her, took her hand. She looked up at me, sharp and quick. There were slashes of green in the honey color of her eyes. She asked, "Why do people always return to who they were when they knew someone last?"

I was not sure of what her question meant. Was she asking me why I made her feel like a child or why I hadn't changed? I paid for the check instead of answering. I felt the sweat start to collect under my arms and at the small of my back. I couldn't end it like this. "You want to go down the street for another drink?"

Mara checked her phone, trying to find an excuse, I could tell.

I HEAR THAT scream from before. From behind her eyes, rushing past my ears. It is acute and sharp, but it doesn't stop. My stomach drops. I am falling, falling.

"It's the memories." Mara put her phone down, finally, to look into my face. "Every time we change, the old versions of ourselves are saved and tied to all of the memories that self lived. When I see you, I remember everything I felt when I knew you."

Walking down the street with Mara, I remembered the feeling of Layla's hip against my knuckles. The rain pouring down. The smell of fresh bread. Back with Mara, I said, "I think we constantly carry our memories around, but I don't think we change. I think we repeat the same patterns over and over. The memories just shift our perception."

We pondered on barstools next to each other. Mara spoke first. "Would you do it again?"

She didn't say the words, but I understood what she was asking me. I looked over at her, and her eyes were as wide as they had been that night in the dark. I told her the truth: "I don't know."

Mara sighed. "You used to act like nothing mattered. Whether you lay in bed all day and drank or whether you got up and went to work. Whether it was me in your bed or any other girl. It all seemed the same to you."

I sighed this time. She was right, and I wasn't sure how to assuage her. I saw Mara as that six-year-old girl again, before the laughter; I saw her jumping down from that stool and walking out. I felt my child's heart skip a beat, and I knew then I would not survive the loss of her. It wouldn't be the total of the losses in my life. I had lost and I would lose again. I just knew I would dream about her, all day and night until I couldn't tell what was real. When memories of Layla's gold irises and Kit's fire hair fell away from me, Mara's memory would remain; the scent of rosemary would haunt me. Losing her would not send me off of a small bridge over a lake, it would demolish me. I would sit up in bed one day and simply shatter into pieces.

Shaking, I offered my hand to her. "Mara. We create meaning, and I thought I was a non-thinker, but I need to live my life by my own means, and you are part of that meaning." I rushed on before she could accept or deny my offer. "All I have done is dream about you. I can't even imagine my life without your song in my body, I—" I couldn't breathe, couldn't control my tears.

Mara stood and held me to her chest. I wept.

When I finished, we walked outside and she looked up at me. "You don't see that this is what you did with Layla? You are putting all your money on one bet. Again."

I picked Mara's hand up, brought it to my lips, and told her the obvious. "People don't change."

Mara looked away from me. "So, if I hurt you, you will find a bridge to jump off of?"

I looked away this time. "If you leave me, I won't need to. I'll shatter into thousands of pieces."

Mara laughed. "A bit melodramatic, no?"

Hearing that laugh was like tasting happiness in the back of my throat instead of bile. "No. You are my past, present, and future. That will always be the case."

Mara gave a half-smile. "You believe in fate, then?"

I smiled back. "With you, yes."

Mara's smile twisted mischievously. "Then what about Layla and Kit?"

I chuckled to myself. She wasn't gonna make this easier. "I needed them to give me enough memories to shift my perception so I can be here with you now."

Mara was quiet for a few moments. We continued to walk. I heard my own breath. Quick and hesitant. I was waiting for a sign from her. Any sign telling me she would stay by my side, her knuckles brushing mine every once in a while. It started to rain. She looked up and closed her eyes. I turned and kissed her.

MARA
2018

I RECOGNIZED HIS KISS, WHICH WAS THE SAME, WITH AN undercurrent of patience. He took his time with the kiss. Before, he'd been rough and shaking and biting. With that kiss, he started softly. Longingly. It ached, his kiss. He pulled my body to his. I grabbed his shirt, tight, needing more. The embers of the kiss grew into a fire, and his hands had my hips pressed against a wall. I wrapped a leg around his waist, and I knew he would love me the way I wanted, but I pushed him back.

I gave him a chaste kiss on his cheek and took my phone out to order an Uber. It was not yet the night. A night would come. I told him this in a kiss on his right shoulder before I slid into my Uber and closed the door.

DAI
2018

I STOOD ON THE STREET, WATCHED HER GET INTO THE Uber, and waved as she was driven away. I hoped it wasn't our last kiss. I thought through the night, picked out details like pieces of candy, and stored them in the back of my brain. The smell of rosemary on her neck. The soft firmness of her hands in mine. The deep, low laugh of hers that rose higher and higher the more she laughed. Her honey eyes slashed with green. How beautiful her face looked when she cried: the flush in her cheeks lighting up her face, the vulnerability making me feel as though I could reach out and touch her. I ran these details through my mind all night, so I wouldn't forget them.

THE NEXT MORNING, I lay in bed, thinking back on Mara climbing into the Uber and driving away from me. I cursed myself for all the time wasted. I had had my chance. Her body in my arms. Her song in my kitchen. The smell of her love wrapped around me.

That night, I could not sleep.

Nor the day after. Every creak in my apartment made me jump up from my bed. I'd press my eye against the peephole in the door, though Mara would have no idea where I lived now. Every time someone climbed the stairs or walked past the door, my heart stopped.

ON MONDAY, I called in sick to work. I hadn't slept all weekend. I felt like that kid barely out of his teens, who lay in bed all day and worked only twice a week, who had jumped off of that bridge.

I FOUND MYSELF at the grocery store where I had seen Mara, standing, staring at a jar of pickles as though she had wronged it in some way. I paced the produce aisle, looking for her, until an employee asked me if I needed anything. In a panicked answer to his question, I grabbed two or three peaches, so he wouldn't think I was suspicious. I paid for the peaches and rushed to the coffee shop.

AT THE COFFEE shop, I saw the smiling lipsticked girl from Friday evening. Seeing me, her smile dropped. She looked at me, scared. I cleared my throat, ran my hands through my hair, and tried to relax before walking up to the counter.

I only had to say I was looking, and then she gave me a knowing smile and pointed diagonally. I was so flustered that I looked at the finger pointed as though Mara had shrunk and sat on the tip of it. I strained to hear what the girl was trying to tell me.

"Her shop is down the street."

I spat out a quick thanks and ran out of the coffee shop and almost ran past it—"Music in the Kitchen," the name of her bakery. I pushed open the door, and the heat inside rushed into and around me. My desperation melted and started to pour from my eyes. I laughed as I tried to juggle the bag of peaches in between my hands, wiping away tears. I looked up, and there she was: Mara.

She walked up and put her hands on either side of my face. I felt her pinky finger brush the barely visible scar on my throat. Her hands smelled like cinnamon. I laughed. Then I cried. For the absurdity. For my loneliness. For my guilt. For my love. She let my tears fall, every one without interruption. My face was cupped between her hands. She stood on her tiptoes until our foreheads touched. She hummed quietly. My tears ran down and over her hands.

When I was done, she kissed my lips, light and airy. Then again, like she'd been waiting for me. Thought of me in the back of her mind. She bit my lip at the end of the kiss, so I knew this wasn't a dream. Then she looked me in my face with those "I love you" eyes, and I thought she would give me another open-mouthed kiss filled to the brim with longing, but instead, it was a peck on my bottom lip that felt like years of forgiveness all in one kiss. Then she was smiling up at me, hands still on either side of my face, and I felt as though this was our new beginning.

I picked her up in my arms and spun around while holding her close to my chest. Her arms were wrapped around my neck and we were laughing, laughing.

A Lockheed YO-3 flies overhead, silent.

I woke to her song, rolled over, and listened to it for a few seconds. It dawned on me that I had never heard her song exactly right. I had heard the first few notes and assumed the rest of the song, but simply listening to it, it was far sadder and far more beautiful than I had remembered.

I got out of bed, walked up to her kitchen doorway, and watched her hips swing and the bones in her back move. I walked over to her, and I didn't hesitate or fear her. I walked right up to her and slid my arms around her waist. She continued to sway, and I swayed with her, to her rhythm.

She started the song from the beginning, and I hummed the notes I knew. I listened to the rest. Her high, sweet alto was almost a soprano, but at the last second refused to be and stubbornly took the lower note. When she finished the song, it was with a note that was flat, seemingly discordant, and perfect. The note mixed with the smell of rosemary in her hair was intoxicating. I was drunk on her. I kissed her shoulder, then the back of her neck right in the middle of the bouquet of baby's-breath. She sighed. The potential of the moan behind it made my heart speed up.

MARA
2018

I TURNED THE STOVETOP OFF AND MOVED THE PAN OF bacon and eggs to a cold eye. Dai's lips grazed the back of my neck again, and I shivered. I turned around and rubbed the bristles in his not-quite-beard. I chuckled to myself, looked up into Dai's eyes to chuckle some more, and saw an intensity that made my heart pick up a beat. He had a wildness he hadn't had before.

He kissed my throat, nibbled after, and his hands were in my hair, massaging my scalp, and before I could let my moan out into the air, he took it. Put his mouth on mine, sending electricity down my spine. Dai grabbed my hips and lifted me; I wrapped my legs around him. He carried me to my bed, turned around, and fell back. My stomach dropped for a second and I squealed, laughing.

Dai growled in my ear after we landed, and it was clear his meaning, but I wanted to hear it. Needed to. So, I nipped the lobe of his ear.

"Say it."

Dai smiled against my throat. "I love you."

I ran my fingers through his hair. He moaned in his throat, low, so it sounded like a growl. I felt his moaning growl as a hum in my throat, like it was coming from me. "Say it again," I said. Dai smiled against my throat again; I felt the smooth hardness of his teeth against the skin at the hollow. He grazed his teeth along it and said it again: "I love you."

DAI
2018

MARA LAY ON MY CHEST. HER HAIR TICKLED MY face and arms. My right arm lay across her back. Our breaths were in sync, but my mind wandered back to Kit's followers making love to her as a group, as one. For a moment, I missed my and-hood. I felt the loneliness two have between them.

Mara sat up on my hips, then. "What is it?"

I looked up at her. "What do you mean?"

Her wide honey eyes searched my face. "Your breathing changed and I just got the feeling something was wrong."

"You can hear me, can't you?" I waited for her answer. I wondered whether she got what I was trying to communicate. She bent down and kissed my nose. She reassured me with her hands smelling like cinnamon on the sides of my face, which felt like just the right thing. It felt like my mother picking me up and spinning me around while holding me tight against her chest. Then Mara answered me, "Yes."

It flowed out of me before I could stop it. "I have never loved anyone as I love you."

MARA
2018

I LAUGHED. "CORNY MUCH?" BUT IN HIS EYES, I SAW IT. Myself. In his eyes, I saw his version of me, reflected, and I didn't want to look away because I knew he needed to see himself through my eyes, and I was afraid I would show him nothing but death.

He looked hurt, and I was unsure which thing he was hurt about. I saw the little boy in him, the child that needed to be held. I stood on the bed and pulled him up by his arms so that he sat up. Then I sat on his lap and held his head to my chest.

"Try again."

And he did. With his hands and mouth. I apologized in kind, and then we were clinging to each other, with sweat and moans and I-love-yous. We stopped only when we were so tired and hot, we could only lie next to each other, breathing heavily.

We looked over at each other, and we laughed.

SITTING IN THE car outside of my dad's house, I felt déjà vu. All the hairs on my arms stood up, and it felt like I would cry. Dai leaned over and squeezed my hand. I was thankful I had chosen to wear my navy-blue dress; it felt like another beginning.

When we got out of the car, Dai grabbed my hand again and let me lead him around to the back of the house. My dad stood up when he saw us. He walked around to the front of the table and leaned against it with his hands in his pockets, so he could greet the first person to join us at our family table since Mom had passed.

I ran up to my dad and threw my arms around his neck. He pulled his hands out of his pockets, wrapped his arms around me, and twirled me in a circle. Then set me down and kissed my forehead. His salt-and-pepper mustache was stretched wide, like we hadn't seen each other in some time, though this was a weekly occurrence.

He looked behind me. Remembering we were not alone, I looked over my shoulder, apologetic, and extended my hand for Dai's. Dai cleared his throat nervously and put his hand out. My dad stepped forward and put his hand out for Dai's. I dropped my hand, realizing this was a new rhythm the three of us would have to get used to.

We sat. After a few minutes of small talk, my dad went inside for the steaks. He started grilling them, smoke rose up, the smell of cooking meat drifted, surrounding us, and there was Sailor with her smile, coming back home after her overnight business trips. *How* that smile had chased away my guilt-induced nightmares. My dad's voice brought me back, rose, and covered me like a blanket. I looked over at him and he smiled. I smiled back, and my voice joined his. I looked over at Dai. He was listening. He listened and watched us back and forth, trying to get the rhythm just right. Then he joined us, and we were, all of us, in one accord.

After we sang, talking was easy. We ate steak and laughed at the little things. One of us would start singing, then the other two would join in. My dad reached out and squeezed my hand, approving.

When we cleaned up, my dad asked if I had met Dai's parents. I looked over at Dai, who cleared his throat and told my dad he hadn't spoken to his parents in quite a while. My dad shook his head and placed his hand on Dai's shoulder.

"Son, death comes for all of us eventually. That journey out of life is done alone, even with someone beside you. What do you gain by living your life alone?"

Dai looked at him and replied, "The more people I have, the lonelier I will feel on that journey."

My dad laughed, a good-hearted laugh that seemed to start in his chest and rumbled throughout his body. "The older you get, the more you will see that this world is a lonely place with constant reminders of that journey, the only respite being those we love and who love us." He nodded in my direction. Then he took out his pack of cigarettes from his shirt pocket and offered one to Dai. Dai accepted, and they stepped to the side and smoked together, standing companionably. They were nearly shoulder to shoulder, and I had a vision of both of them in tuxes, waiting for me to come around the corner in my wedding dress.

Before we left, I hugged my dad. He held the sides of my face, looked at me, and said, "M&M, I love you." Then he kissed my forehead, between my eyebrows, the way he had done when I'd been a kid. My dad looked at Dai and put out his hand. Dai shook it. My dad patted his shoulder and held it firmly for a moment. Then Dai and I turned and walked toward the car.

As we walked away, I looked behind me and saw my father standing, watching us. He looked fragile, like he had just given me away.

DAI
2018

I KNOW WITHOUT A DOUBT IN MY MIND THAT MY FATHER IS *inside of it. Armed with only a camera, he is still more accomplished at my age than I.*

Mara sat in the car with the keys in her lap, looking like she might burst into tears. I didn't know how to comfort her, so I asked her what the second M in "M&M" stood for. She looked up at me with tears glimmering in her eyes, and she giggled. A small sound that never left her mouth but sat inside with the secret name. She leaned over, grabbed my chin, and kissed me.

"I'll never tell." Her eyes sparkled, and I didn't mind her keeping secrets, as long as that smile stayed on her face.

WHEN WE WERE almost home, I asked her, "Does it bother you that I haven't introduced you to my parents?" She looked over at me quickly, then away. That was how I knew she would lie to me.

"I've met them. No big deal."

Then I was back in that hospital, and my mom was sunken in on herself, tears coming down her face, pain etched into her shoulders. She was holding her arm up like it might fall off all of a sudden. My father, protective, wrapped himself around her the best he could. He led her away. How had I never seen them like that? How had I not felt my mother's pain?

I sighed.

Mara offered her hand. I took it. She squeezed my hand lightly. "Dai, I know not everyone has the same relationship with their parents as I have with my dad. There is no rush."

I lifted her hand to my mouth and thanked her with my lips.

DAICHI
1975-2019

AKIRA AND I SPENT FIFTEEN YEARS AFTER OUR DAUGH-
ter left running our company together. Publicly,
we used Ueno Daichi's name. Privately, we would
walk beside Kumoba Pond together, hand in hand, as the
sun set each evening. She would whisper my real name
into my ear, and I would dip her like I had seen American
heroes do in the movies and kiss her passionately. Then
we would laugh and I would know she loved me outside
of Ueno Daichi.

IN THE SPRING of 1990, Akira was diagnosed with cancer. I put
as much money as I could into her treatment, but she died in
the spring of 1995. I was alone again at the age of 75. Though
Sayuri had not mentioned it in my dream, I knew I was fated
to lose everyone I loved as punishment for the many things
I had done during my life: abandoning my father, bringing
fellow workers to their deaths, stealing the jar, my selfishness
during the war, taking over Ueno Daichi's life.

NOZOMI CAME TO pay respects to her mother, wearing a white silk kimono. My grandson stood beside her in jeans and a T-shirt. He stood just below his mother's shoulder, yet he grasped her hand tightly, unsure of the people around him.

I approached him, and he did not bow. I patted his head and told him, "Like this," then bowed to him to show him how to approach his elders. He let go of his mother's hand and stood stiff like a soldier. He bowed as I had, and then he lifted his hand to his head in a salute. I smiled down at him and kissed his forehead. Then I looked to my daughter, who greeted me the traditional way and then hugged me like an American. My grandson hugged me as well, and I regretted only making my daughter promise to stay if I'd died before her mother. After the seventh day, my daughter and her son flew back home.

I WALKED THE path near Kumoba Pond, where I had walked supporting Sayuri and then laughed with Akira, alone. I had not had time until this point to consider my place in this greater world outside of family and country. I thought, *Would it even matter if I walked into this pond?* Are not these stories we tell and prayers we give simply cultural imperatives to keep our families moving forward, to keep us from being frightened of the unknown? I did not know the answers to these questions. I started reading. I needed to understand my place in the world. I started with Neo-Confucianism and spent a year reading books I could find in Japan and abroad that might help me understand my place. When reading philosophy and metaphysics was not enough, I invited experts to talk to me about them. I traveled overseas to listen to lectures.

AT THE END of two years, I found there were no certain answers. I found myself once again beside Kumoba Pond. I looked over the edge and at my reflection. I saw a 77-year-old version of my father. He had done his best to provide everything he could for me: a roof over my head, food to eat, water to drink, and a livelihood to take on when he'd died. His hands had clutched the dirt not because he had wanted to work until the end, but because he had not been ready to leave me. I wept on this realization, silent and alone, as I imagined my father had done lying between our sugar beets, dying.

I remembered how my father would sit against the wall near the stove in our one-room home, and he would watch me until I fell asleep. Until the age of twelve, I'd slept peacefully, knowing he watched over me. Silent and honorable. Teaching me to live the same way.

I HAD NEVER asked my father for forgiveness for my lies, for the many bodies I had sent to rot, for my abandonment. Nor had I honored him after death. I spent the next couple of years searching for evidence of him in his homeland. It was hard, then. America had done its best to destroy my father's home country through air raids and bombings, but I found Nakajima Genkai. He stood next to my mother, Nakajima Hana. My mother wore a cotton yukata standing next to my father, who wore American trousers and a cotton shirt. My father smiled wide with his arm around my mother, who stood somber and dignified next to her new husband. They were farmers coming to America for a chance to escape an economical caste system, only to be forced into a caste system based on race. I framed the picture and set it beside my bed on the nightstand so I could wake in the morning and pay my respects to them, and so I could do the same before I went to sleep.

MANY YEARS PASSED, and Nozomi decided I was too old to be by myself. Though I could still walk by myself beside Kumoba Pond, and I could still clearly see the leaves on the Mongolian oaks and the narcissus flycatchers soaring over my head, I agreed with her. Once again, I walked the path by the pond with someone to talk to. This time, I leaned on her, and she described the scene around us. I watched with pride as she took over the Ueno company. She hired new innovative scientists and engineers to replace those of my generation who were dying and retiring. She brought in new contracts and expanded the company. She brought honor to the Ueno name.

THE ONLY SUBJECT my daughter hesitated on was her son, my grandson. When I asked, she would tell me he was studying in America and would return when he graduated. At night, I would hear her crying in her room and know she lied to me. I knew from experience that my grandson was fighting his own war in America, whether he realized it or not. When he was ready, he would find his way back to his family to pay his final respects.

MARA
2019

DAI JUMPS FROM THE BRIDGE. HE FALLS THROUGH the air for a few seconds, and then into the lake below. The lake is still before he hits the water. Not a ripple. When he hits the water and as it swallows him, it remains still; this is how I know I am dreaming. Out of the ripple-less waters rises Kit, naked and pregnant. She holds her swollen belly with both hands as though at any second, she will birth her child. Then she lays eyes on me. They are big, green, and accusing.

I WOKE. MY stomach was chaotic. My hand flew up to soothe it. I sat up and shook Dai awake. I searched for his hands in the covers. I grabbed his hands, held them, and squeezed for dear life, so he knew how serious his answer would be to me. I calmed my breathing so I only had to ask once. "Are you the father of Kit's child?"

WHEN WE PULLED up to the farmhouse in Indiana, Dai was nervous. His hands shook. His back had a lake of sweat seeping forward. He had no idea how this would turn out. I didn't either. How could we know? This tumultuous woman—part myth, part human, a goddess who could be touched and pleasured, who would grab you and offer her lips as though she had no idea how powerful she was—I hated her. Though, perhaps, I loved her. I didn't think I would have had the courage to kiss Sailor without her exigent kiss. Had I needed her kiss? Had she freed me from myself? Had she freed Dai for me? Had she the goddess gotten involved between us frail humans simply to bring us together? Perhaps I was giving her too much credit.

I nodded at Dai, signaling that I was ready to walk up to the house. We got out of the car and held hands, squeezing as we approached.

On the porch, Kit lay in a wooden rocking chair, head thrown back, a quiet snore escaping her lips. Her arms were wrapped protectively around her swollen stomach. And I knew I had loved her.

We stood for some time, watching Kit sleep, afraid to wake a sleeping goddess. Meddling in the lives of common folk was tiring, I supposed. I wanted to laugh at my joke but feared waking her, so I bit my lip and swallowed the laugh.

Dai held my hand so tight it was hot, and I imagined my hand burned when he let it go; it wasn't, and the squeezing didn't hurt.

A man came to the door dressed in worn jeans and a heavily mended T-shirt. Wrapped around his left arm was the tattoo of the rose vine covered in thorns. His hair was no longer blue but looked as though it was prematurely graying. He wiped his hands on an old dishrag. Dai and I both looked up, startled, as though we had been looking through Kit's underwear drawer and had been caught. He gave us a pleasant smile, as though coming outside and seeing a couple holding hands while watching a pregnant goddess sleep was a normal occurrence for him.

"She is beautiful," he said. There was no question—of course she was, and in the reverence I heard in his statement, I knew he saw her as the goddess we all saw her as.

I squeezed Dai's hand, as the question was not mine to ask, but his. Only his. He cleared his throat the way he did when he was uncomfortable. Dai asked if we could take a picture of Kit, for later. The man didn't laugh at Dai's joke. He put the rag into his back pocket and stood as though Dai hadn't spoken. Dai cleared his throat and asked if we could stay until Kit woke up.

The man, whom I now recognized as the blue-haired boy who had caught Dai as he'd passed out at the party, said, "Yes, but the kids and the rest of the community will be back in an hour, and it will be hard to get quiet time."

Dai opened his mouth, like a fish, then closed it, which meant all of this was over his head. He got like that sometimes. He hit a breaking point. I remembered myself in front of my mirror, buzzer in-hand, and Sailor with limp hair and never-ending tears.

I spoke for him, or started to. The man gave a knowing smile when I asked, "How many kids live here?"

The man addressed Dai, who could not look him in his eyes. "None of them are yours, brother. We decided, since you went off on your own, it was not right to tie you to us. We bind only willing parishioners."

The invitation sat among the four of us.

I put my head down. Nausea hit me hard. I fought the urge to grab my stomach, turn, and vomit. I swallowed bile, squeezed Dai's hand, and glanced in his direction using my periphery. Dai nodded and dropped my hand. My stomach did a freefall, and I couldn't breathe for a moment, but he turned and walked to the car, and I knew he was responding to the information and not the invitation. He stumbled into the car and closed the door behind him.

I thanked the man. He shook my hand and asked that I have a good day. I responded in kind and followed Dai's path to the car. Dai was ghost-white. My stomach did flips. This time, my hand rushed up to it, protective. I asked Dai if he was okay, and he stared out the window at nothing. I thought of Sailor doing tai chi, full of anxiety but giving me space until I had been ready to approach her again. I took a deep breath, dropped my hands to the steering wheel, started the car, and waited.

HALFWAY HOME, HE reached over and squeezed my leg. It hurt. I yelped. I was going to yell at him, but when I looked over, his face was red, almost purple, looking bruised. Then the tears. Next came the sound. A heaving. Then an intake of air as loud as a vacuum cleaner. I didn't need to ask whom he was mourning. I leaned over and grabbed his hand. He squeezed mine hard, and all I wanted at that moment was for him to burn through my hand with his. Anything to make his pain go away.

WHEN WE ARRIVED home, a wave of nausea hit me so hard I had to sit in the car for a moment to keep from vomiting.

DAI
2019

*I*F I LISTEN HARD ENOUGH, I CAN HEAR THEM, OR IT.

When we got home, I got out of the car and lay like a starfish on our bed, like I'd used to do when I'd lived alone and the lake water from my jump had felt like it was sloshing around in my lungs. Lying there, my mind wandered and settled.

This world is a fucking joke. You are driven to become a man. It itches underneath your skin, burns and itches until you make a major move, but the punchline is, it doesn't matter what you do. You just wake up as an adult one day, no matter what, but in those moments before that day, when the itch is getting so bad you just want to flay the skin off of your body, you don't know that. You just keep feeling the itch, the incessant itch, and all you can think about is making it stop, and when I'd felt it, made my move, and she'd shot me full of bullets, it had felt like the only choice I'd had was to get rid of the itch—to jump off of that bridge and onto that impossible hill in my dream, because it had been better than facing that itch. Myself. My mistakes. My fear.

Seeing Kit lying in that chair, pregnant and powerless, I'd seen she was human, but instead of embracing her humanity, like her followers, she had chosen sheep-hood, a collective where she didn't have to make decisions. She hadn't even chosen to give up the pregnancy. It had been decided. Kitand had done me a service by releasing me and our baby, but I knew I would always hate them for this.

MARA
2019

I STOOD IN THE SHADOW OF THE DOOR, WATCHING DAI FALL
before my eyes. Once again, I was powerless to stop
it. The high-pitched tone—in my ears, a pinprick of
a tone—sounded. I could barely hear it, but it was there.
Coming toward me. Faster and faster came my breath. It
was my death I heard. My heart sped up, too. A cold sweat
came over me. I fell to the floor. Carpet fibers bit into my
knees. I vomited, then clutched the carpet to keep myself
from falling any lower. I looked up, and Dai was kneeling
beside me. In his eyes, I saw myself. I was still alive. In his
eyes, I saw worry. I sat back on my heels. A cool current of
air swept by. I took a breath in. And let it out. Dai took my
hands and helped me up.

We stepped over the mess.

He brought me a cup of water and some new clothes from
our dresser. He got a bucket and filled it with soap and water.
Then he cleaned that carpet, scrubbing it as though it were
his passion in life. When he finished, he washed his hands and
opened the window next to our bed.

I took the air into my lungs and nodded at him, appreciative.

He sat next to me, picked my hand up, leaned over, and
kissed my forehead. As he pulled away to look into my face, I
saw it: a seam in the middle of his throat that I had not seen

until then. Death was coming for Dai, too. I reached over and traced the line. He flinched, letting me know he had intentionally hidden this sign of his oncoming death from me. He took my hand and put it down into my lap. This was his private pain, so I left it. I knew two things in that moment: that love is sitting next to a person you cherish, knowing death will come at any moment, and that I was pregnant.

DAI
2020

*B*UT *I BELIEVE...*
    I stirred the too-bright yellow macaroni and cheese. The gaudy color reminded me of my day trips with Kitand. In this crazy universe, it was the only thing Mara would eat. I felt her warm hands on my bare hips.

She sniffed. "Smells like artificial cheese and butter. So good."

I turned around and put my hands on her naked, swollen belly. We called our daughter "Dango" because we had not agreed on a name, but we would in time. I massaged Mara's hips. She smiled up at me with the pained smile of someone who is tired of enduring. I kissed her forehead, thanking her, asking forgiveness. Then I got on my knees, lifted her stomach, and spoke: "Dango, my sweet dumpling, whenever you are ready."

Mara looked down at me with that pained look in her eyes again.

I stood up and whispered into her ear, "May, any day now, she will come."

Mara looked up at me with feigned annoyance. "I regret telling you."

I smiled back at her. "No, you don't."

PART III

Death

DEATHBED
2021

THEY SIT ON AN AIRPLANE OVER THE SPARKLING Pacific. There are three of them in this family. Mara, Dai, and their sweet Dango—May. At this moment, all that can be seen through the small porthole of the window Dai is looking through is an expanse of clouds below and an endless blue sky above. They are flying to Japan to pay their last respects to Dai's grandfather. Dai's parents will meet them at the airport to take them to his grandfather's home and deathbed. Dai knows this means his father will be picking them up. He heard it in the distracted, overly friendly way his mother had told him, "We will come to get you." He sighs.

Mara switches May to her other shoulder and reaches her hand out for Dai's. She grasps it and squeezes. She knows that sigh is a sign of trouble. She suddenly can't wait to land so that she can call her father and hear his deep rolling laughter to calm her anxiety.

Dai scoots down in his seat so he can lean his head against Mara's shoulder. He closes his eyes, shutting out everything but her shoulder under his head. It is firm and consistent, everything he needs to keep from falling. Mara continues to squeeze Dai's hand. From afar, the group seems to be preparing for something dire.

May, lying on her mother's shoulder, stirs and reaches out her hand to her father, sensing this is needed. Dai opens his eyes, feeling her tiny palm brushing his nose. He smiles and lets go of Mara's hand. He cups his daughter's palm in his and kisses it. Mara rubs May's back and kisses her cheek, reminding her she is still a baby. May curls back into the ball she has grown accustomed to over the past ten months, and she falls back to sleep.

Dai looks back out the window of the plane.

Mara looks over at Dai, worried. She is not sure where he is—if he is falling off that bridge once again. Running from choices he will have to make, the pain he will feel, his grandfather's death, his parents' pain, the unknown before the three of them. The scar on his neck is invisible from this angle, and Mara has the impulse to reach over and find its unnatural smoothness slashed across his throat. The absence of the proof of its existence makes the enemy, death, seem elusive. It scares her—the enemy's intangibility.

Dai looks over at her and offers his hand. Mara looks up at his neck and sees it, this time. There it is. Of course. She places her hand in his. He squeezes, this time, reassuring her: I am here. Mara smiles back at him, but her heart beats wildly in her chest, betraying her. She looks out the porthole so that her face will not lie any more than it has to.

When they land, Dai walks out first. The sun blinds him for a second, and he is back on the battlefield in his dream; he feels as though at any second, a bomb will go off and send him flying to the purgatory of that hill. May starts to fuss, and Mara, who is right behind Dai with the baby and diaper bag, puts her hand on his back, encouraging him to move forward.

Dai comes out of his reverie and steps down the stairs. People are shuffling into lines to await the bus that will take them to their gate. Dai has not been to Osaka since his grandmother's funeral. He was five, and Japan seemed like a magical place where his giant of a grandfather lived and where he himself somehow belonged. He had spent days practicing the bow in front of his bedroom mirror so that his grandfather could be proud of his American grandson, but he messed it up, and his grandfather kissed him on his head like a small child. He didn't speak after that, not until he was back in the States.

Dai walks toward the temporary outdoor baggage claim and grabs the luggage they checked. Then he stands in line. Mara follows close behind while trying to calm May, who is still upset and unable to tell her parents it is too humid, her ears are refusing to pop, and the jiggling is hurting her stomach. Mara, to her credit, gives the jiggling up and searches the diaper bag on her shoulder for a bottle. When she cannot find one, she pulls out a pink binky that says "Cutie Pie" and puts it into May's mouth. May calms as her ears pop. Dai and Mara look at each other, relieved. Perhaps this trip won't be as stressful as they feared.

When they finally arrive at the baggage claim, Eduard Kühn stands from his slouched sitting position in the airport waiting area. Dai immediately notes that his father's shirt is two sizes too big, wrinkled, and that his father is half the weight he was when he last saw him six years ago.

When Eduard visited his son at the clinic, he was rational with him. He would pay for his son's stay in the clinic and would secure a temporary apartment for Dai once he left the clinic, but neither of them would tell Dai's mother he had committed himself.

Though his words were unemotional, Dai remembered his father's eyes drifting to his throat and watering. Dai didn't accept any other visiting requests from his father after the first, and after a month, his father went back to Japan to help Dai's mom care for her ailing father. Now, Eduard's eyes are gaunt, like they exist at the end of a long, tired tunnel.

Eduard walks toward his son with a grimace that he is trying desperately to turn into a smile. He gives up once he approaches his son, and he hugs him. The simultaneous sound of both men patting each other's backs is audible. They step back and nod at each other. Eduard looks to Mara and then the baby, his granddaughter, but he decides it's best to take it slow. He puts his hand through his hair in a similar fashion to his son, and then he puts out his arms for a hug. Mara, seeing the familiar action, senses he wants more than he is asking for and hands him the child instead. Eduard is taken aback and holds May at arm's length, not knowing what to do with her.

May stirs at the commotion and opens her eyes. Eduard brings her to his chest, remembering what it felt like to hold his son when he was this small. He holds her close and kisses her on her cheek. May raises her hand and grabs Eduard's nose. Eduard does not smile, but the right corner of his mouth lifts.

In the car, everyone sits quietly—dead quiet. Even May's chest rises and falls in her sleep without a sound. Dai looks out at the skyscrapers, the cars, and the people rushing around that look like him but do not feel familiar. He watches as the buildings peter out and more and more mahoganies and Mongolian oaks appear. Then they are surrounded by trees and Mount Asama stands hulking in the distance.

Eduard lowers his window and pulls out a cigarette, placing it in his mouth. Mara coughs as a sign to Dai, but he does not hear her, as he is trying to figure out what to say to his mother once they get to the house. Eduard remembers Nozomi correcting him politely in this same manner and puts the cigarette back into his pocket. With nothing else to do outside of driving, Eduard speaks. "Dai, be patient with your mother. All of this is hard for her."

Dai looks at his father and nods. He thinks, *What I wouldn't give for a cigarette or a drink at this moment.*

When they pull up to the house, Dai is in awe of the hulking white mansion in front of him. He gets out of the car and stands below it. He laughs to himself, thinking of how his mother always described his grandfather as traditional. Smelling burning tobacco in the air, he pulls out a cigarette himself and walks over to his father's side of the car. Eduard leans against his door, already smoking his cigarette, quickly, before taking his son in to see the mother he has not talked to in eleven years. Both men stand side by side, refusing eye contact, standing soundless.

Mara sits inside the car, watching May sleep, hoping the squared battle-ready shoulders of both men standing outside the window are not a foreshadowing of what is to come.

When Eduard is finished with his cigarette, he walks to the back of the car and opens the trunk. He pulls out the suitcases and walks toward the house. Mara gets out of the car with May, who is still sleeping in her car seat. They stand in front of the house that seems as big and insurmountable as Mount Asama in the distance. Mara sighs, then follows Eduard. Dai flicks his filter, puts his hands in his jean pockets, and walks toward his grandfather's house.

Walking inside, Dai notices a large portrait of an older woman in a silk kimono sneering at him. He passes the picture of his great-grandmother and clears his throat nervously. His mother sits with her back to the door in the living room. A large hospital bed sits in front of her, with his grandfather lying prone. Next to the bed is a heart monitor, beeping constantly. Pictures of grim-looking men and women in kimonos and yukatas sit on a shelf above his grandfather's bed. The room smells like antiseptic and decay.

Eduard walks up to his wife, bends down, and kisses her cheek. Nozomi puts her hand on the other side of her husband's face and returns his kiss without turning toward him. Mara walks up with the baby and bows the best she can with her arms full. Nozomi does not acknowledge her. After a few minutes, Mara walks over and stands next to Eduard, who clears his throat and leads her upstairs to the guest room.

Dai stands next to his mother's chair and stares down at his grandfather. Nozomi says nothing. After a few minutes, she turns her cheek up toward Dai, indicating that he should greet her. Dai leans down and kisses her cheek and gives her a side hug. Nozomi motions her head toward her father's sleeping form, indicating that Dai should greet his grandfather, as well. Dai ignores his mother.

Nozomi waits and then motions for Dai to greet his grandfather again. When he does not, in an even voice, without looking at her son, Nozomi asks, "You would wait to give your final respects to your grandfather until he can no longer speak, bring a stranger to his deathbed, and then refuse to offer him the respect he deserves in his own home?"

Dai replies, "Mara's my—" But, realizing he does not have a satisfying title that represents who Mara is to him, he says, "Mara is the mother of your granddaughter."

Nozomi looks at her son, whom she has not seen in eleven years. "And did you bother to introduce us? To ask for my rings? To have a ceremony? How did I raise such a selfish son? First you—" Nozomi cannot go any further.

"What, mother? What did I do?"

Nozomi does not answer. She remembers her mother saying *Tears are not for us. We are stronger than that.* She takes a slow, careful breath and motions that he should follow her into the kitchen. Dai stands watching her walk out of the room, as though she is expecting him to follow, as though he is tethered to her. He waits until she passes over the threshold and turns around, so she can see he is not his father. Nozomi stands waiting, impatient, but she knows that in order to win, she must remain calm. Like her mother taught her when pulling out her too-loose stitchwork. *Love is not careless. Love is patient.* Dai lets his mom stand in the kitchen, looking at him, for three seconds. One. Two. Three. Then he takes a leisurely stroll toward her.

Nozomi does not speak until her son stands in front of her. When he arrives, she takes a step back so he can stand on the white tiled floor with her. Dai refuses and stands in front of the threshold, creating a barrier between them. Nozomi looks up at her son. "Dai, I called you when your grandfather first became bedridden. He asked for you; he wanted to tell you the things you needed to know to become the next patriarch. You are the oldest son. It is tradition."

Dai ignores the guilt trip. "I didn't come because it was an act, Ma. I'm a drunk, and grandfather was far from traditional."

Dai barely stands taller than his mother, but he cannot escape her eye. Their tie. Even with the barrier between them, even though he looks down at her, he feels as though she is towering over him. He steps back. Nozomi sees her son stepping back onto the ledge of that bridge, and this time, this time, he will not climb back out. "You think I don't know what you were trying to do? You think you can just smile at me and I will forget everything? Your father said you were only drunk, being stupid up on that bridge in the middle of the night. The doctors believed it was just a drinking problem, that you just needed to sober up and go to A.A. But I knew. I knew that you climbed up there to die. And you didn't even recognize that you were trying to kill me with you. Your grandfather. Your family. How could you not remember that you are us? Did I not teach you to write your name 'Ueno Dai'? Yet you *still* so carelessly jumped."

"Mama," Dai cries out, and Nozomi hears the cry Dai made as a baby when he had a fever. The fevered cry that would rush her to his bassinet in fear. She pulls him into her arms, holding his head to her chest. Dai stoops down awkwardly. Nozomi wants to sing the lullaby she sang to him to calm him down but decides against it, fearing he will not ask her to sing it again, like he did when he was a happy child, sharing with her their ties to this country, this home.

"You should have come home earlier. It is your duty as patriarch."

Dai sighs. "Ma, nothing about our family is traditional. You married Dad, moved away, I don't speak Japanese, and we all took grandfather's last name. You were meant to be the matriarch."

May starts to cry upstairs. Dai lifts his head from his mother's chest and goes upstairs to get her. Nozomi walks back into the room her father is dying in. She is unsure of what to do. Dai comes back with May and offers her to his mother. She puts her hands up as though in defense of herself. She is not ready.

Dai sighs and holds his daughter to his chest.

Nozomi wrings her hands and sits back in the chair next to her father's deathbed. Dai stands next to his mother, looking down at her. Nozomi does not look up at him; he is accusing her with his eyes, she feels it. She turns the wedding band on her finger, a nervous action Dai has never seen his mother do. She pulls down her hair and combs her hands through it. Dai looks away, embarrassed at seeing his mother so vulnerable.

Nozomi speaks: "My mother told me a story once about my father. She showed me a picture of a man, slighter than your grandfather and a foot shorter. She told me this was Ueno Daichi and that I had two fathers. The man in the photograph had died before she could become pregnant with me. The man I called father was named Samson Nakajima. His father had given him a Christian name so that he could fit into American culture easier, but it hadn't helped him. America did not think he was American enough to be treated as such. When he came to Japan, he was seen as an outsider because he was Nisei, an American-born Japanese. Thankfully, though my mother was Nisei, she was trained to run the company by Ueno Sachiko, the head at the time, and her mother-in-law, my grandmother. My mom ran the business for twenty years and brought partners that were trustworthy and willing to work with your grandfather.

"When I found out about the lie, I was angry. I stopped wearing house slippers. I had my feet bare even when visitors came. I stopped bowing. Upon meeting a person, I looked them straight in the face, and if I liked them, I put my hand out to shake theirs, like I had seen Americans do. Your father was simply a happy accident—a sweet, bumbling American reporter who came to interview my father. I felt bad for him after their first meeting and just wanted to comfort him, but then we were laughing, and anyway, I was more than willing to move overseas, to succeed where my father had failed, but it wasn't easy. They didn't put Japanese in camps anymore. The prejudice was quieter. Non-white faces were still treated as though they could not be American, whether they were born there or not. I kept my head down, and when I had you, all I wanted was to share with you everything that made you special and good. I used the kanji for 'big' or 'great' when naming you. I hoped you would be bigger than all of this here. I did not want you to get confused and think your being Japanese was a bad thing because you were born Japanese in America instead of white, either. But I failed. I didn't tell you about your grandfather. I didn't have you pay your respects to Ueno Daichi so that he could protect you."

Dai sighs. His mother flinches as though he has raised his hand to smack her. May stirs and starts to fuss. Dai jiggles her, trying to calm her, and May becomes more agitated, fussing louder. Without her father's secret, Nozomi feels empty. She sighs, stands, and takes her granddaughter from Dai. She holds May in the crook of her arms and rocks slowly from side to side. She sings the lullaby she sang to Dai as a baby and that her mother sang to her. May settles and falls back to sleep. Nozomi raises her arm up so she can kiss May's head, but May stirs, and Nozomi's heart skips a beat, and she knows she will teach her Japanese and the correct way to tie a kimono, and she will walk with her beside Kumoba Pond, pointing out the narcissus flycatchers gliding overhead and the primroses in bloom.

This time, Dai whispers, "Mama."

Nozomi cannot deny her son. She looks into his face.

Dai clears his throat. "Mama, I thought my story was to grow up, find a girl, and fall in love. But this isn't a story; I'm not some romantic who just needs time to grow up to recognize the happiness that's been in me all this time. Mama, I'm an alcoholic who struggles every day to find happiness in the things and people I love. Every day. And that is never gonna change. I am not going to change."

Nozomi looks at her son, and she lifts his daughter toward him. "And what about your daughter? Would you leave without even considering her?"

Dai sighs again.

Nozomi has no idea where to go from this, so she sits in the chair with her granddaughter and reaches out to hold

Samson Nakajima's hand. Though he has not yet passed over, she pleads with him in a whisper to protect his grandson.

Dai cannot take any more, so he turns and walks outside so he can think. His father stands next to the front door, finishing a cigarette. Dai stands on the other side of the door. Eduard flicks the filter away and pulls another cigarette out. He puts it in his mouth and offers one to Dai. Dai slides it out of the pack and puts it in his mouth. His dad lights his and then his son's. They both take a moment to take in the nicotine.

Eduard turns to his son. "You all right in there?"

Dai nods.

"She missed you, you know."

Dai nods, not wanting to start a fight.

His father goes back to smoking.

Dai turns to his dad. "You tell her?"

Dai's father shakes his head no. "You'll learn women have a sixth sense for when something is wrong with their child."

Dai nods.

Eduard wants to tell his son that one day, his daughter is going to hurt the woman he loves worse than anyone else has ever or will ever hurt her. That Mara will spend many sleepless nights worrying about a careless child who will treat her with derision even as she tries to make life easier for her, that it is a miracle his mother is still standing, because she should be dust. Instead, he finishes his cigarette, drops it, and crushes it. Then he pats his son on the shoulder and walks into the house.

Dai stands for a moment on the left side of the doorframe and finishes the cigarette he received from his father. When he finishes, he flicks the filter to his left, steps on it, and then decides to go for a walk. He soon finds himself next to Kumoba Pond. It reflects the chestnuts and Mongolian oaks on its surface, the narcissus flycatchers are flying over it, and the primroses and anemones lean over it. But his face is strange to him because it is his mother's face, not quite his dad's and never his grandfather's. It is upsetting, but it is the truth. Looking at life and its reflection, it seems easy. His mother holding up May: *And what about your daughter? Would you leave without even considering her?*

Dai remembers the feeling of the wind burning his face as he fell, and though he does not feel it at this second, he hates himself for not knowing when it will come again, or if he will win the battle next time.

A hand slips into his. Mara looks out at the pond as she stands next to Dai, giving him the space he needs. Dai wonders why it has never occurred to him to offer his name to her, his family line. He wonders if he has denied May her birthright. He sighs, trying to keep his mother's face out of his mind.

Mara looks up at him. "You all right?"

Dai nods. Then he turns to her. "Do you want to get married?"

Mara half-smiles. "You asking?"

Dai shrugs.

Mara looks quickly at him and then away. She sighs so that she sounds casual and the lie seems genuine. "I never thought about it. What we have works."

Dai relaxes and nods. He squeezes her hand, appreciative.

Mara squeezes his hand back. "Let's walk."

Dai hesitates and follows. They continue around the pond. Mara slows so they are walking side by side. She leans over and kisses his arm. Through the cotton material of his shirt, she can feel his arm and can imagine how it is connected to his shoulder, which has rounded out the way a man's should, but out of the corner of her eye, she can see the scar. She looks ahead of her.

"She loves you, you know."

Dai nods.

They continue walking and he feels it coming, what she has been turning over in her head while walking over. She stops walking. He stops beside her. Then she speaks. "Love, you weren't alone and aren't alone. When you jumped off that bridge, you jumped with me, your mother, and your father. We were all beside you. We all had lake water in our lungs and clay under our fingernails. Our lives are connected to yours, in life and death, because we love you. If you have a battle to fight, whether it is tangible or not, we—I—will fight by your side."

Dai releases Mara's hand. "I get it. I'm an asshole for trying to kill myself. I hurt everyone when I jumped. Do you think I don't feel guilty about it? The thing is, it wasn't about you guys. It's this absence of feeling. This disconnect from everything around me. Like nothing matters. Maybe we create meaning in this world, but most days, what it actually feels like is a losing battle. Like I'm constantly trying to create meaning to counteract the fact that nothing in this world matters."

Mara turns away from Dai so he doesn't see the fear on her face.

He looks back at her. "It's absurd, isn't it?"

Mara feels his eyes on her; the heat of them is so sharp that she must look back at him. His eyes are crazy like at the party, like at the hospital. Mara hears the beating of her heart and the high-pitched tone of death coming closer and closer.

Dai pulls Mara close and wraps his arms around her. He can feel her heart beating triple-time through her temple. He leans down so his lips barely brush her ear, and he whispers, "Marry me."

EDUARD KÜHN
1975

THE WORLD IS A STRANGE FUCKING PLACE. I ONCE believed life to be purposeless. That nothing mattered. It made me feel as though I could do anything.

Despite my beliefs, I still drafted for my father's sake. "It's the only way a man can prove himself nowadays. The Vikings of yesteryear are gone" is the last thing he said to me before I got on that bus. The bastard died a week later on the floor of his T.V. room. They didn't find his body for another week.

By then, the cosmic joke was already on its way to the punchline.

The United States government sent me to Japan during the Vietnam War to interview a businessman and write an article about his company to increase good relations between America and Japan, and to ensure he continued to sell us radio parts. The very same radio parts that had replaced the ones we'd used during the air raids in Japan during World War II. The radio parts we would be using in our planes to communicate with each other when we flew over Vietnam, so we knew where to drop our bombs.

But the joke is on me.

Mr. Ueno's driver takes me to Mr. Ueno's home, instead of to his office. Unlike in Osaka, with the buildings packed next to each other, the balconies and windows stuffed with people, surrounded by honking cars that speed by, and the constant noise, here, it is quiet.

I look up, and I can see the stars above me that my grandfather pointed out. He told me the stories about the constellations in German.

When we arrive, I get out of the car and stare. The house is overwhelming. Overpowering. It seems as though it has a secret inside it must protect at all costs. I am not sure what to do next.

The driver motions that I should follow him. I grab my camera bag from inside the limo, put it over my shoulder, and follow. I have been warned that Mr. Ueno is traditional and tall. When I received the intel for this meeting, they laughed. "How tall is tall there, five feet?" So, they sent me. At six-foot-one, they figured I would tower over the supposed Japanese giant of technology.

Looking at his home, I am not so sure anymore.

The driver presses the doorbell and steps away. A moment later, the door is opened. A woman stands at my height in a navy silk kimono with white peonies blooming along the hem. Her hair is pulled back in a chignon. She looks me straight in the eyes without blinking. I am speechless.

She nods, deadpan, and I am unsure of what to do, so I nod back. She turns, and, like I have a string around my waist, I follow.

I hear the naked slap of her feet against the marble floor, and I can't remember whether I am supposed to take off my shoes or whether she should have slippers on. The little bits of Japanese I know are flying out of my head. I follow her to an office in the back of the house. It is as large and commanding as the front of the house. There are murals in big gold frames, a wall of filing cabinets, and in front of me, a large redwood desk, imported, behind which is a wall of windows facing a large pond, and above it, Mount Asama. Behind the desk sits a large man in a suit, writing, as though there is no one in the room but him. The woman who opened the door turns to me and introduces her father. All the English words go out of my head, too. Only a few handfuls of German words and the stories about constellations in German remain.

There is a laugh like thunder in front of me; the man at the desk stands and searches my face for an answer to a question I am not privy to. I walk toward him and stop once I am standing in front of his desk. Mr. Ueno stands at least a half-foot taller than me. He stands with his hands in his pockets, waiting. I remember I am supposed to greet him, but I can't remember how, so I stand straight and extend my hand. He looks down at it and then back into my face, still searching for the answer I am not sure how to give. I drop my hand after a few more seconds, and he turns toward his wall of windows and looks out at the pond. He stands with his hands still in his pant pockets, breathing evenly.

When he finally turns around again, he faces me with a smile. He extends his hand this time, and I take it. His grasp is hard, and I have to work not to pull my hand away too quickly once he releases me. He tells me in English that he is honored I have flown all this way to meet with him. He switches seamlessly to Japanese and tells me he hopes I will stay for dinner and introduces his daughter as Nozomi. Then he switches back to English and repeats everything he said in Japanese and adds that I am welcome to stay the night so that I do not have to pay for a hotel in Osaka.

I nod. I am a few seconds behind, but I understand what he is telling me. I am still unable to translate my thoughts into any other verbal language outside of my grandfather's native tongue.

Mr. Ueno nods at his daughter. Then he turns and sits at his desk, returning to his work.

Nozomi walks out, and I am attached again; I follow. This time, she takes me upstairs, and we stop in front of the second door to the left. In the doorway of the guest room, Nozomi lays her hand on my shoulder. Then she gives me a glimpse of her smile, and there it is: language. I smile back and tell her in Japanese that I am thankful for the opportunity to interview her father. Her smile is wide, and I know I've made a fool of myself, but I don't care because her smile is everything I came for. Everything I drafted for. The reason I take pictures. I fumble for my camera to capture her, but then we are laughing and laughing and I have to put my camera down so I don't drop it.

When we calm down and she has wiped the tears of laughter from her eyes, I ask her what was so funny in the first place, and she laughs again. This time, I take my camera out and take a series of pictures of that smile.

When she stops laughing, she stands straight and brushes off the front of her dress. For a moment, her hand rests on her stomach, and my mind travels forward in time, and she is resting her hand on her barely swollen stomach as she tells me we will have a child.

And I come back to my time, and I am breathless and forgetting I am no longer in the future, and I put my hands around her waist and bring her to me. I lift my hands to her cheeks, and then my lips are on hers and thanking her for an event that hasn't happened yet.

We are breathless. Or breathful. Our shared breath between us. Our lips a movement away from ecstasy. Our foreheads touching. This is as natural as breathing in the oxygen in the air and breathing out the carbon dioxide our bodies produce.

Her hands are grasping my upper arms as though she will never let me go. I lift my head and look into her eyes, and I am thankful, because I can see she was with me, too. The present version of her was in our shared future.

But in the second after our eyes meet, we also remember we aren't there yet. She slaps me. We jump apart. I am so flustered that I trip over my camera bag and fall. She looks down at me on the ground, twisted in my camera bag, and she laughs. I expect her to throw her hands over her mouth as I've seen other girls do, but she doesn't. Her mouth is wide and her hands are out to help me up. I put my hands out for her, and she helps me up, and I just say it.

"Marry me."

She drops me. Her hands fly up to her mouth. I jump up, and because I will not allow her to be every other girl, I take her hands in mine. She is so surprised that she starts to cry and laugh, and it is the most beautiful moment I've seen, and I know there is no way I will be able to capture this moment with my camera.

The trap snaps shut. The punchline is, of course, that I want—need—her to be my purpose for living.

We do not tell her father. The next day, I interview him. The day after, I type up the report and place it into a manila envelope and into my bag to take back with me, and then at the end of four days, the American government tells me it is time I come home.

ONE DAY, WHEN I was still a kid, my grandfather placed a plate of beef rouladen in front of me, then pulled up a chair beside me. He patted my leg and told me, "*Enkel*, grandson, a Frenchman once said, 'There always comes a time when one must choose between contemplation and action. This is called becoming a man.' Dear grandson, life is not always about choosing to act. It is choosing when not to act. Life will get complicated and you will feel as though you must act, but you will have to learn to stand aside."

MY FATHER WAS bitter and sardonic, born German in the wrong lifetime. He drank down disappointment until he couldn't see straight; all he could do was feel around with his fists. Put so many holes in his plaster walls, he decided his son's face would save him some money.

His father was a quiet man, a librarian, and a cowardly wallflower.

My great-grandfather was an angry man. A working-class Lutheran factory-worker-turned-minister, whose father was a farmer and whose brother stayed a factory worker. He moved to the States in a rage because his fatherland had failed him, his father, and his brother. The Liberals could not agree on a plan and the Kaiser worried about foreign policy more than he did the everyday working man. With all the anger inside him, with all the bitterness, my great-grandfather figured, why not carve a place for himself and his fledgling family in the land of opportunity. It was a great time to be a German outside of Germany. In America, at the turn of the century, thousands of books were written in German, including the Good Book. Movie stars looked cool smoking cigarettes and speaking our language.

My grandfather attended a German-speaking kindergarten in a small rural community in Illinois. He lived in a community with other kids that played, learned, and loved in German. My great-grandfather opened a Lutheran church in his backyard. Everyone in the neighborhood would come on Sundays to hear him speak in their shared native tongue. Then, like a family, they would break bread and eat together. My great-grandfather had everything he had spent his life fuming about, so it was only a matter of time before his cosmic joke played out.

As the Great War approached, more and more neighbors started to disappear. He would see them in town, and they would not look him in the eyes. Later, he would ask after them and find out they'd changed their names to better fit in. They no longer spoke the language of our fatherland. They became cowards. My great-grandfather would not be moved; this moment in history would pass. He started offering lessons in the German language on weekdays.

Then they hung a man in Ohio, a German man who simply loved his fatherland. My grandfather took this as a sign; he was only a few years from 18 and decided to move to a tenement apartment in Chicago, where he could find work. My great-grandfather continued to fight even harder. He started to preach in German outside of his house, loudly, with the good book split open in the palm of his hand. He would stand outside every day. He started to walk around the woods, reading the Good Book, then walk into town and yell the good news at anyone who passed by. Some days, he would have to take a day off from proselytizing when he was beaten in the streets. Most days, he would go home and down enough schnapps to help with the pain and come back the next day so he could give the world the love of God in his father tongue.

ON A TUESDAY in April, my grandfather found my great-grandfather with a luger in his right hand and his brains splattered behind him like someone had lost their patience and thrown a bowl of goulash at the wall.

My grandfather *became* quiet, I think. No man is born without an anger in him, a drive to reach out to the world around him and grasp it to his chest. But a man can lose that drive. Bit by bit, if the world he seeks to reach out to shrinks from him. Spits at him. Tells him he is nothing as long as he is himself. A man has to quiet the anger or let it all out and have nothing left.

When Nozomi appeared at my doorstep with her father's conditions for our marriage, I thought of the weeks I had spent looking longingly at the pictures of her I had developed, of the shared future *we* had seen. I thought of my grandfather learning day after day how to give up his fatherland, his father's dreams, waiting day after day to be able to be himself, whoever that could have been. I thought of my grandfather and his holding tight to the last thing he had left, the last part of his father's dream. His last name. Kühn. Bold.

I agreed to the terms. I have stood quietly by Nozomi's side as best as I can. What else is there for me to do? I was helpless and am, and that's what my grandfather was trying to tell me. You have to know when you must stand aside and hope for the best. *Hoffen.*

A FUNERAL
2023

THE BLOSSOMS ON THE ROWS OF APPLE TREES ARE mostly snow white and coat the ground, the trees, and the roof of Mara's childhood home for the occasion. Not all of the blossoms are white. One tree in the yard has pink blossoms, like a drop of blood mixed into a bucket of white paint. Seeing this, standing between his future and his past, Dai feels a quivering just below the surface. He clears his throat, pushing it down. His hands start to shake. Dai brings his shaking right hand, holding a cigarette, to his mouth, and pulls on it, long and deep, to keep from hyperventilating, which feels like a possibility, though he cannot explain what has started this. His stomach quivers and he knows it is in anticipation of the fall. It is coming again. Another battle. And there will be nothing he can do to stop it. He will only be able to weather it.

Mara's father, Ezekiel, sees his future son-in-law's left hand shaking and clenched into a fist at his side and the shaking right hand bringing his cigarette to his mouth. The air is chilled despite the festive colored blossoms lying on the ground and on the trees. The early frost may stunt the harvest for this year. Ezekiel will have to remember to come out after the ceremony and wrap the trees to keep them from getting too cold. He pulls on his cigarette and figures his son-in-law cannot be cold, as the rest of his body is not shivering, only his hands. He must be nervous, then. Ezekiel smiles to himself, remembering his wedding day. Mary stressed every day until the wedding finally arrived. She threatened to call it off twice; she broke down crying the week before because her cousin had called and told her they would miss the ceremony and would only be able to make the reception; she lost twenty pounds and then gained it back stress-eating. But Ezekiel was calm. Took everything in stride. That morning, he bit into an apple and chipped his tooth. His heart wouldn't slow, and he feared he might have a heart attack before he could marry. Then he didn't. Mary walked down the aisle, and everything was okay.

Ezekiel pats his son-in-law on the back. "It'll be okay, son." Dai nods at him and goes back to his cigarette.

Eduard finishes his cigarette, throws the butt to the ground, and puts his hands into his pockets. Dai glances over at him, his eyes wide like an owl's. Eduard chuckles inwardly, thinking of Dai before his competitive chess matches back in high school. He would be anxious and shaking, but once the match started, his shoulders would relax, and his eyes would focus on the board instead of flying all over the room, looking to be saved. He would be fine. Eduard nods at his son and pulls out another cigarette in solidarity.

Dai watches his father pull on his cigarette and blow the smoke off to the side. He remembers how big his father used to be. How much he towered over Dai when he was a kid. How his father had to bend down to his level to pick him up. Eduard coughs, and Dai fears, watching his father, that the skin stretched thin and bulging at his throat will tear at the next cough. Dai blinks, forcing back his body's urge to break down at the evidence of his father's mortality. When his father nods back at him, he wants to tell him that he has had a premonition and that he loves him, but it gets stuck in his throat under the oncoming battle, and instead, the best he can do is a nod in return.

A phone buzzes. Dai nearly jumps out of his skin, then pats himself down, looking for the offending object. He pulls the phone out. The voice is not audible to Eduard and Ezekiel, but Dai's face calms, and he flicks his cigarette to the ground and hangs up. He tells the two men he will be back. Then he strides away and goes into the house, where a verbal fight can be heard. One voice is young and high-pitched, but loud and adamant. The other voice is older, calmer, but obviously agitated. Dai goes to the door the voices can be heard behind. May turns when her father walks through the door, and she runs up. She grabs and holds on to Dai's leg.

"Daddy, Baabaa said I couldn't go out. I said, 'It's Pop Pop's house.'"

Dai smiles at his headstrong three-year-old daughter dressed in a purple kimono. Her hair has apple blossoms braided into it and is pulled up and back into a chignon. He squats down to her level, and she throws her arms around his neck. He stands and spins her in a circle. He does not look at the frown he assumes is etched into his mother's face.

"Sorry, Ma. Little Miss was told to behave herself, and obviously, she is not." Dai pretends to be a monster. He makes a loud roar and then play-attacks his daughter. May giggles, roaring back, and, between hysterics, proclaims her fingers were crossed when she made that promise.

Dai looks over at his mother to give her a real apology, and she is smiling at them. Nozomi walks up and puts her hand on his elbow. "You're sweet to her, just like your father was with you." And Dai hesitates, not being able to recall a moment like this with his father. Will his daughter remember this?

Nozomi leaves the room, and Dai follows with May in his arms. Outside, Nozomi motions to him to put his daughter down so she can walk with her. Dai follows his mother's orders and watches her take May's hand as she shows her how to walk down the stairs in a kimono.

When they approach Dai's father and father-in-law, the two men put their cigarettes out and exclaim how beautiful May is. She beams, and everyone inwardly sighs. After a moment, May starts to jump up and down, asking where Mommy is. Dai looks at his mother and motions in the direction of the neighbor's house, where Mara is getting dressed. Nozomi reaches down and offers her hand to her granddaughter. May takes it and starts walking as though she is really dancing. After a few steps, Nozomi leans down and tells her granddaughter, "*Mago*, granddaughter, we are ladies, and we will walk as such."

May looks up at her grandmother, nods, and starts to walk the way her grandmother showed her when she was by the stairs. Then she looks up at her grandmother again. "Can I dance later, at the party?"

Nozomi smiles. "Yes, love, as long as it is like a lady."

May sighs as though deeply troubled. "Baabaa, I'm a child, not a lady."

Nozomi replies, "But you will be, and that's why you practice now."

May sighs again. "Baabaa, how will I know when I'm a lady and it's real-time instead of practice?"

Nozomi sighs, this time. "You won't know, love. One day, you will wake up and you will look in the mirror and will ask yourself, 'Is today the day'? And everyone will treat you like a grownup, and you will pretend, because it seems wrong to correct everyone. The secret, *mago*, is that everyone is pretending to be a grownup. Even me. If you know that, then life will be easier."

May walks silently, as she usually does after one of their talks. Then she squeezes her grandmother's hand and looks up at her and says, "Baabaa, I'm not going to pretend. I'm gonna be a kid as long as I want until I'm ready to be a lady."

Nozomi squeezes her granddaughter's hand, leans down, and kisses her forehead. "Then you are wiser than us all." May smiles, then starts to dance-walk once again. Nozomi tries to do her granddaughter's dance-walk and almost trips. They stop and laugh and laugh.

DAI TRIES TO calm his beating heart, standing in the bathroom stall. He focuses on details to calm himself: the forest-green color of the stall door and sides. The bright white tile floor below his feet that seems like it belongs in a personal bathroom in someone's home instead of a public bathroom in a funeral home. The yellow glue-like substance hardened on the back of the toilet. Urine or glue? Dai pulls out the mini bottle of Jägermeister from his jacket pocket, opens it, and gulps it down. It tastes like burned black licorice. He shakes his head from side to side afterward, as though that'll get rid of the taste. It doesn't, but after a few minutes, it doesn't matter. Dai pulls out a business card. On it is written, "Jerry Mitchell." No titles are listed. His old therapist used to tell them in group, *We title ourselves.* Even when someone gives us a title, we decide whether to take it or to refuse it. Jerry decided not to title himself at all. Dai is not sure what that says about him.

Dai holds the card in his shaking hand, and, for the thousandth time, reaches into his jacket for his phone. He puts the numbers in, and his thumb hovers over the "Send" button. He hears footsteps and puts his phone to sleep and slips it into his jacket pocket. Dai pulls out two pieces of gum and throws them into his mouth. The card gets put back into his wallet. He clears his throat and flushes the toilet. Then he walks out of the stall and toward the sinks to wash his hands. The attendant tells him they are ready to start toward the cemetery. Dai nods, washes his hands, and follows the funeral attendant to the front room so that they can carry his father out to the hearse.

They walk back into the main room of the funeral home. Standing at the door as they walk in is the funeral director. He doesn't say sorry; he gives an encouraging smile and asks Dai if he can get him anything. Dai thrusts his hands into his pant pockets and shakes his head no. He continues down the aisle of the showroom. His father's casket sits closed, now, at the end of the aisle. Five men sit in the front pews or stand next to the casket. Some, Dai knows from family functions, and a few work for the funeral home. As Dai walks in, everyone seems to perk up. They stand at their assigned handles. Dai's is at the front right-hand side. He slips on the white gloves he is handed and leans down and grips the gold-colored brass handle.

The casket is made of the same color of mahogany as the chessboard Eduard and Dai played chess on when he was a child and his father was the King to his wife's Queen. The game of chess Dai played with his father was called Kriegspiel. Dai's father learned it from his grandfather. Eduard taught it to Dai. Kriegspiel required three people: two players with a board between them like the game Battleship and a person standing between the two people, acting as an umpire of sorts, seeing everything that was happening below. His mother was always the eye in the sky. Dai sat on one side, trying to figure out what his dad was doing on the other side. His father sat silent and brilliant on his side. Dai would always think: *I'm so close this time*. His heart would speed up, his palms would sweat, and his mother's face would be bright and excited, but inevitably, he would make that move. The mistake that ensured his loss. His mother's face would cloud over in disappointment, and he would know the game was lost, so he'd start to make stupid moves on purpose. He'd throw key players into the line of danger and go out of his way to save pawns. His mother would shake her head in disappointment; she had no words.

His dad would stand up after he won and extend his palm for a handshake with his son, with a hand on top of the handshake for comfort. Then he'd kiss his wife with his hands on either side of her face, a loud smacking kiss, like this was the first time he had won and he had trained his whole life just to beat his son.

And now his father is dead.

His mother was the one to call him. It was five a.m., thirty minutes before Dai's alarm clock was to go off, which meant it was six p.m. in Japan; Dai remembered doing the mental calculations for the time. His mother's voice was even and calm. He had to ask her again because the tone of her voice surprised him. "Did you say Dad's dead?"

They are burying him back home. He wanted it that way and said so in his will, much to his wife's surprise, which means Nozomi will have to choose between being buried with her father and mother in Japan or with her husband in the U.S. when she dies.

The funeral attendant on the front-left side of the casket counts to three, and they all lift the casket at the same time. The casket is lighter than Dai anticipated it would be, but, thinking of his father's wasted figure when he saw him at the airport three years ago, Dai thinks perhaps he should have known. The thought makes him want to reach into his pocket and smoke a cigarette, to call out to the funeral director, who is still standing at the door and giving practiced empathy to the mourners, to get him another drink, except he already feels numb, like after his father's wins. He would watch as his father celebrated, and he sat having failed, wondering when it had all gone wrong. Was it the moment he'd made the wrong move or the moment he'd sat down at the board to play?

As Dai walks down the aisle, sweat rolls down the sides of his face. He holds the casket with one hand and swipes his forehead with the other. It's not the fifth of Jack he had for breakfast, the couple gulps of mouthwash he had after he brushed his teeth, or even the Jäger he had in the bathroom; it's the nauseating stomach-in-the-throat feeling he knows he has, though the liquor is covering it. At night, he is dreaming about the hill again. The thought of it makes him nervous. He holds the casket again with one hand and runs his other hand through his hair, which feels greasy with the amount of sweat on his scalp and forehead.

As they walk through the door of the funeral parlor, Dai sees Mara standing across the parking lot with her father. She is leaning against him, swollen with their second child, her hands clutching a tissue to her eyes as she audibly sobs. Her father has his arms wrapped around her and rubs her back. He seems to be either singing quietly to her or making the same sound she used to make to May when she was a baby. *Ssssssbhhh.* Dai can see that his father-in-law is shriveling, too. He is not paper-thin like Dai's father was, but it is coming. And will Dai be able to hold Mara and comfort her when her father dies? Who will hold her when he inevitably gives up his fight? His mother, perhaps? Dai snorts at this. The attendant next to him looks over and gives him a sympathetic look. Dai nods at him with the best impression he can make of a grieving son. The attendant looks away, having done his job of comforting the grief-stricken.

The group approaches the hearse and slides the casket in. Then they all get into the limo behind it. Dai looks out the window as Mara's father leads her to the limo with the rest of the immediate family. Mara looks back in Dai's direction. Dai looks away before she can catch his eye. He sighs. He wants to be everything he can be for her. He wants to win this battle; he wants to promise they'll be one hundred years old, holding hands in matching wheelchairs. But he can't help but fall. He wants to blame it on his mom's even voice the night she called and told him his father was dead, but it started before that, at their wedding. The happiest day of their lives, his hands wouldn't stop shaking; even that night, when he finally had Mara alone and in his arms.

That night, he started dreaming about falling onto the hill again. He woke in the morning queasy, his stomach in his throat. He joked with Mara that perhaps she was pregnant. A month went by, and she missed her period. By then, he was having night sweats. By month four, he could barely get out of bed, and Mara kept telling him to go back to therapy. He would tell her he was fine. "I'm not a morning person." Which was partially true. Around month five, he started staying up until three or four in the morning. He figured his brain was tired of the dream.

Around month six, early one morning, after a sleepless night spent blankly gazing at the T.V. on mute, he dragged himself upstairs and into bed. He closed his eyes; they felt as though they weighed fifty pounds each. Then little foot-steps came running down the hall and pushed the bedroom door open. May jumped onto the bed on his side and hugged him as best as she could from the side while singing a song about it being morning-time. Mara rolled over, her stom-ach lying on Dai's arm. She laid her head on his chest. And there was the old vision, of being trapped under Kitand, of being trapped on that hill. Eyes trapped open and no place to go. He started to hyperventilate. May stopped singing and started to cry. Mara shifted herself up and pulled Dai up, as well. They hobbled out to the car. He leaned on her, hobbling as best as she could, carrying both their unborn daughter and him. May ran behind him, pulling on his pant leg, insisting he was okay.

"You okay, Daddy? You're okay, Daddy. Right? You're okay?" Next to the car, Mara nearly fell to her knees in pain. Dai snapped out of it. He helped pick her up and got her into the car. He picked May up and got her into her booster seat. Mara clutched her stomach, crying; the contractions were too early.

"Bedrest. No stress" was the prescription from the doctor. After that, Dai got up every morning, closed the bathroom door, drank a mini-bottle's worth of whiskey, brushed his teeth, then woke up his daughter to get her ready for pre-school, drove Mara to "Music in the Kitchen," and then got to work himself. He could not afford to lie in bed as he had done as a kid; he had to be an adult.

Dai pulls out a cigarette and puts the window down. He lights it and doesn't look at any of the other pallbearers for approval as to whether he can do this. He's grieving.

The baby in Mara's womb shifts. Mara rubs the bottom of her stomach, soothing her. She is not sure how to soothe herself.

You can't ignore this forever. He's obviously drunk. What about May and the baby? What happens when he gets too drunk and gets in a car accident or forgets one of them in the tub?

Mara knows her mother's voice that has come back once again is right. Of course it is. When her father came to stay after hearing about Eduard's death a week ago, he merely glanced up at Dai and then at her. He looked back at his newspaper and finished his black coffee, but she saw it in his eyes. The reality of them. He got up, kissed May's forehead, and went out back to smoke his morning cigarette, but there was no mistaking it. Her father was a silent man, but he did not lie to himself or to her.

When she woke the next morning, Dai came out of the bathroom, and his hair was shaggy and greasy-looking, and his eyes were glassy and refused to settle on her face. There was no denying the truth, so when Mara's father asked her to come and stay with him for a spell, she agreed. Then she called Nozomi. Though they were not close, Mara knew the only way to do this would be with Dai's mother's help. Nozomi only asked that when she came stateside, her granddaughter would come and stay with her the few days before the service and for the duration of her time in the States. Mara agreed.

Mara's youngest daughter jumps within her. She hums to soothe both of them.

Nozomi opens the limo door and places May in the booster seat next to her mother. Then she leans down and kisses her granddaughter's forehead. May smiles up at her grandmother, showing her missing front tooth. Nozomi pulls the seatbelt over her booster seat, buckles it, and turns to close the door. May reaches up and grabs her grandmother's sleeve and tugs. Nozomi looks back, and May motions for her to come closer. Nozomi leans down next to her granddaughter's face. May motions that she come closer. Nozomi leans down next to her ear. May whispers, "Baabaa, I love you." Then she throws her arms around Nozomi's neck. Nozomi remembers the feeling of her son's arms around her neck, and the sound of his voice when he cried out, *Mama, again.*

Nozomi kisses her granddaughter's forehead, then holds her granddaughter's face in her hands and whispers to her, "Baabaa loves you, too." She kisses May's cheek. Nozomi gives

Mara a brief nod, then closes the limo door, walks to her own car, and drives to the burial site.

Nozomi turns the A/C down as she watches her son stumble toward the car, his hands shoved into his pockets, his hair long and oily, his face sweating. He looks up at the car, bleary-eyed. He looks unsure but still continues to walk toward her. Nozomi barely recognizes him. She leans over and opens the passenger door. Dai stands in front of the car door and leans down, refusing to meet his mother's eyes. "Ma, where are they? I looked away to lower the casket, and when I looked up next, the limo was pulling away."

Nozomi looks straight ahead, gripping the steering wheel. "Get in, Dai."

Dai chuckles to himself, thinking how Mara and his mother have somehow banded together, Thelma-and-Louise-style, to plan whatever this is. His chuckle turns into a maniacal laugh by the time he is sitting next to his mother, who is not in on the joke.

Nozomi is unsettled. She grips the steering wheel, staring ahead at a row of magnolia trees flowering next to the entrance to the cemetery, and behind it, her Eduard, the man she always knew would stand by her side. Her son finally stops laughing. Nozomi mentally puts the pain in a box in the back of her mind and pulls out of the parking lot.

Dai reaches into his jacket and pulls out a cigarette and a lighter. He puts the window down and sticks the cigarette into his mouth. Nozomi coughs lightly, warning her son to put the cigarette away. Dai ignores her. He cups his hand in front of the cigarette as he lights it so the air rushing past will not put it out. He sucks on it and blows the smoke out in front of himself, instead of to the side. Nozomi opens the window behind Dai. She continues looking ahead. She alternates gripping and relaxing her hand on the wheel so that it sounds as though it is creaking, protesting in its way. Dai clears his throat and sucks on the cigarette for a full sixty seconds. Then he turns toward his mother and blows the smoke into her face. Nozomi puts down her window. Then, without looking at her son, she speaks as calmly as she can manage, though she is angry and the words come from behind her teeth.

"Your father died from lung cancer."

Dai takes another puff and blows it out the window on his side. "Dad still thought it was worth smoking until the day he died."

"He was already dying."

"We're all dying, Mom."

They sit in silence. Nozomi grips the steering wheel. Dai looks out the window, remembering the drive with his dad from the airport in Osaka. It felt as though he were preparing for war.

"Ma, where are we going?" Dai asks this question without looking over at his mother.

Nozomi peers at her son, who looks like a stranger solemnly staring out the window. "To the clinic."

Dai's only reaction is a slight slump of the shoulders, as though he has been carrying an invisible load and has decided to drop it. "You know which one?"

"We asked around for good clinics."

Dai continues looking out the window. He reaches into his pant pocket and pulls out his wallet. From the wallet, he pulls out a card. He hands the card to his mother. Nozomi takes the card and glances at it.

"Is this where you want to go?"

Dai continues staring out the window, ignoring his mother's question. He reaches into his jacket pocket and pulls out a mini-bottle of Jack Daniels. He opens it and drinks it down, then puts the empty bottle back into his jacket pocket. They continue to ride in silence.

When they arrive at the clinic, Nozomi shuts down the car and sets her keys in her lap next to the worn business card. Dai sits with his hands in his lap. He does not know what to say to his mother. He wants to say that he is sorry that he is not as strong as his grandfather or his father. He wants to tell his mother he loves her. He wants to ask her to care for Mara like this once he inevitably loses his battle. Instead, he says, "Thanks, Ma," then gets out of the car and goes into the clinic.

Nozomi cannot make herself go in. The facade of the building seems benign. Brick and mortar. At the same time, it is a sinister, breathing thing, inflating and deflating, the sickness hidden inside of it struggling to come out. This scares her, this place, the sickness inside it, the sickness her son admits is inside of him.

A knock on her window makes her jump. At the window is an older man with wisps of white hair like wisps of fog floating in the air. He waves. The sky blue of his eyes is almost translucent. Nozomi lowers the window.

The man sticks his hand out. "Hey, didn't mean to scare you. I'm Jerry, the inpatient psychiatrist here. Dai said you were out here, and I know this process can be stressful, so I figured I'd come out and make sure you were okay."

Nozomi looks up into the translucent pupils gazing kindly into her face, and she starts to cry. Jerry stands patiently, giving her the time she needs. When she calms, he hands her a card. On it is written a different name and address than the card her son handed her. She shakes her head. "I'm fine, really."

Jerry nods. "Maybe, but we all have bad days."

Nozomi nods and takes the card. Jerry smiles and gives a matter-of-fact nod and turns away.

Nozomi reaches out and grabs his arm. "Tell him when he is ready, I want to come to see him."

Jerry nods in confirmation, turns, and walks inside.

Nozomi reaches back, pulls her wallet out of her purse, and slips both cards into the wallet before replacing it in her bag. Then she picks up the keys off of her lap, starts the car, and pulls out of the parking space.

THE END
2025

MARA SITS IN THE STARK WHITE HOSPITAL ROOM in a canvas chair, next to a bed that takes up most of the room. Her dad lies in the bed, prone. His arms are placed on top of the folded-over sheet and blanket on top of him. His face is slack, relaxed, but, to Mara, already looking like death. She reaches out with her left hand to take his hand. He does not respond. She blinks back tears and, in an effort to comfort herself, starts to sing a song she remembers her mom singing to her a long time ago. Gloria Gaynor flows out of Mara's throat, accompanied by tears. Then there it is, the telltale high-pitched tone, getting louder, preparing her for the tornado, the harbinger of death. Death is coming. Always coming. There is absolutely nothing she can do about it but watch it take everyone she loves and one day succumb to it herself.

MARA WAKES TO a hand squeezing hers. Her father struggles to sit up in bed. Mara stands up abruptly to help him, but he puts a hand out, letting her know he will do this on his own. Once he is sitting up, he beams, or rather half of his face beams while the other half sits stubbornly in the same slack position it had while he slept. He pats her hand. Mara throws her arms around her father's neck. He wraps his arm around her. They hold each other for a few moments until he pats Mara's back.

Mara swipes a hand over her face to catch any tears, then sits down next to her father once again. She reaches out and grabs his hand to hold it in both of hers. She is unsure how to look at her father. It is a struggle to see his face, as half of him looks as she remembers him, and half looks how she imagines he will look in death.

Ezekiel asks his daughter, "How are Little Miss and Gloria?"

Mara holds her hands balled up in her lap, like a child trying to hide a small bird from the prying eyes of a parent. "The girls are fine, Daddy. Worry about yourself."

Ezekiel, seeing his daughter's distress, tries to comfort her. "M&M, how do I look?"

Mara looks away and lies. "You look fine, Daddy, just fine."

Ezekiel smiles as best as he can. "Darlin', who knows if I will leave this hospital."

Mara bursts into tears. She throws her hands over her face because she can't stand the sight of his face in death right next to his face with a smile on it. Ezekiel lets his daughter cry for a few minutes, knowing how important this time will be after he passes. When she calms down, Ezekiel speaks to his daughter, though her hands still cover her face.

"You know, M&M, death is not sadness. It's not some big bad coming to get me or you. It is simply the end of our journey here. The thought of the end is frightening, but for me, your mom is waiting on the other side. Hopefully, anyway. I guess I'll see." Ezekiel chuckles to himself.

Mara thinks: *But Daddy, I'm falling through the air and I am looking at the ground that I am hurtling toward, that you will hit any second, and I am scared.*

Fatigue comes over Ezekiel. He sighs and seems to be getting visibly smaller. Shrinking into himself. "M&M, I'm tired. I think I'll close my eyes for a bit. Go home, dove; come back tomorrow."

Mara puts his hand back on the folded-over lip of blanket and sheet. Then she helps him adjust until he is comfortable enough to sleep. Ezekiel closes his eyes. Mara sits back down at his side, watching.

LATER THAT NIGHT, Mara sits on the side of her bed. The fear is still with her. The feeling that everything is temporary. That she is alone, her existence tenuous. The galloping sound of her heart sounds like thunder in her ears. She closes her eyes and breathes, counting to four. The tears come and she allows them. At this moment, she knows she is alone and it is the truth. Of course it is.

When the tears subside, Mara takes a few more breaths until her body no longer shudders under the truth. She opens her eyes, and Dai is standing in the doorway in front of her, his hands stuffed into his pockets. He clears his throat, which she knows he does when he is uncomfortable or unsure. Dai takes his hands out of his pockets and walks toward her; his hands are balled up at his sides. As he approaches her, he opens and closes them as though to remind himself not to ball them up. He stops in front of Mara.

Mara reaches up and grabs each of his hands. She curls them both back into balls and kisses each as though to tell him she will love him no matter what. He sits beside her, his hands still clenched into fists and extended in front of him, wrists up, as though he is unsure what to do with them.

"I'm supposed to be comforting *you*, Mara."

Mara smiles to herself, gets up, and squats in front of him. She opens both of his hands from their clenched position and kisses each palm. She looks up into his eyes. "Dai, this moment is everything, and that scares the shit out of me."

Dai puts his hands out, palms up. Mara places both of her hands in his. Dai closes his hands around hers, loosely, like a cup. In her eyes, he sees how the green has settled in like distant moons on a distant planet. His heart speeds up looking at the alien landscapes, and for a second, he is afraid, but he knows what comes next, and he knows: he cannot fall without her. He clasps her hands and pulls them back so she is pulled toward him. He braces himself for the impact, which slows his fall, the brace. For a moment, she is falling up toward him, and he remembers the lonely blue sky and the numb lack of the hill. He reaches out and grasps her hips to remind himself he is not alone in that dream. Tugs her toward him, so she knows she isn't alone. When their galaxies collide, it knocks the air out of him, but he doesn't have time to react because they are falling back faster. And Mara sees his scar, an absurd smile carved into his throat. She wants to look away, to pull away from it, but there is no escape. The air is rushing past their ears, and this is inevitable. So, she relents, raises her lips, and kisses death. She smiles to herself, getting it. The absurdity of fear. Then Dai is lifting her chin, and in his eyes is a world for her.

And when she feels her stomach dropping from the fall, she is laughing against death. Her arms are wrapped under Dai's shoulders, her hands are placed on Dai's upper back, her nails are entrenched in his shoulders. Mara licks Dai's scar. Drags her wet, rough tongue over the unnatural smoothness of his mortality. Then continues to laugh and laugh. It's coming for them, quick—she sees it in the corner of her eyes if she chooses to—but she closes her eyes and laughs with tears running down her face instead. And Dai throws his head back, laughing with Mara, enjoying the sharp pain of reality on his shoulders. His arms are wrapped around her waist, tight, so she is as close to him as possible. By the time the back of Dai's head comes to rest, they are clinging to each other for dear life.

ACKNOWLEDGMENTS

Thanks to Joshua Isard, my sisters, Muse Writers Center, and SFK Press.

ABOUT THE AUTHOR

Rebekah Coxwell lives in Virginia Beach, VA, with her two brilliant babies. She currently teaches at Muse Writers Center, a local nonprofit in Norfolk, VA. She has been published in a few literary magazines. This is her first novel.

FURTHER READING

"1866-1920: Rapid Population Growth, Large-Scale
 Agriculture, and Integration into the United States."
 Calisphere. Los Angeles Public Library. calisphere.org
 /exhibitions/essay/5/population-growth/.

"Asian American History." *Japanese American Citizens League*.
 jacl.org/asian-american-history/.

"California's Little-Known Genocide." *History.com*. A&E
 Television Networks. www.history.com/news
 /californias-little-known-genocide.

Camus, Albert. 2001. *The Myth of Sisyphus, and Other Essays*.
 CNIB.

Camus, Albert, et al. 1965. *The Fall & Exile and the Kingdom*.
 The Modern Library.

Eliason, Grafton T., et al. "Existential Theory and Our
 Search for Spirituality." *Journal of Spirituality in Mental
 Health* 12, no. 2 (2010): 86–111. https://doi
 .org/10.1080/19349631003730068.

"History of Japan, Between the Wars, 1920-36." *History
 of Peru, Mass Politics and Social Change, 1930-68*.
 motherearthtravel.com/history/japan/history-9.htm.

"Japanese - Rebuilding a Community - Immigration . . .
- Classroom Presentation | Teacher Resources - Library
of Congress." *Planning D-Day (April 2003) - Library of
Congress* Information Bulletin. Victor. www.loc.gov
/teachers/classroommaterials/presentationsandactivities
/presentations/immigration/japanese5.html.

JAPANESE FUNERAL STYLE 3. www.osoushiki-plaza
.com/eng/eng3.html#4.

"Japanese Funerals." *Coming of Age Day | JapanVisitor Japan
Travel Guide*. www.japanvisitor.com/japanese-culture
/japanese-funerals.

"Migratory Workers." *The Columbia Encyclopedia, 6th Ed.*
Encyclopedia.com. www.encyclopedia.com
/economics/encyclopediasalmanacs-transcripts-and
-mapsmigratory-workers.

Nielsen, Chris Stewart. 2007. "Whiteness Imperiled: Anti-
Asian Sentiment in California, 1900-1930." University
of California, Riverside.

Notehelfer, Fred G., and Kitajima Masamoto. "Japan."
Encyclopædia Britannica. Encyclopædia Britannica, Inc.
www.britannica.com/place/Japan
/The-bakuhan-system#ref319502.

Okada, John. 2007. *No-No Boy*. University of Washington
Press.

Olmstead, Alan L., and Paul W. Rhode. *A History of
California Agriculture*. University of California

Agriculture and Natural Resources. s.giannini.ucop. edu/uploads/giannini_public/19/41/194166a6-cfde-4013-ae55-3e8df86d44d0/a_history_of_california_ agriculture.pdf.

Royde-Smith, John Graham, and Thomas A. Hughes. "World War II." *Encyclopædia Britannica*. Encyclopædia Britannica, Inc. www.britannica.com/event /World-War-II.

"Tobacco Leaf Harvesting, Curing, and Fermenting." *Red Rose, Fronto King, Hot Grabba Leaf, Fanta Leaf, and Other Tobacco Leaf Types for Sale at Leaf Only*. www.leafonly .com/tobacco-harvesting-curing-fermenting.php.

Wolf, Jessica. 2017. "Revealing the history of genocide against California's Native Americans." *UCLA Newsroom*. newsroom.ucla.edu/stories/revealing-the -history-of -genocide-against-californias-native -americans.

Yoo, David. 2000. *Growing up Nisei: Race, Generation, and Culture among Japanese Americans of California*, 1924-49. University of Illinois Press.

SHARE YOUR THOUGHTS

Want to help make *Falling* a bestselling novel? Consider leaving an honest review of this book on Goodreads, on your personal author website or blog, and anywhere else readers go for recommendations. It's our priority at SFK Press to publish books for readers to enjoy, and our authors appreciate and value your feedback.

OUR SOUTHERN FRIED GUARANTEE

If you wouldn't enthusiastically recommend one of our books with a 4- or 5-star rating to a friend, then the next story is on us. We believe that much in the stories we're telling. Simply email us at pr@sfkmultimedia.com.

Do You Know About
Our Monthly Zine?

Would you like your unpublished prose, poetry, or visual art featured in *The New Southern Fugitives*? A monthly zine that's free to readers and subscribers and pays contributors:

$40 Per Book Review

$40 Per Poem

$40 Per Photograph or Piece of Visual Art

$15 Per Page for Prose (Min $45 and Max $105)

Visit NewSouthernFugitives.com/Submit
for more information.

ALSO BY SFK PRESS

CPSIA information can be obtained
at www.ICGtesting.com
Printed in the USA
LVHW030922201221
706601LV00001B/48